TWO WOMEN AND THEIR MAN

NOVELS BY MERVYN JONES

John and Mary
A Survivor
Joseph
Twilight of the Day
Lord Richard's Passion
The Pursuit of Happiness
Nobody's Fault
A Short Time to Live

TWO WOMEN AND THEIR MAN

A NOVEL BY

Mervyn Jones

St. Martin's Press
New York

To Bernice Rubens

Copyright © 1981 by Mervyn Jones
For information, write: St. Martin's Press,
175 Fifth Avenue, New York, N.Y. 10010
Manufactured in the United States of America

Library of Congress Cataloging in Publication Data

Jones, Mervyn.
Two women and their man.

I. Title.
PR6060.O56T8   1982   823'.914   81-18212
ISBN 0-312-82754-7   AACR2

Dear Mr Jones,

I have received your letter of the 7th. I am afraid I must say categorically that I cannot grant your request. I do not read novels, and to be frank with you I do not know what useful purpose they serve; I therefore feel no obligation to provide you with 'material', as I believe it is called, for a work of this nature. Moreover, the idea that the 'material' should be derived from the most painful part of my own life is extremely distasteful to me. The events to which you refer occurred more than forty years ago. They have been recalled to the attention of the public because Samuel Pritchard is now a famous name (a fact which I find extraordinary) and presumably you wish to profit from this morbid interest, but I can hardly be expected to sympathize with such a motive. So far as my past actions are concerned, I have long ago paid my penalty under the law. I am an old man now, I have managed to rebuild my life, and I think I can say that I enjoy the respect of my neighbours. Thus, I consider that I have a right to be left in peace. If you are determined to write on this subject, I cannot prevent you, but it will be without my co-operation.

> Yours faithfully,
> David Hughes-Talbot.

Dear Mervyn,

How lovely to hear from you again! I really think friends ought to keep in touch more, now we're all getting older. I'm sixty-five, you know, though I find it hard to believe. We don't often come to London, but Cornwall isn't all that far now there's the motorway, and of course we'd be delighted to put you up. Can we tempt you? We live pretty comfortably, if I do say it myself – Alex at long last is selling his work in a big way – might even, the way things look, rise to the Sam Pritchard price-level!

You must have guessed somehow that I'd want to leave on

7

record the truth about what happened in 1939. But you don't know yet how different the truth is from the legend. I started the legend, though at the time the last thing I was concerned with was the distant future. I lied at the trial. I've been lying ever since, at least by implication. I dodge interviews whenever I can, but this just helps to build up the legend. The last article I saw talked about my 'unhealed wound', which made me feel that I've been striking a cheap pose all these years.

Until fairly recently, I wasn't bothered. The thing was a forgotten sensation, buried in old newspaper files. I had told Alex what really happened, and that seemed to be my only obligation. (Alex merely remarked 'How curious' or something of that sort, and we never talked about it again. He realized, naturally, that marrying him enabled me to make a fresh start.) But since the Pritchard boom, and the relentless growth of the legend with me as the central figure, I've felt rather trapped. I won't say that I've worried desperately, and I might well have done nothing about it, what with my natural idleness and my real contentment in life with Alex. Still, now you're giving me the chance to put things right, I'm glad to take it.

I don't expect you'll get a word out of David. As a man of integrity – he was always that – he can't very well give you a version that isn't the truth. The lies were mine, not his. On the other hand, the truth involves behaviour that he's probably still ashamed of. That, in fact, made me hesitate a little before saying yes to you. But, considering what I did for David, I don't feel that I still owe him anything after all this time. I just want to say, he is not to be judged. Whatever he did came from within himself, the man he was: I was always clear about that, and Estelle was too. No villain need be, passions spin the plot – you know?

I've never seen David or written to him since the divorce. Fortunately, Ann accepted Alex happily as a stepfather. (Ann is my daughter with David – not the one you've met, she's my daughter with Alex.) She's never wanted to get in touch with her father, either when she was a child or since she grew up. Actually, Ann is a great believer in the legend. I'm sure she'd like to claim Sam Pritchard as her real father if only she could make the dates fit.

Nor have I ever been back to Bala, although I still have a sister living there. I went back just once, after the trial, to collect some things from the house. A woman I used to know quite well shouted 'Bloody tart!' as I came out of the station. I daresay the same thing would happen now.

You say you're surprised that David went back there. Well, if ever a man was attached body and soul to a patch of earth, it's David Hughes-Talbot. Besides, everybody sympathized with him. Now he's old, I gather that he's very withdrawn and solitary and generally regarded as sort of hallowed by suffering. He never married again. My sister says that when he came back he was already grey-haired and stooped though he was under forty, so he was no great catch for a woman, whatever the sympathy. And I suppose, considering what had happened, he was through with women.

Estelle – yes, I've got Estelle's address, I'll dig it up before I post this. She is now Mrs Straus (her fourth husband!). I hope she'll help you, but she does make a big thing of having turned her back on Europe. You say you've met her once – that's useful. I'll also write to her and urge. We were out of touch for ages, then she read one of those articles and wrote to me. The result was that she came and stayed here, and we spent a weekend with her when we were in the US in 1974. Once we get together, it's as though we'd seen each other last week. She lives (of course Mr Straus lives too, but he's a rather self-effacing character) in an enormous house on the coast of northern California, which is quite like Cornwall, I thought. One of the odd things about Estelle is that she gives the impression of being a very urban sort of person, and always dresses as if to go shopping in Bond Street, but really she hates towns and loves remote places.

I stayed awake half last night wondering how I was going

to manage this job. I can remember the David of 1939 and the Estelle of 1939 quite vividly – the one who slips away is me, the Martha of 1939. I don't feel sure of what she thought, what she felt, or how she would have told the story. Some scenes, which I know were crucially important, float elusively at the edge of my mind and I recall them only as one recalls dreams. Other scenes do come back as though they'd happened yesterday, but even that isn't quite so; it's as though they were in a book I read yesterday or a play I saw yesterday, not in my own life. There's a lot I'll have to try to pin down, to test and test again before I pass it on to you as the real thing. Don't hurry me, please. I'm never a systematic worker, and I know this won't be easy. I'll do my best.

Love,
Martha.

Dear Mervyn Jones,

Thank you for your letter. I've also heard from Martha, who speaks warmly of you. I do indeed remember meeting you in New York – was it really as far back as 1961, almost twenty years ago? Things don't happen to me at the same rate they once did. I should be thankful for that, no doubt.

I didn't reply at once because I had trouble making up my mind about your request. Not out of reticence, I assure you. I've never been one to care greatly who knows about my personal life, and at my present age it would be ridiculous. In any case, Martha tells me that she intends to let all the cats out of the bag. My doubt was rather whether any account, however frank and truthful at the factual level, can convey the meaning of what happened. As you're a novelist, I needn't say to you that truth is seldom convincing. Martha and I were sincere friends at the same time that I was in love with her husband. It was difficult right along, and it ended in what's conventionally called a tragedy. The logical deduction is that both Martha and David would have been far better off if I'd never appeared at Bala.

And yet, we all needed each other. I'm not sure if Martha sees that, although our friendship has endured. David, I'm sure, will deny it. His account, if he gives you one (unlikely, I'd say), will be the least truthful, though not deliberately. Well, that should be forgiven – he carried the can. But it's true, and it's the meaning of the story, and I finally decided that even if I can't say so effectively, I ought to try.

From my angle, I'll have to explain why I needed David as a lover and Martha as a friend at just that time. It has much to do with my being an American and with my experience of Europe. I was saying a long farewell, and trying to carry away some reward for the hope and trust that I'd brought. I think I must begin at the end, the way novelists often do, and put down a marker with my departure. It was a sad departure, but not empty-handed.

Something will be in the mail to you fairly soon.

All good wishes,
Estelle Straus.

Dear Mr Jones,

Your second letter places me in a difficult situation. I have not changed my view that your project is contrary to the most elementary standards of decency, but I can no longer protect myself by silence now that you have the promise of narratives from my ex-wife and from Estelle Mavros (or whatever she is called by this time).

Martha is a fine woman and you will see, when you are acquainted with the facts, that I have cause to be profoundly grateful to her for her conduct at a vital moment. However, she also harbours an acute resentment against me, for which the influence of the man who became her second husband is doubtless responsible. For example, she has consistently refused to allow my daughter any contact with me.

11

Inevitably, therefore, you will received a biased and distorted version of events from her. The position is much worse in the case of Mrs Mavros. I must warn you that she is a malicious, untruthful woman, with few or no notions of morality, and you should treat whatever statements she makes with the utmost caution.

However, I cannot prevent these accounts from reaching your eyes. My hand, consequently, is forced. It is necessary for me to provide an accurate and objective record of events which I should greatly prefer not to recall to memory. I propose to embark on this unpleasant task without delay, in order to put it behind me as soon as possible. I shall not hesitate to be entirely frank and to admit to conduct which is to my discredit, and which I shall not attempt to excuse, although it has hitherto been shielded from public scrutiny. From me, at all events, you will get the truth, the whole truth, and nothing but the truth.

Yours faithfully,
David Hughes-Talbot.

ESTELLE

I sailed from Liverpool, on a British ship bound for New York, in November 1939. The war had begun. I had stayed on to be with Martha through David's trial. I booked my passage as soon as we knew that he'd been reprieved; but I still felt guilty about going, because Martha would have nobody who loved her and didn't hold her to blame. I tried to persuade her to come to America with me, but she said that she didn't want to be a refugee on top of everything else. So I was leaving her to go through the war; besides, I had several friends who were – or soon would be – in the British or French Services. There was no fighting yet, and (to everybody's surprise) no bombing, but one sensed incalculable miseries to come. The blackout, the ration coupons, the order to carry gas masks: these spread an atmosphere not only of gloom but of menace.

Yet I couldn't hide from myself, or from Martha, that I was glad to be going. Because I had left America young and innocent, memories of innocence – sodas in the corner drugstore, fumbling kisses on the porch, white dresses on high-school graduation day – returned to me across the chastening experiences of my eight years in Europe. More immediately, I was going to the bright lights and the fat steaks, to a nation safely at peace. I didn't believe that the US would get into the war. Why should we be that crazy, twice in twenty years? Here I may say that I've always been a bad guesser. I was astounded by Pearl Harbor, even more astounded than other Americans, because the world for me consisted of America and Europe, and I'd given no more thought to the Japanese than to the Eskimos. Later, I expected the cold war to explode irresistibly into World War III. This was a reason, reinforcing other reasons of my own, why I didn't return to Europe for many years. It was strange, when at last I did retrace my steps, to travel in a Europe at peace while America was floundering in the idiocy of Vietnam. But I must get back to Liverpool, 1939.

Martha came to see me off. She was living, very provisionally, with her brother, who was a teacher. He had worked in London but, anticipating the war, had transferred to a country school, I think in Cheshire; he limped for some reason and wouldn't be wanted by the Services. His attitude to Martha was coldly censorious but he couldn't refuse her shelter, and his wife was kinder – her attitude, Martha said, was intrigued and curious. Martha intended to get some sort of war work and support herself, anyway when Ann was a bit older. She brought Ann to Liverpool. The sister-in-law would have looked after her for the day, but Martha didn't want to be beholden for any extras.

It was a cold, raw day, the beginning of what – so Martha told me when we looked back years later – was a very hard winter. The ship was jam-full, naturally, and the passport formalities took hours. Our feet froze as we shuffled slowly through a vast shed, a sort of limbo that made time endless. When we emerged, and had to cross an open space to reach the gangway, it was dark and the blackout had started. The shed was one mountainous hulk without visible outlines, the ship was another, Liverpool had ceased to exist. We groped our way aboard. (Friends seeing passengers off were allowed on ships.)

We went to my cabin, but there was literally no room for us. I was to travel in a cramped third-class cabin with four berths, all that I could afford. So we went upstairs again to the lounge, too late to get seats. Children were scampering about everywhere; the ship was carrying more children, being sent to America for the duration of the war, than adults. Ann got the idea, apparently, that she was making the journey too. She was bright but she was less than three years old (I think – check with Martha) and the whole scene was so strange, so unlike anything in her little life, that it couldn't be explained to her. She stood very still, clutching Martha's hand, with an air of being deceived and trapped. Then someone hurrying past jostled her, she started to cry, and she couldn't stop though she tried to be brave. I said to Martha: 'You'd better go.' She shook her head, but a minute later the loudspeaker ordered non-travellers to leave the ship. We kissed each other. I remember that Martha's face was cold, and that seemed appalling, as though she had begun to die, or ceased to be the Martha I had known. We said nothing. She picked Ann up and went into the darkness, not looking back. We both felt – knew, we should have said – that we would never see each other again.

As for the journey, it was horrible. What made it worse than it need have been was a determined imitation, which could only come across as a parody, of a peacetime crossing: lavish food, organized games, dancing to the gramophone. This enforced jollity contrasted with the misery, seen constantly in hurt eyes, of people going unprepared into the unknown, women parted from the men they loved, lonely and bewildered children. Some kids had mothers with them, but many didn't; these soon escaped from unhappiness by becoming boisterous, rushing around and yelling, forming into uncontrollable gangs which presaged (I thought) the gangs of the homeless and parentless who would rove the ruined cities of Europe. There were some women – nurses or teachers, I don't know – who had the job of looking after the unaccompanied kids, but they couldn't keep an eye on them all. Once, there was an alarm because a boy was supposed to have fallen overboard, and the ship turned back to search for him. He was found, giggling diabolically, hiding in the crew's quarters.

It was best not to think of how all these wild children could be got into the right lifeboats in case of disaster. One similar ship had already been torpedoed. But the danger, though it was real, didn't impose such an unrelenting strain as the uncertainty of the journey. There was no set arrival date, and the ship kept changing course to evade the rumoured U-boats, heading sometimes north, sometimes south, and even east if my sense of direction hadn't deserted me. Add to this that the weather was foul. We began with days of fog, clammily sinister like all fogs and also frightening because one imagined a German warship right alongside. The ship moved at a snail's pace, sounding its hooter every few minutes – no sound in the world is more melancholy, more despairing. Later, we ran into heavy storms and it was impossible to tell whether we were changing direction deliberately or being blown off course. The storms did at least put an end to the obligatory dancing and the rampages of the kids, and the ship seemed less overcrowded when most people were being sick in their cabins. Being a good sailor, I spent a lot of time on deck, gripping the rail, watching the gigantic waves (not giving much, I assure you, for the chances of survival if we did get torpedoed) and quite often drenched, but better off than in rooms pervaded by the infectious stench of nausea. After about ten days, I think, of this journey, I was scarcely able to believe it when, on a bitterly cold but calm and clear day, I made out land on the horizon. We were reaching Halifax, Nova Scotia. Some Canadian passengers disembarked, and on the spur of the moment I decided to follow them although I was booked to New York. I made it by train, inconveniently but contentedly, to Toledo, Ohio, which is my home town.

That wartime journey was, I'll agree, something special. I describe it because it clarified, by taking it to an extreme, the essential quality of every Atlantic crossing by sea: a quality difficult to explain to the air generation. When I eventually – thirty years later, and at an advanced age for any 'first' – got on to a plane from New York to London, I was amazed to see the other passengers taking their seats as casually as if they were on a bus from Toledo to Cleveland. I realized that many of them went to Europe often, even regularly. In the days of the sea crossing, that would have seemed fantastic. There were, it's true, a few wealthy eccentrics who revisited the liners as they revisited grand hotels; and there were diplomats and businessmen to whom the crossing was no novelty, although those who were really important committed themselves sparingly to the five or six lost days. For most people, an Atlantic crossing was a rare event.

Before the sailing date, you said goodbye to all your friends and probably gave a farewell party. You spent days packing. You arrived at the ship with a couple of weighty trunks (such trunks no longer exist, unless immobilized in attics); a rich first-class passenger might have a score of them. Leave-taking was an emotional business: kisses, tears, pledges not to forget, and finally waving between deck and quayside as the ship slowly carried you away. The gradual diminishing of the land, and the sight of the waves reaching to the horizon, linked every traveller with the immigrant ships, the Pilgrim Fathers, even Columbus. A phase of life was closing, another was opening. America – or Europe – would be not a spectacle but an environment, at least for months, perhaps for years, perhaps for ever. You would return, if you returned at all, a changed person. So that was the quality of the Atlantic crossing: a quality of significant decision, of expectation intensified to the pitch of solemnity.

I was in my early teens when I made up my mind that Toledo, Ohio, wasn't where I belonged. One of the first books that I read without being advised by my parents or by a teacher was Sinclair Lewis' *Babbitt*. It struck home, not least because Babbitt was a real estate man and so was my father. The Babbitt world, it was revealed to me, was stupid, shallow and crude to an intolerable degree. Yet I was living in it, and I would always be living in it unless I made my escape.

In my innocence, I regarded *Babbitt*, which was a best-seller, as a piece of underground literature, and imagined that I was the only person who took in its message. But I actually was the only one, so far as I ever discovered, in our Babbittish suburb or in my high-school. I kept my thoughts to myself, having the temperament of a dodger rather than a fighter. I passed successfully, up to the time of my escape, for a nice, quiet, ordinary girl.

Most girls like me – there were plenty, though I didn't know it, in the America of that time – were thinking of getting away to the big cities, New York in particular. This didn't tempt me; for one reason, I was never fond of cities. Chicago, the biggest I'd seen, had appalled me. With a breathtaking sense of reaching for the stars, I fixed on Europe as my goal. At school, I noted (and secretly marvelled that nobody else perceived it) that, while we were exhorted to take limitless pride in being American, we were taught that all the greatest books and plays, the most beautiful music, the masterpieces of architecture, and even the laws of science were the products of Europe. I thought of Europe as a civilization that had grown and matured, instead of being hastily pieced together. My visions were of graciousness and beauty, of old houses built round courtyards, of rooms lined with leather-bound books, of men who wore cloaks and kissed ladies' hands with impeccable courtesy.

After I graduated from high school, I started work as receptionist in a doctor's office. In those days, it wasn't usual for girls to go to college unless they had some definite career purpose. Secretly, I taught myself French, German and Italian; I have a quick mind for languages, and enthusiasm did the rest. I had no idea of the pronunciation, so that I arrived in Europe able to read literary magazines and unable to buy train tickets, but I soon put that right.

The doctor paid me well, for that time, and I never asked my father for money. He must have been grateful; the Depression had set in and presumably it hit the real estate business. But it wasn't considered proper to talk about financial problems in the family, so the Depression affected me no more than a foreign war. What I noticed, mainly, was that prices dropped and you could get bargains everywhere. I saved money steadily. I was living at home, and my daily expenditure was car fare and a lunch of ham on rye and a glass of milk. I was paid for at the movies, for I always had as many dates as I wanted, and didn't let them suspect that I was dreaming of European men. For a time, I even had a steady boyfriend, which didn't mean what it means now. I worried a bit that he might ask me to marry him, since it wasn't unusual for a girl to be married at nineteen or twenty, and resolved that I must get across the Atlantic before that happened.

Finally, the day came when my savings account reached my target: the fare to Le Havre on a French ship plus a hundred dollars. It was spring, 1931; I had just passed my twentieth birthday. I informed my parents that I wanted to spend the summer in Europe. Nowadays this would be a perfectly conventional idea, and might well be pressed on a girl if she hadn't suggested it herself; then, it was startling. But, once they picked themselves up from the shock, my parents were too fair-minded to oppose me. I had never made any other demands or caused them any trouble; I was considered to be a sensible girl, likely to survive the dangers and temptations of foreign lands; I was paying my own fare (of course, I didn't say that it was a one-way fare) and my success in saving it up had to be accounted for virtue; and the doctor was prepared to hold my job open.

My mother murmured something about going with me, which would have scuppered the whole design, but my father must have vetoed this on grounds of expense. All she did was to accompany me to New York and wave fondly as the ship departed. I stood on deck for hours gazing at the Statue of Liberty, the Long Island coastline, and at last the empty horizon; I had never seen the ocean before. Then a young man invited me to join him for a drink. It was my first alcoholic drink, as I'd grown up under prohibition. The young man, who spoke with a delectable French accent, was my first European. My head whirled.

I reached Paris, but I didn't stay long; though manifestly in another class from Chicago, it was nevertheless a city. Some girls had hooting taxis and crowded cafés in their dreams of Europe, but not me. I read the want-ads in the Paris *Herald Tribune* and clicked with a French family who had a villa at Grasse and wanted a *jeune demoiselle, parlant anglais*, to look after the kids for the summer. The kids were little beasts and resisted being taught English, but Grasse was lovely. On my free days, I walked for miles. The terraced hills, the villages clustering round old churches, the stone-built farmhouses with their red roofs, the twisted pines, the ancient rocks, the sudden glimpses of the blue, blue sea . . . this was it, this was what I'd come for.

My next job was in Menton, as companion to an English lady who spent the winter there. Her title, the Dowager Lady Hitherleigh, was enough to enchant me. She told me frankly that she wouldn't have taken on an American if she hadn't been left in the lurch, and she spent much time correcting, by which she meant de-Americanizing, my English and generally trying to civilize me, for which I was sincerely grateful. I was grateful, too, when she wanted me to carry on next year, back at Hitherleigh. 'Funnily enough, I've taken rather a shine to you, my dear,' she said. Hitherleigh was a dream too: log fires in Adam fireplaces, a stately butler, stables with grooms, dogs all over the place. I fell in love with England, not knowing that I was seeing an England that was giving its final performance to an audience tiptoeing away.

The job lasted until Lord Hitherleigh ambushed me between the bathroom and my bedroom. I fought him off at the cost of a painful bruise on my thigh. I didn't consider my virginity precious but I wasn't about to lose it this way, with Lady Hitherleigh just along the corridor and only fifteen minutes to go before the dinner-bell. I didn't explain to the Dowager why I was quitting, but I didn't need to. She said coldly: 'Perhaps you haven't come across many men like my son, but you will.' In the train to London, I reflected that I'd seen the flip side of all that graciousness and beauty.

Over the next two years I had three more jobs, choosing them for the places they took me to: Capri, Salzburg, and Oxford. I built up a network of friends, meeting them in employment agencies or on train journeys or in the mail line at Poste Restante. They were girls of all nationalities, living my kind of life. Since I saved whenever I worked, and Europe was cheap once you knew the wrinkles, there were longish spells when I didn't need a job. I would find out which of my friends were similarly placed and we'd go for a holiday together, picking out a *pensione* in some Italian fishing port or maybe a *Gasthaus* high up in the Austrian Alps. The holiday lasted until the cash ran out. Each of us could have had a holiday of a different kind, travelling first-class wagon-lit instead of sitting up on the wooden seats, and staying in classy hotels. But a tacit rule of the club, and pride in our independence, forbade it. 'Once you start that kind of thing . . . ' said Rosemary (she was English, a magazine-cover blonde) after reporting on one of her offers. We nodded; there was no more to be said.

We were not – I'd better make this clear – in any way the forerunners of the beatniks or the hippies or whatever they're called now. We never thought of ourselves as Bohemian (that word was still in use). We dressed conventionally, and as smartly as we could afford, and paid our bills. The men whose dinner invitations we accepted were more likely to be sanitation inspectors than poets or artists. We weren't political, either. For us, it wasn't the decade of the Five Year Plans and the Spanish civil war; indeed, we seldom looked at the newspapers. I know, and I knew at the time, that both the artistic avant-garde and the politically committed were around, advertising for recruits and making plenty of noise. I take no pride in failing to join them. But at least one memoir of the thirties should record that there were young people like us too. We were simply girls with an aversion to permanence and a preference for living abroad. Today, I suppose, girls like this become secretaries in UN agencies. Or air hostesses.

As for my virginity, it was disposed of in the nicest possible way. Of course it isn't true, as some people think nowadays, that all the girls were condemned to enforced chastity before the dawn of liberation. What is true is that a girl made her own choice; I'm sure that several of my friends were virgins all the time I knew them, and presumably to the wedding night, and weren't accused of being retarded or frigid or (horrid modern word) uptight. My own attitude was that I was prepared for anything but I insisted, especially after Lord Hitherleigh's assault, on being asked courteously. I was fortunate, therefore, to meet Luigi.

He was employed as secretary – secretaries were often men in Europe at that time – to an elderly scholar who had a villa at Capri; I was looking after kids in the villa next door. Luigi's intentions were clear from the outset, but he favoured me with seduction in the classical European style: three weeks of evening walks and moonlight boat-rides, of flattering speeches in beautiful Italian, of kisses progressing by measured steps from hand to forehead to cheek to lips. I was grateful for being treated with respect and given time to decide. In the end, I felt that Luigi had taken a lot of trouble and deserved to be rewarded.

I should have become a different person, according to the books I'd read, but after carefully examining myself I saw no sign of it. What was pleasant about my little affair with Luigi, in fact, was that life went on just the same. I continued to do my job, it came to an end on the agreed date, I had a holiday, I looked for another job. Clearly, there was no reason why I shouldn't sleep with other young men if they attracted me and if they asked me nicely, so I did. I expected, so far as I thought about it, that life would go on like this indefinitely, or at all events as long as I was young. Instead, just three years after arriving in Europe, I got married to Mavros.

Mavros was Greek; I always called him Mavros because his first name had about eight syllables and I couldn't learn to pronounce it. He was – or his family was – immensely rich. He had never done a stroke of work in his life, and if he'd been forced to look for a job he'd have had no idea where to start. I found this odd, but amusing. Only rich Greeks succeed absolutely in assuming as an article of faith that the money is unlimited, that it can't possibly be spent as fast as it comes in. I once asked Mavros where it came from. He looked puzzled and said: 'Oh, land . . . buildings . . . some ships . . . things like that, I believe.' I noticed at once that he didn't ask the price of anything he wanted to buy. He would produce a wad of bills, select one that looked as though it might suffice – he didn't grasp the relative values of francs, lire, marks and so forth – and then shove the change into his pocket, bills and coins together. But generally he paid with cheques, which no shopkeeper or hotel manager ever dared to query.

I married him because he was unbelievably beautiful, with a perfection as rare in men as it is in women, and also because he carried about with him a conviction – of which his wealth was a pre-condition, I'll admit – that life could be pure pleasure. I had never met anyone who believed that it was unnecessary ever to be unhappy or frustrated, even in the smallest way, but this is what Mavros did believe, and it was simply intoxicating – more intoxicating than the champagne which he started pouring into me within an hour of our first meeting.

This was in the Hotel Georges V in Paris, where I had gone to be interviewed for a job. Mavros was living there, so far as he could ever be said to live anywhere. We met in the elevator. He said 'Bonjour', I said 'Bonjour', and then he asked me to have lunch with him. I was low on money at the time, so I accepted. He took me to an absurdly expensive restaurant from which I emerged, dizzy with champagne, at half past four.

From then on, he never left me alone except at night. By night, I mean the hours between four in the morning, when he delivered me to my hotel in the *Quartier Latin*, and twelve noon, when he appeared with a lavish quantity of flowers and plans for lunch. Time passed in a haze of elaborate meals, extravagant spending in luxury shops, floating around Paris in a chauffeur-driven Rolls-Royce, night-clubs in which the dancers and singers were always practically on top of our table, and champagne, champagne, champagne. The first time I was strictly sober was at our wedding. What I remember best was that we were always laughing. The least silly little thing would set Mavros off, and therefore set me off too. When I showed him a letter telling me that I'd got the job I was applying for, we laughed hysterically. Of course, I tore the letter up.

I wasn't taken completely by surprise when Mavros asked me to marry him. One pointer was that he had made no effort to get me into bed, although he must have realized that I wouldn't have any strong objections. Another pointer was that he talked recurrently about places he wanted to take me to, including a house he owned near Cannes and also the family home in Athens. In those days, men and women did everything they do now except that – outside the ranks of the Bohemians, and Mavros was definitely no Bohemian – they didn't live together. Affairs were conducted from separate bases; no matter how often or how regularly a girl went to a man's residence, it was always a visit, and in theory an unforeseen yielding to persuasion. If you were committing yourself more than that, you got married.

Mavros asked me to marry him, ten days after we'd met, under a tree in the Bois de Boulogne. I'd guessed that something unusual was in the offing when he stopped the car and suggested a walk; normally, he never walked anywhere. I said yes at once. Probably I'd have said yes on tomato juice, but the champagne I'd consumed at lunch made it easier. He kissed me and tried to fasten a diamond ring on my finger. It was too tight – I don't have delicate hands. We both laughed helplessly. Then he summoned the car and we went to the Pré Catalan to drink more champagne.

We were married in a Greek church in Paris, with the beautiful Orthodox ceremony. It was to be the worst of my marriages, but it was by far the best of my weddings. The Mavros parents showed up, and a host of cousins, filling a coach of the Orient Express. I went through it in a bemused trance, just able to follow the whispered instructions from the priest.

Before we took the night train for Cannes, the Greek Consul gave me a present I hadn't expected – my Greek passport. Lying in the wagon-lit, I switched on the little reading-light and examined it page by page. I thought: now I am a European.

The house, crowning a headland overlooking the sea, was as beautiful as Mavros had promised. Inside, the furnishings were luxurious and impersonal; nothing had been chosen by Mavros himself. Although he spoke of 'my house', I believe it was a family possession. Living there was like living in a hotel. Servants came out of the woodwork and I was never able to pour a drink for myself. But then, living in a hotel was what Mavros preferred.

I spent my time swimming from our private beach, sunbathing on the roof-terrace, or going for walks. Mavros disapproved of all three activities. He didn't swim and (as I've said) didn't walk, and he was displeased when I was out of his sight or, worse still, off the premises. As for sunbathing, he was horrified when he found me in the nude – 'Estelle, the servants!' He was convinced that I would get sunstroke, too. He always kept in the shade when out of doors; I guessed that he was proud of his white skin.

Mavros' idea of having a good time was to move from place to place. I was fond of travelling too, but I did think that making something of your home was an integral part of marriage. I was just making plans to shift the furniture around, and maybe get painters in to change the colour schemes, when he announced that we were going to St Moritz, because nobody stayed on the Côte d'Azur in July and August. So we went to St Moritz, and then Munich, and then Venice in September. I was keen to go to Athens if we did have to keep on the move, but he said there was plenty of time for that. It occurred to me that his parents, who had been no more than polite to me at the wedding, weren't too pleased about his choice of a wife. He admitted that this was so. 'They'll change their attitude when you have a baby,' he said.

By this time, I knew a lot more about Mavros, or it would be truer to say that there was nothing to know. Nobody can keep laughing for ever, and beyond the laughter was an utter vacancy. Being with him all day and all night was a bore, then a torment. He had no conversation except little guessing games or chatter about the other hotel guests, yet he could never keep quiet. I like to read sometimes, though I don't class myself as an intellectual; he read nothing. I found myself making schemes to be alone for a few hours, seldom successfully. It rained a lot while we were in Munich, and we used to sit facing each other in the large room of our suite, waiting for the church clock across the road to strike the hours, until he said: 'Well, we could have dinner soon. How about venison tonight, d'you think?' I began to face the truth: I was married to a grown-up child.

Being married was just the trouble; if we'd been having an affair, now would have been the time to call it quits. All the more so because Mavros turned out to be sexually under-powered, and on disappointing nights I couldn't help remembering Luigi and others. When there's not much else, this gets to be important. Perhaps unfairly, I figured that it was why Mavros hadn't tried to get me into bed before we were married.

Venice is a claustrophobic place, the worst place we could have gone to at that stage. There were many times when I wanted to scream. There were times when I did scream. We had rows. Once, I told him I couldn't stand Venice, and he asked where I wanted to go. I said: 'I wish I could go back to when I got into that elevator in Paris. I wish to Christ I'd taken that job.'

Thoughts of the future kept me awake at night while Mavros slept like a child. With a few more years of those enormous meals he wouldn't be beautiful any more, just fat and flabby, and the drinking would soon be a problem. Somehow, I had to get free. I realized that if I started a baby I'd be trapped; the succession obviously mattered in his kind of family. We weren't using any birth control. Actually I'm not the fertile type – two children in four marriages has been my final score – but I didn't know that yet.

Our marriage limped along for another couple of months. We went back to the house in France, where there was more space than in a hotel and co-existence – it was no longer living together in any real sense – was more feasible. I changed my mind several times, resolving to accept the commitment and make a go of it, then deciding that I just couldn't. As a hopeful gesture, and to fill my time, I started teaching myself Greek. Mavros wouldn't help; he took it as a criticism of his French, which was the language we spoke together.

Finally, I told him that it was all over so far as I was concerned. The way I put it was: 'We'd better recognize that we made a disastrous mistake.' I didn't want to hurt him, or I'd have said a ridiculous mistake.

To my great relief, he sighed and said: 'Yes, you're right.' I'll never know why – because his new toy had ceased to amuse him, because he was dimly aware that he was unequal to the effort of coming to terms with a different personality, because letters from his parents were having an influence, or because I wasn't pregnant. We parted without drama. He bought my ticket to Paris, depositing me where he had found me. I stayed one night and went on (third-class, and enjoying it) to London. England was the country where I hadn't been with Mavros.

The divorce was astonishingly easy, considering how slow and complicated one expected it to be then. Perhaps Greek law is different, or perhaps it was just that money on the Mavros scale smooths all paths. Anyway, all I had to do was sign a few papers. I didn't get alimony, but I got a considerable lump sum – my pay-off. Together with the proceeds of selling the jewellery that Mavros had given me, I had enough to last me for as far as I cared to look ahead.

My first thought was to take up with my friends. A couple of the girls were working in England, and Rosemary happened to be at home with her parents for a spell. There were also other English people I knew, married couples whom I'd met on holiday and who had urged me to look them up. I got on the phone. 'This is Estelle,' I'd say. It took me some time to grasp that I wasn't the same Estelle. Through the five more years that I was to spend in Europe, I was somebody else: Mrs Mavros.

For purposes such as registering at a hotel, it didn't occur to me not to use my married name. I travelled on my Greek passport, though I still had US citizenship. Friends like Rosemary knew about my marriage because I had written them ecstatic letters before doubts set in. And when I met new people I was introduced as Mrs Mavros; first names weren't divulged on casual acquaintance, as they are now.

With some experience, I could reconstruct the conversations to which I gave rise:

'Greek, is she, that woman?'

'American originally, I think. She married a Greek.'

'Wasn't he with her, then?'

'They're divorced.'

'Oh, I see.'

Divorcee – I don't think the word is used any more. There are too many, presumably, for it to be a special category. But when I became a divorcee, it still served as a description of a woman. Unconventional? Obviously. Immoral? Most people would have denied thinking so, at least without knowing the particular circumstances and who was the 'guilty party', but it was what they felt. They were closer to the early years of the century, when a divorced woman was automatically barred from respectable society, than we are now to the 1930s.

And then, there was a paradox. The divorcee was regarded as bold and courageous; I saw admiration, not to say envy, in the eyes of some married women and even of men. But she was also considered to have made a failure of an adjustment which other women managed; therefore, she was unstable, wayward, or just plain incompetent. Most people didn't try to reconcile these contrasting attitudes, but fused them into a general conclusion that the divorcee was someone who had broken away from the herd.

I couldn't rebuild my friendship with Rosemary and the other girls as though nothing had happened. They were glad to see me, but we didn't talk openly, spontaneously, as we used to. I was no longer in the club. I had broken the rules by marrying a rich man and then rapidly leaving him with a good pay-off; it wasn't precisely 'that sort of thing', but it was possibly worse. I found myself getting along better with the married couples who were five or ten years older than I was. They were already living in closed circles, so they got a kick out of knowing somebody who retained the capacity for the unpredictable, who appeared and reappeared at intervals. I had to be careful, however, not to assume that I was always welcome. If the wife decided – rightly or wrongly – that I was a danger to her, I was in no position to argue.

These people assumed, I noticed, that I was the same age as they were. It was unheard-of to be divorced at twenty-four. I became resigned to this assumption, and took to dressing and making up in an 'older' style than before. I behaved in an 'older' way, too; as Mrs Mavros, I hadn't the right to be girlishly high-spirited. It was only when I was alone – walking along the country lanes in a tartan skirt and hockey socks, or swimming in a cold sea in the early morning – that I could still be Estelle.

I had told Mavros that I wanted to go back to the moment before I'd stepped into that elevator in Paris. Now I had freed myself from Mavros, but I still couldn't go back. When I tried to get the same kind of job that I'd done before, the agencies had nothing for me. I applied through the want-ads and was interviewed two or three times – again, no dice. In a later decade, I should have trained for some kind of career, or

29

at least become a student. But it wasn't possible then for someone in my position – a foreigner, without the British School Certificate or the French *bachot*, and past the standard age – to walk into a university.

I didn't fit in anywhere, it seemed. If I had any identity, I was a woman of independent means. Well, there are worse things; I decided to make the best of it. I read a lot, went to museums and galleries, attended lectures if I was in Paris or London long enough to follow a series.

For the first time in my life, I was able to have a home of my own. I didn't want anything permanent, anything that would hold me down. But a place where I could move the furniture around, put up pictures of my choice, maybe stay long enough to plant flowers in the garden and see them come up – that attracted me. It wasn't difficult to find small houses to rent by the month. In France, especially, they could be dirt cheap away from the *zones touristiques*. My happiest spell was in a little village on the edge of the Camargue, which was already a nature reserve but drew only a scattering of visitors. I became a serious bird-watcher, crouching for hours in the bushes and disturbed only by wild horses who trotted up to see what this odd motionless creature could be.

I preferred to live in the countryside, indeed in remote places; but I was drawn at times to the cities by the need to see friends, or to be near a particular man. The best compromise was to find a place twenty or thirty miles out with a good train service. Neither Paris nor London spread its tentacles as they do now; the other world of quiet roads, clean streams, and unofficial footpaths began at a defined frontier, which I always crossed with joy. I remember Saint-Michel-sur-Orge with affection; Cobham, too.

At Cobham, on summer evenings twice a week, I walked across two fields to the bend in the road where I met Arthur. My cottage was a mile and a half from the station. Rabbits lived in those fields; after he'd climbed over the stile and kissed me, Arthur used to clap his hands to imitate a gun and make them scamper for their warrens. He was a cipher clerk in the Foreign Office. Tuesdays and Fridays were the nights when he wasn't on call. In the morning, I walked with him to the stile, but no farther. I understood that it wasn't proper for him to have an irregular liaison with a person who, apart from anything else, was an 'alien'. The last evening, when he told me that he was engaged to be married, he said goodbye at the stile and took the next train back to London. I clapped, but it didn't sound like a gun and the rabbits took no notice. I gave up the cottage at the end of the month.

It was with men, especially, that I felt the effects both of my supposed age and of being a divorcee. They imagined me to be – this, I suppose, is how they would have put it – an experienced, sophisticated woman. I didn't myself consider that some intermittent light-hearted experiments and a rash, foolish marriage amounted to much in the way of experience. But for these men who desired to be lovers of Mrs Mavros, I was what they wanted me to be. I never tried to explain myself to them.

A man defines a woman by the manner of his approach to her. I wasn't likely any more to be grabbed in the Lord Hitherleigh style; it did happen occasionally, but I had learned that a derisive laugh was an effective defence and saved me a bruised thigh. But I couldn't expect, either, to be coaxed gently along, as an innocent who above all mustn't be scared, in the Luigi style. Defining me as a virgin of possible promise, Luigi was the first man, and also the last for years, to see me as I really was. Looking back as Mrs Mavros, I realized that Luigi had himself been fairly innocent, pursuing a strategy derived less from experience than from an Italian education, or perhaps from the reminiscences of his employer. I was now beyond the range of such sweet, charming boys; they didn't aspire to divorcees.

The style considered suitable for Mrs Mavros involved the use of signals in an understood code: the hand cupping my ass with easy confidence as we stood side by side, the kiss (sophisticated) on the back of my neck. The words selected had the effect of placing a responsibility on me; where Luigi had said 'I adore you', men now said 'You fascinate me' or 'You're irresistible'. The end in view, though it wasn't indecently rushed, wasn't expected to be long delayed. The scene of action, in the first place, was generally a hotel managed in a tolerant spirit. It was assumed that the procedure was familiar to me.

I don't mean to imply that I had what was called 'an endless string of lovers'. I'm not, thank goodness, a woman for whom the wrong man is better than no man at all. I was perfectly happy, as I've said, during that peaceful spell in the Camargue, when my closest intimacy was with an ugly one-eared cat to whom I gave a corner of my quilt. But meeting a man whom I could think of as a lover always made me feel doubly alive, and I knew well enough that I had no reputation to lose. If numbers matter, there were five men between Mavros and David. Each is still very clear in my mind's eye, although at this distance I might list them in the wrong order; it wasn't a period in which anything 'led to' anything else for me. I suppose that, from the first of these affairs to the fifth, I did become more what I was imagined to be. Through experience, after all, one becomes experienced. Yet there remained, so near the surface that the discovery could have been made by any man who had cared enough, the girl who hoped to be treated courteously and feared to be hurt; and who was seeking patiently, though with dwindling hope, for an ideal first glimpsed in high school back in Toledo.

That girl was unreasonably surprised when she found that most of the men who signalled to her were married. It was, once again, partly a question of age. Arthur – twenty-nine in that Cobham summer – was reaching the limit at which a man who was attractive to women was likely to be still a bachelor. But, I reluctantly recognized, there was something else. Mrs Mavros was just right for men who had been married long enough to get bored, and wanted the sharper flavour of an adventure. (Incidentally, this was why my affairs didn't last long; it wasn't a parallel set of habits and comforts that the men sought.) Without in the least intending it, I had become the ideal mistress. The invisible girl had no hope of spoiling the fun.

For me, an affair with a married man was never the same as an affair with someone unattached. While we made love, I imagined the wife contemplating us from the foot of the bed, a presence not to be denied. It wasn't important whether she knew or didn't know, except for practical reasons; in any case, she was involved. I'm not saying, precisely, that I felt guilty. I shouldn't have become this man's mistress if I hadn't been extremely fond of him, and I thought that I deserved some pity for holding a secondary part in his life, so a sense of doing the wife an injury didn't come naturally. Besides, he had become as ready for an affair as he had for marriage at an earlier time, and if his mistress hadn't been Mrs Mavros it would have been someone else. But none of this made it possible to pretend that the wife didn't exist. We were, ineluctably, three and not two. I was always intensely curious about the wives, seeking to make them as real as they were undoubtedly significant, and I couldn't help asking questions about them although I knew that it was bad form on the part of a mistress.

The men – all my married lovers, of whom there were three before David – took the line that their marriages didn't concern me: 'I don't know why you want to worry about her, my sweet.' I was given to understand, briefly, that the marriage had become meaningless through the extinction of love, or had been a mistake in the first place; it was being maintained for reasons of respectability and career and for the sake of the children. I had an obvious motive for accepting the truth of these accounts, and indeed they weren't improbable. From my own blunder, I knew how people rushed into marriage and how a dazzled infatuation with beauty created an illusion of love. In those days, it wasn't rare for a man to propose marriage to a girl because he had an overwhelming desire to sleep with her and couldn't do so on other terms. One of the wives I had seen, across the teacups; she was beautiful in a pale, delicate way and it was easily credible that she was the type who went in for wounded feelings and paralyzing headaches. At another time, I had a passionate affair with a man of exceptional virility who told me that his wife was a polio victim and confined to a wheelchair. I never made up my mind whether this was true. If it wasn't, he deserved high marks for ingenuity.

Marriage . . . I am really, I can claim, rather good at marriage. Only my first attempt was an unqualified disaster. Perhaps it's truer to say that I'm good at marriage with American men. I married a wonderful man six months after my return to Toledo; we were deeply in love, with every prospect of enduring happiness, and I almost went out of my mind when he was killed on Iwojima. My third marriage lasted for fifteen years. The male menopause, and an uncontrollable passion for a young dancer with admittedly phenomenal legs, put an end to it, but I don't think that was my fault and I'm content to remember what went before this typically American mischance. With Andy Straus, finally, I'm sure it's till death us do part.

So it seems extraordinary, looking back, that in my twenties I believed myself disqualified from the race by my fall at the first hurdle. Yet that was how it appeared. Not one of my married lovers contemplated leaving his wife to marry me; it was obvious that the idea never crossed their minds. The two men who were bachelors regarded me, just as obviously, as an indulgence to be relished before life became wholly serious. Between a well-qualified mistress and a suitable wife, they drew a firm distinction. In the Bohemian world, it might have been different. An affair might have merged into living together, and into marriage when children were desired. But although my life was irregular, my men were conventional; and I must say that I liked their good manners, their educated English or French, their predictable habits, and their clean underwear.

I didn't accept the justice of my situation, but I won't pretend that I often worried about it. Since I couldn't do otherwise, I lived in the present. The beginning of an affair – the moment of acceptance – filled me each time with a trembling joy. Whatever others may have thought, for me it was never a routine, but always as unique and unprecedented as the first time with Luigi. Each of these affairs gave me some happiness, and still gives me happiness in memory. The hours that we had together were sweetly, but not tragically, too short. The talk was good, as it must be between two people who don't see each other so much as they would wish, and the love-making was good for the same reason. I was always eager for the next meeting with my lover, but I wasn't tied down as I had been with Mavros; I had time to see my other friends, to read, to do my gardening or whatever. There is a charm in this kind of affair that young people nowadays, who start living together as soon as they've been to bed, are missing – the expectancy, the thrill of meeting, the sudden delight of voices in a room that's been silent for two or three days, the game of domesticity that one knows to be a game, the poignancy of parting. It doesn't give what marriage gives, but it gives what marriage lacks.

All the same, there were times when I thought of the future and could see nothing ahead of me but more and more of these three-month or six-month affairs, until it really did become a routine and I grew cynical and hardened. I'd be older, I'd be less 'fascinating', and the quality of the men who were interested in me would decline. Instead of choosing, I'd be searching – making the advances, offering myself. Perhaps, I thought, I had no right to think myself better than a prostitute who begins as a luxury call-girl with a select clientèle and ends as a pleading street-walker. This comparison was the more unavoidable because the money I'd received from Mavros, and therefore my independence, wouldn't last many more years. It was a point of honour with me to accept nothing but small presents from my lovers. Sooner or later, I'd be counting on them to pay my rent.

Once you start that kind of thing. . . .

By 1938, I had a growing sense that I was drifting without a rudder. I could reassure myself, however, with the knowledge that my current lover was a distinctly high-calibre man. His name was Georges Lecourbe and he was an assistant professor of law in the University of Grenoble. I met him on the ski slopes. I had decided to get into winter sports and I hoped to acquire some real skill, as much as with my bird-watching. At that time, leaving aside a few resorts in Switzerland, ski-ing was for enthusiasts, not for dabblers in a fashion. There were places with magnificent slopes but without cable-cars and chair-lifts – you had to do it the hard way. The hotels were simple and cheap. Once you'd bought boots and skis, which were quite cheap too, there was no further expense. You didn't take lessons, you made friends with people who knew how to ski.

I stayed at a hotel for a couple of weeks and then managed to find a family in a mountain village who would rent the upper half of their house to me. The country was spectacularly beautiful and I could see that it would be beautiful in summer too, and marvellous for walking. Even before I started my affair with Georges, I reckoned that I might stay indefinitely, or as long as I ever stayed anywhere.

Georges was endowed with that rare, astounding bodily perfection, like Mavros. Unlike Mavros, he was strong and muscular and kept himself in splendid shape. His skin was permanently bronzed because he ran six kilometres every day in nothing but trunks, even in freezing weather. Naturally, he was superb on skis and won most of the season's races. He used to terrify me by heading down a precipitous slope at top speed with every intention, it seemed, of smashing into the wall of a house. Physically, he was completely fearless. His other sport was motor-racing; years later, he was killed crashing on a bend.

We began by spending nights together in ski-huts in the course of expeditions, but after that I went to his house in Grenoble. This was possible because he was estranged from his wife. He came from the Bordeaux region, on the other side of France, and had been married at the age of twenty-one to a girl he'd known since childhood. It was more or less an arranged marriage, uniting two claret-producing properties. They were never in love, by his account, but hoped that they might get along together reasonably; however, they didn't. The job in Grenoble provided a plausible excuse for them to live apart. Madame Lecourbe looked after the vineyards. As they were practising Catholics, and highly respectable people, divorce was out of the question. Indeed, Georges went back to Bordeaux for the month of August and shorter visits at other times. He and his wife slept in separate rooms, he assured me.

It was a fine summer, the days almost always sunny but the heat tempered by the mountain air. I used to take the afternoon bus into town and stroll about until evening; Georges didn't like me to come to the house until the cook and the maid had gone home. When term ended and he had more free time, he picked me up at my village and we went to the high places we remembered from winter, with Georges driving like a madman in a car that roared up hills as though it were about to take off and jump.

I missed him badly while he was away in August, and when he came back in September I had a feeling that things weren't the same as before. He didn't often spend the day with me, although the new term hadn't started. At his house, where we used to talk incessantly and he made me tell him everything I'd been doing since our last meeting, he now didn't listen to what I was saying. If I asked him what was on his mind, he said quite crossly: 'Nothing – nothing.' I thought that perhaps he'd had a difficult time with his wife. She was devoutly religious, and if she'd guessed about me she would take it badly in spite of the hopeless state of the marriage. More likely, I told myself, he was worrying about the danger of war. It was the time of the Czechoslovak crisis. Georges was a reservist officer, and he would have to go to the Army at once if war broke out. His politics were right-wing, he was inclined to admire Hitler, and the idea of fighting Germany in alliance with Communist Russia was certainly enough to depress him. In any case, a war would be a most unwelcome interruption of his comfortable life.

One evening, I went to his house and rang the bell as usual (he'd never given me a key). There was no answer. I stepped back and looked up; the house was dark. Though I hadn't taken special note, I could have sworn that there'd been light from the windows when I arrived. I rang again, and banged the heavy antique knocker in case the bell was out of order, but there was still no sign of him. It was very strange. Georges disliked social occasions and wasn't interested in films or music, so he seldom went out in the evening. Anyway, he was expecting me. I sat in a café for an hour; then I tried again, but the house was still dark. I had no way of getting back to my village, so I took a room at a cheap hotel. I didn't sleep much. I was scared that Georges had had an accident with his crazy driving.

In the morning, I inquired for him at the university. Teaching hadn't started, but he was in his office. I walked in. He was astonished to see me and obviously far from pleased – he never liked me even to phone him there. I explained what had happened, and said I'd been anxious about him.

'But why did you come last night?' he asked. 'I'm expecting you tonight.'

'No, it was last night.'

'I'm sure I said Thursday.'

'No, Wednesday. Anyway, where were you?'

'I went out with some letters, to catch the late post. You must have come at just that time.'

As soon as he said this, I knew that it wasn't true. I hadn't mentioned that I'd gone to the house twice. But I'd have known in any case from what I can only call his shifty manner. After a sort of cross-examination, which I found as wretchedly embarrassing as he did, he admitted that there'd been somebody with him. She was a secretary at the university. It had been going on for quite a while and they'd managed to spend a week of August together. I understood, more clearly than ever before, what it must be like to be the wife of a man like Georges. I said: 'It's breaking the rules, being unfaithful twice over at the same time.'

He came round from behind his desk and took me in his arms. He didn't care about the girl – I was the one he loved – he would get rid of her. But I was sure that he'd try to keep both of us in hand, even if he meant what he said at this moment. And if anyone was dropped it would be me, because I was last season's model. I told him I would have to think things over, and I would prefer not to come to the house that night. Relieved to get me out of the office, he said: 'Very well, we'll be in touch.' I took the bus to the village and stood for a while staring at the mountains, which I would never see white with snow again. Then I packed my cases.

After the break-up with Georges I did some hard thinking, not only about him but about all the men who had given my life its ragged, aimless shape. I held no grievance against them, for they hadn't promised me more than they gave. Yet I wished that one of them – just one – had been willing to make a venture without pre-ordained limits. They always calculated, while I never did. They made the rules – that we should meet only on certain days of the week, and that we shouldn't be seen together in public. Especially, they coolly assumed from the outset that the affair would last for no more than a matter of months.

But when the break-up came, they couldn't look me in the eyes. I found that this hurt and angered me more than anything else. Arthur standing by the stile and peering at the ground as though he'd dropped a shilling, Georges pressing my face into his shoulder . . . it was always like that. At the beginning, they had foreseen this necessity much more clearly than I had. They had calculated that I wouldn't mind too much – I was used to it. When the time came, however, they flinched from the recriminations and the tears which they should have known me better than to expect. They turned the statement of an inevitable truth into an embarrassing, unpleasant, dishonest little scene.

I've said that I didn't explain myself to men. What I didn't explain, because it must be either useless or unnecessary, was the spirit in which I welcomed a man as my lover. I made no demands or conditions; yet I was ready each time for my life to be utterly changed, enlarged beyond earlier bounds. I was ready to travel anywhere, to live with him openly if he wanted, or to go through an infinity of secret meetings if he wanted that. That was the spirit. It was a spirit that none of the men matched or sought to match.

I wasn't looking for a wild, romantic recklessness. I had seen, with Mavros, how shallow and evanescent that could be. I was looking for courage; for generosity; for seriousness; for depth of feeling; I would dare to say, for greatness of soul. Maybe the best word would be dignity.

They had failed me, these men. But a woman who allows herself to believe that men have failed her because they are men – worse, that all men are bound to fail her – is lost. I came to the conclusion that Europe had failed me.

This was hard enough to accept, when I had spent seven years in the pursuit of an ideal bound up with my vision of Europe. But I had been forced to observe, in many ways, a dwindling of those grand traditions which had seemed to promise a finer, more ample life. Wherever I went, I saw noble old buildings being knocked down or allowed to decay; the new ones were cheap and shoddy, or vulgarly ostentatious. That was a symbol of an inner decline. People were often selfish, they were mean and grasping about money, they stooped to petty swindles. Often they were afraid of the future, clinging to pensionable jobs at the cost of subservience and humiliation. Loyalties had come to matter less than the calculation of advantages. The trivial, malicious gossip that gave most people pleasure was the shabby remnant of a heritage of stylish wit. It was all a closing-in, a shrinking of the heart.

That September, we were going through a war scare. I had

no views on whether it would be right to fight for Czechoslovakia. But if war was coming, I wanted to see people prepare themselves for it with dignified resolution. Europe seemed no longer capable of that. All I could see was selfish anxiety, stopping not far short of panic, and – when the crisis was over – selfish relief, both in France and in England. The Munich deal was fixed up a couple of days after I left Grenoble. Georges must have felt that both his problems were solved. But I was saddened by the contrast between his physical fearlessness and his lack of moral courage.

Passing through customs, I presented my Greek passport without pride. (The homeland of democracy was now, like most European nations, a dictatorship.) For the first time since I'd joined in the pledge to the flag in junior school, I was glad that I was an American. There had to be reasons, other than ambition or the escape from poverty, why millions of Europeans – including my grandparents – had crossed the Atlantic in the opposite direction from me. They must have sensed what was coming.

I thought of my parents with a degree of affection and respect that I had been unable to muster in youth. They had never reproached me for anything, even for deceiving them about my 'summer' in Europe. It must have worried them when I married a man I'd just met who had no job or profession. My next letter, barring postcards from here and there, announced my divorce. They took it in their stride, merely sending me good wishes on the former occasion and sympathy on the latter. Since then, they'd continued to write regularly to Poste Restante in places they'd never heard of. I skimmed through their boring letters, scrupulously filled with news about births, marriages and deaths in the neighbourhood and about Toledo civic improvements, and threw them away. I wrote back at long intervals, briefly, and of course evasively; but my letters, I could be sure, were re-read and cherished. A couple of times a year, Daddy informed me that the real estate business was healthy (despite President Roosevelt's reckless policies) and if I needed money I mustn't hesitate to ask. I didn't even thank him for the offer, but Christmas and my birthday always brought a sizeable cheque 'to spend on whatever you fancy'. Christmas also brought a bundle of cards from neighbours in the suburb and friends from high school, faithfully keeping up with my movements. Daddy's most recent letter said that, if this talk of war in Europe was serious, I could cable for my fare any day. He had never pressed me to come home. Only my welfare and safety concerned him.

All this came to my mind, evidence of what I had spurned and left behind: decency, kindliness, unselfishness, maintained in good order and kept fresh like a regularly sprinkled American lawn, or stocked up to meet my requirements like an American ice-box. If there was no nobility in my native land, there was at least integrity. And it was a place where I could be recognized as Estelle, not introduced as Mrs Mavros.

But what I'm presenting as conclusions were really no more than feelings that rose to the surface and sank again. It was a wavering time for me. I don't think, so far as I can recall, that I ever made up my mind in 1938 to return to America. If I did, I soon unmade it again. It isn't easy to admit to a mistake persisted in for seven years. Since the crisis had ended in peace – 'peace for our time,' Neville Chamberlain said, and for all I knew he was right – the obvious motive for leaving Europe had been removed. There was no hurry, at all events. It made no sense to get into the stormy, brutal winter of the Middle West.

I went to London after a few days in Paris. As before, it seemed natural to make for England after a break-up in France. Rosemary was now married, with two children. Her husband was a quantity surveyor, whatever that meant, and they lived in the outer suburbs. She didn't invite me to her home, but we lunched together in the sort of restaurant patronized by ladies in town for a day's shopping. She looked sedate and placid, and had put on quite a lot of weight; gone was the girl to whom men had offered holidays in classy hotels. I looked drawn and nervous, I suppose.

We were still close enough for confessions. I told her that I'd just emerged from an affair with a Frenchman who had ditched me in favour of a newer girl.

'What are you going to do now?' Rosemary asked.

'I don't know. I think I want to be alone for a time.'

'Until you're ready to look for another man?'

'I don't look for them, Rosemary. Well, I certainly don't want to look for one now.'

Rosemary concentrated on her food for a few minutes and then told me that a friend of her husband's, who had been ordered to Singapore for business reasons, owned a cottage in North Wales. He would accept a token rent if he could find someone to light fires in the winter and see to any necessary repairs. It was isolated and perhaps rather primitive – 'but you don't mind that, do you?'

In the state I was in, any definite prospect was a guiding light. I met the man and signed a lease, for six months but renewable. I had never been to Wales. I had a vague idea that the people were artistic and I could interest myself in some traditional craft, or perhaps learn to play the harp. It might be possible to ski in the mountains (I was wrong about this, it turned out). The man mentioned that the local people spoke Welsh. I could learn the language, anyway.

The only other thing that I'd heard about the Welsh was that they were all Methodists or Baptists and had strict moral principles. There would be nobody in those mountains, or in the small town with the curious name of Bala, likely to invite me to start an affair. I was wrong about this, too.

DAVID

My home, Craig-derw, is three miles from the town of Bala and only a mile and a half from the nearest point on Llyn Tegid, the lake on which that town stands. These distances, however, give a false impression if they suggest an easy proximity. The ascent from the lake-shore is extremely steep, with a gain in altitude of almost five hundred feet. It was customary for a rider to dismount and lead his horse, and the first car that I owned was apt to finish the climb with a boiling radiator. The road leads to a plateau, on which Craig-derw and some other farmhouses are spaced at wide intervals. To the west, my home commands a magnificent view of unspoiled country, crowned by the imposing peak of Arenig Fawr. To the east, the town and the lake are invisible because of the steepness of the escarpment. In winter, I have known the plateau to be snow-covered while only rain has fallen in Bala. In summer, the lake may be shimmering in heat while the air of the uplands is fresh and invigorating. It is no exaggeration to say that Craig-derw is in a world of its own.

Visitors – I have no visitors now, but they appeared sometimes when Martha lived at Craig-derw – used to say: 'It's so quiet.' True, we did not hear the traffic on the main roads; nor the trains which, until the closure of the railway lines in recent years, converged on Bala from three directions; nor the outboard motors of the fishermen on the lake; nor even the sound of voices, for Craig-derw is separated from its closest neighbours by a belt of woodland as well as by ample distance. But if one knows how to listen, it is not quiet. The land is criss-crossed by streams, all making a rapid descent and racing from one small waterfall to the next. There is not a spot anywhere near my home where one could fail to catch the sound of running water. The wind, although it may be fierce or gentle, is incessant even on days that would be perfectly still down by the lake, and the attentive ear can always discern its rustling in the trees and bushes. These sounds of wind and water are the voices of Nature itself, continuous and unaltered since they were heard by our earliest ancestors. They must have been audible at the moment of my birth in the large bedroom of Craig-derw, and they will not be interrupted by my death. Except for a brief interlude of happiness, my life has been lonely, alike in youth and in its long decline. I sometimes think that it might have been unendurable, had not these consoling voices relieved an empty silence.

Craig-derw, as a place-name, is undoubtedly of great antiquity. It means 'the rock of the oaks', and there is indeed an outcrop of grey rock, surrounded by oak trees, a hundred yards from the house and in a declivity somewhat sheltered from the winds. The oaks growing there today must have been planted by my grandfather, for I estimate them to be eighty years old. They will outlive me; unlike a weak human, a tree has no allotted span. However, the wood of the oak was formerly a material in constant demand, and the trees were doubtless cut down and replaced many times across the centuries. When Craig-derw first acquired its name, it must have been a holy place; the grove was consecrated to the mysteries of the Druids, and the rock was reddened with the blood of sacrificial victims. This is of course a conjecture without positive evidence, but it is a belief firmly held in our family and I see no reason to doubt it.

When the first farmhouse was built at Craig-derw, I do not know. There are others in the vicinity attested to be five hundred years old. The first name in our family Bible is that of Gareth Hughes, who died in 1786. It is likely that the family had already been established for a number of generations, but the parish registers were imperfectly kept, and Hughes is such a common name in Wales that it is impossible to be certain which of the entries relate to my ancestors.

My great-grandfather was the first to use the name of Hughes-Talbot, which he assumed on marrying a Miss Talbot. The Talbots, I need scarcely say, are an illustrious family in Wales and the Marches; Talbot is the surname of the Earls of Shrewsbury, a title conferred as the reward for valour during the Hundred Years' War. There are many collateral branches, and the bride who came to Craig-derw was certainly not an Earl's daughter. Nevertheless, Hughes-Talbot was a name that inspired pride. I shall be the last to bear it; I cannot deny that this is a sad reflection.

The first Hughes-Talbot raised the family fortunes to a level of some prosperity, perhaps with the aid of a Talbot dowry. Bala is a sheep-farming region. The soil is too thin to support cereal crops but the grass, nurtured by the heavy rainfall, is excellent. When there was no refrigerated lamb from New Zealand to compete with our Welsh mutton, and no synthetic fabrics to compete with wool, raising sheep was a lucrative business. The Hughes-Talbots owned more land, and consequently more sheep, than any of their neighbours. It should be remembered, however, that Wales is a country of small family farms. Our holding of fifteen hundred acres – including meadows, rough grazing, and timber – would not have been considered anything remarkable in the richer counties of England.

My great-grandfather demolished the original farmhouse and built the present Craig-derw, which attained the proportions of a Victorian gentleman's residence. The construction followed a plan often favoured at that period, with two large gables and a central porch placed between protruding bay windows. Estelle Mavros was once kind enough to inform me that it was a frightfully ugly house. I believe that it is no longer fashionable to despise Victorian architecture, and Craig-derw would now be admired if I cared to attract attention to it. But its visual merits do not concern me; it is simply my home.

Martha found the house impressive, even somewhat daunting. I suspect that she never quite got used to being mistress of it. It was, of course, considerably more ample than the house over the bakery in the High Street of Bala which had been her home until our marriage. As well as the house, she was impressed by the contents: the chairs and tables of carved oak, the Persian carpets, the silver candlesticks which dated from my great-grandfather's or at least my grandfather's time. She sometimes asked me what these objects were worth. I could give no answer, since I should not have dreamed – nor should I dream now – of selling them. I thought then that we should have a son to inherit them; fate was to decree otherwise, and when I die they will presumably be disposed of at auction, but I cannot stop thinking of myself as the trustee of a heritage. My indifference to the market value of such possessions gave Martha the idea that we had no need to care about money. She teased me about my meticulous checking of the household accounts, which was in fact a necessity.

Altogether, Martha had an exaggerated notion of what the ownership of Craig-derw meant, and this will doubtless be reflected in her account of our circumstances. Her imagination converted me into a wealthy landowner, almost into some kind of feudal magnate. She liked to gaze out of the west-facing window and marvel at the extent of what she called 'the estate' (I preferred to think of it as the farm). When Arenig Fawr was hidden in the mists, as was frequently the case, all the land that was visible was our property, and Martha found this an exciting thought. Ignorant of conditions in other parts of Great Britain, she could not realize that there were scores of farms larger than ours, nor that there were scores of manor houses or mansions larger than our home. Moreover, farm prices were low in the extremely difficult period that stretched between the two world wars. My love for Martha impelled me to shield her from the harsher realities, but the truth was that our income sufficed only to ensure a modest standard of comfort, and even this was not to be taken for granted.

My family history had taught me forcefully enough that happiness, as well as material prosperity, is inevitably precarious. The Hughes-Talbots had shared to the full in the self-confidence, or the complacency, that was general in the epoch ended by the shock of 1914. I remember my grandfather as a jovial old man, fond of laughing at his own jokes. He was a popular figure in the neighbourhood, I believe, and probably he had no anxieties. He must have supposed that the world he knew would endure for ever. With my father, the shadows began to close in.

I did not have a happy childhood, except for my first five years which of course I recall only dimly. I was born in 1909. I have memories of being kissed and cuddled by my mother, of lace tickling my face and soft hands stroking my hair. She spoiled me, I imagine, so far as the customs of the time permitted. I was the only child, and perhaps she foresaw that she would have no other. My grandparents, too, treated me with indulgent affection. But I also have memories of being shut out of my mother's room and weeping miserably outside the door. Her health was delicate, and I can hazard a guess that she had one or more miscarriages.

When I was five, she died in childbirth. My brother or sister, whichever it was, also perished. The Great War, as it was then called, had begun shortly before; my father immediately enlisted. During the course of the war, both my grandparents died. I was thus deprived of everyone I had loved. A maiden aunt, older than my father, came to live at Craig-derw and look after me. She was strict and even unkind; probably she resented the obligation imposed on her. I yearned for my father to come home and prayed every night that God would keep him safe.

He was an extremely brave soldier; he won the Military Cross for leading an attack in the face of furious machine-gun fire. I believe that, in his grief for my mother, he did not care whether he lived or died. He seemed to lead a charmed life, for he was not even wounded during two years in the trenches. But if bullets could not harm him, poison gas did. Apparently, he was trapped by a fall of earth in a trench that slowly filled with the noxious vapour. It must have been a nightmarish experience – re-lived, indeed, in nightmares that tormented him for the rest of his life. He was no longer fit for active service, and spent the rest of the war in a staff job at Aldershot.

When he came home, he was a changed man – although, if my early memories are accurate, he had never been either as naturally cheerful or as affectionate to me as my grandfather. He was now consistently depressed and gloomy, and often irritable in temper. In former times, he had been exceptionally strong and active; he had regarded the ascent of Arenig Fawr, which reaches a height of 2,800 feet, as a normal piece of exercise. It was naturally galling to him that he could no longer walk round the sheep-grazing without succumbing to a fit of coughing. What most infuriated him, I remember, was that he could not whistle to the dogs. He was a master of the signals used in rounding up sheep, and had won contests in this traditional skill. Now, the coughing overtook him as soon as he drew the necessary breath. The men whom we employed were perfectly adequate at working with the dogs, and as I grew up I also became proficient. But my father insisted that no one else could give the signals properly, and always got angry with the shepherd – or, later, with me – if a single sheep escaped from control.

He soon quarrelled with my aunt and she left Craig-derw. I was not sorry to see the back of her, but life did not become easier for me. I had to look after myself to a great extent, sewing on my buttons and polishing my boots to meet my father's exacting standards, as well as fetching and carrying for him when he was unwell. Our cooks and housemaids, lacerated by his ferocious tongue, came and went in rapid succession. The training in self-sufficiency was to stand me in good stead in later life, but this I could not foresee. I was afraid of my father, for I seemed to be blamed for everything

I said or did, especially for making the slightest noise when he was resting. I kept out of his way when I could, only to be summoned by his cracked, hoarse voice to perform some service. Craig-derw had become a prison for a despondent man and a frightened boy. We received no visitors except from the doctor and, occasionally, the rector. Before the coming of the wireless, let alone television, evenings and Sundays were interminable. I read books borrowed from the school library. My father, who seldom read anything, regularly condemned my choice as 'trash'.

I went to school in Bala; there was a school in the small village closer to Craig-derw, but my father disapproved of the teacher for reasons which escape my memory, if indeed they were ever explained to me. I had to walk the three miles to the town, toiling up the steep hill as I returned. I found it difficult to make friends at the school, partly because I was not good at games, partly because of a certain social gulf between the Hughes-Talbots and most of the local people, and no doubt partly because unhappiness had induced in me a shy, guarded manner which was interpreted as 'stuck-up'. My best friend – virtually my only friend – was Jacob Hughes (there were six boys in the form called Hughes). His father, Hughes the Bread, was the local baker and was also a Baptist lay preacher admired for his eloquence. At the age of seven, Jacob had broken a leg when the pony-cart, used for deliveries, overturned. He was left with a permanent limp which debarred him from games, and we shared a contempt for football which set us apart from the other boys. Otherwise, we did not have much in common. Following his father, Jacob was a fervent adherent of Baptist doctrines; the Hughes-Talbots belonged to the Church of Wales and my own faith was not at all strong. (I felt that God had cheated me by sending my father back in such a damaged state.) Jacob was a studious boy, top of the class in most subjects; I made no great efforts, since I was destined to manage the farm regardless of my scholastic record. Thus, it would be an exaggeration to say that we were kindred spirits or bosom friends. Certainly I had no inkling that Jacob was to become my brother-in-law. I do not recall taking notice of Martha Hughes, a little girl six years my junior.

When I was thirteen, my father sent me to boarding-school. This was an English rather than a Welsh custom and an innovation in our family. He may have thought it suitable for the son of an officer (since the war, he had always been called Major Hughes-Talbot or 'the Major'); he may simply have preferred to be alone at Craig-derw. I went to a bad, minor public school which I shall forbear to name. I hated it from the first day. I fagged for a sadistic sixth-former who beat me on the slightest excuse, and I was as frightened of him as of my father; it would be best to omit his name too, since he has made a successful political career. When my fagging year was over life became more bearable, but I went through the school in a thoroughly undistinguished way. I was useless at cricket and rugger, which at a school of that type mattered much more than anything else, and no more than average in the classroom. Only in the Officers' Training Corps did I earn a modicum of respect; I have always been a good shot, the one attainment that ever earned me commendation from my father. Eventually I reached the sixth form and was given a fag, a nasty little boy whom nobody else wanted. I think I can say that I did not beat him without just cause, but when I did beat him it gave me a distinct satisfaction.

In the holidays, I spent as much time as possible out of doors, and necessarily alone. My avocations were training dogs to respond to the whistle, shooting partridges, and fishing. My father was gradually becoming an invalid, as the damp climate made his injured lungs weaker and weaker. For days at a time, he did not stir from his armchair by the fireside. His racking bouts of coughing interrupted him whenever he spoke more than a couple of sentences, greeted me when I returned to the house, and kept me awake at night. He was, inevitably, more cantankerous than ever. He had a number of grievances, over which he mulled endlessly and which he laboured when I wanted to read or listen to the wireless (it had arrived by this time).

(1) The collapse of farm prices gave him a fixed idea that he was heading for bankruptcy. He warned me every year that he could not go on paying my school fees, and was not consoled when I replied that I did not care. Refusing to accept that his troubles were caused by general economic conditions, he maintained that he was being cheated by merchants and middlemen. If I could bring him, now and again, to admit that others in his position were doing poorly, this proved that the country was going to the dogs. 'I risked my life every day in the trenches, and what for? Eh? What for?' The Germans had been allowed to dodge paying reparations, the Americans were squeezing us out of world markets, the Bolsheviks were undermining the loyalty of the British working man. If the coughing permitted, he added denunciations of Hollywood films, jazz, modern art, birth control and short skirts.

(2) He believed that he was receiving less than his rightful due as a disability pension. Perhaps he was; the authorities were generally mean towards ex-servicemen. I rather think that, out of pride, he had understated his degree of disability in the first place, and bureaucracy prevented a revision as his condition grew worse. I helped him to write his letters to the Ministry, which occupied much of his time, and tried to interpret the replies, but I never got to the bottom of the question. For him, it was part of the betrayal of his generation.

(3) He thought that Dr Rees – described as 'that bloody quack' – was failing to give him proper attention. I was more than half convinced, indeed, that Rees was not a good doctor. He had allowed my mother and her infant to die, he had set Jacob's leg badly, and he certainly was unable to help my father. But if I urged my father to consult a specialist in London, he merely said that the expense would ruin him.

(4) He regarded all signs of change in the neighbourhood as threats to our traditional way of life. Some houses in Bala

and along the lake had been bought by strangers – retired people, or people with private incomes, from various parts of England. Here and there, picturesque old cottages had been acquired as holiday and weekend residences. Cars appeared even on our narrow local road, inconveniencing people who still went about on horseback. My father violently resented this intrusion. Although he had for years seen very few people, he liked to assume that he would recognize anyone who crossed his path, and that everyone knew and respected 'the Major'. He could never have adjusted himself to the process that has gathered pace in subsequent decades: the transformation of North Wales into a tourist playground.

Once, when I had walked with my father down the drive of Craig-derw to the road, a motor cycle skidded to a halt. It was ridden by a young man in a loud jacket, with a girl on the pillion. The young man asked the way to Llanuwchllyn, mispronouncing it horribly. My father started to reply, but was overtaken by a fit of coughing. 'Spit it up, old cock!' the young man shouted. The girl giggled. My father shook his stick in impotent rage; the machine roared and pulled away in a cloud of stinking blue smoke. As we stood there, I saw tears in my father's eyes.

Often, I felt desperately sorry for my father. His grievances, I had to concede even though their repetition exasperated me, were far from groundless. The world in which he had grown up was, indeed, slipping away beneath his feet. He depended on me although he could not help rebuffing and alienating me; he had no one else and he must have known that he was generally disliked, by his employees in particular. I wanted to feel respect and affection for him, as a son should for a father. Yet the respect was hard to muster, when I could not but see him as pathetic, or even ridiculous; so was the affection, when he incessantly found fault with me. There were times when I hated him, and then I was appalled to find this hatred in my heart. I realized that it would have been better for him – and better for me, though I should never have believed it – if he had lost not his health but his life in the trenches.

When I left school at eighteen, I expected that I should soon have to shoulder sole responsibility for Craig-derw. Dr Rees took me aside and warned me solemnly that my father was not long for this world. But this was another example of Dr Rees's limited medical expertise; my father lived for eight more years.

During those years, nothing changed for the better. I exerted myself to keep the farm going, a task that become harder with the onset of the world depression. I made an effort to keep on good terms with people in the vicinity, sometimes drank in the bar of the White Lion in Bala, and made a few superficial friendships. My father, characteristically, did not concede my right to go where I pleased until I was twenty-one. After that, I was able to take short holidays and find some relief from the melancholy atmosphere of my home. I went for summer weekends to Barmouth, a popular resort not far away. Before the era of caravan sites, its streets were lined with hotels and boarding-houses. At longer intervals, I spent four or five days in London. Jacob, now a teacher employed by the London County Council, guided me round the museums. He would not have approved of the rest of my programme, which consisted of seeing films and the 'hit' musical comedy of the season, and of strolling at night in the animated streets of the West End. Accordingly, although Jacob had a spare bed, I stayed at a modest hotel near Paddington Station.

I must now, since I have undertaken to write with complete frankness, describe the least creditable aspect of my life at this period. Perhaps because I had been starved of natural affection, my sexual desires ever since adolescence had been extremely powerful. In the school dormitory, I lay awake in the small hours conjuring up lustful visions of women's bodies. I had never seen a woman's body, of course, but a glimpse of one of the kitchen-maids through the swing doors of the dining-hall was enough to stir my imagination. Sometimes I felt that I should explode unless the demands of the flesh secured gratification. I might even have descended to homosexual practices, which were far from uncommon at that school, had not my fag been so peculiarly unattractive.

Back at Craig-derw, these urgings became still more intense. The nights would have presented a strange picture to an all-seeing observer – my father miserably wheezing or shuddering in a recurrence of his nightmare, his son convulsively relieving the sexual tension. I meditated seductions of most of the girls in Bala, if I had merely seen them in the street or serving in a shop. But they were all innocent and respectable, or at least I did not know which were not. Besides, I was shy and had no idea of how to strike up the right kind of conversation.

I had greater hopes of Barmouth. I used to stay at a cheap boarding-house, but I drank at the best hotel. The barmaid was a pretty dark-haired girl with a distinctly pleasing figure. I picked up her name, which was Nora; she was an Irish girl from Liverpool. She always greeted me with a smile, remembered what I drank, and exchanged a few bright remarks, but she behaved in the same friendly way to all the customers and I did not venture to imagine that she was especially glad to see me, although she certainly had her place in my fantasies of conquest.

The hotel faced the sea, and on warm summer nights it was my habit, after the bar closed, to linger on the promenade and smoke a cigarette (I did not smoke at home). One night, as I leaned on the sea-wall and watched clouds chasing each other across the moon, I felt a hand resting lightly on my arm. Unbelievably, Nora was with me.

'I saw you from my window,' she said. 'I've seen you other nights too.'

I managed to say: 'It's nice by the sea.'

'It is. But you looked so lonely.'

'Well, I'm by myself here.'

She gave me one of her delightful smiles. 'Girls can be lonely too,' she said.

I must have kissed her very clumsily, having never kissed

anyone before, but also very ardently. She pulled herself away with a gasp and said: 'Take it easy, now.'

We crossed the promenade and went round to the back of the hotel, where it was dark. After some more kisses, she murmured: 'I've got the key to the tradesmen's entrance.' When we were inside, she cautioned me to be very quiet and take off my shoes. I followed her up six flights of stairs to her attic room. The rest can be imagined. I left at six in the morning in a state between exultation and incredulity. As I ate my bacon and eggs at the boarding-house, I could easily have been convinced that the night had been one of my fantasies.

It was repeated on the following night, however, and thereafter whenever I went to Barmouth. Nora's willingness, amounting to eagerness, astonished me. It had never occurred to me that women derived pleasure from intercourse as well as men. I was astonished, too, by her utterly carefree attitude. I had no deep religious convictions, as I have mentioned, but I believed that what we were doing was sinful, or at least I expected a girl to think so. I once asked her if she did not. She laughed and said: 'Hush, darling – that's for priests and old women.' I asked whether she believed in God. 'Of course,' she answered. 'But if He didn't want us to do this He'd have made us differently, wouldn't he?'

When I reappeared in Barmouth after a month or two, Nora asked whether I had been 'keeping it busy' – this was her phrase – with some girl or other in Bala. She found it hard to believe that I had not. 'Go on – a handsome fellow like you!' she exclaimed. 'Those girls must be blind.' I had never supposed that I was handsome, but Nora declared that I had 'lover's eyes', 'kissing lips', and other desirable attributes. My self-esteem increased considerably.

I never asked Nora whether she took other men to her room when I was not available. Common sense indicated that she was far from a novice in sexual matters. Her praise of my virility indicated standards of comparison. She was utterly immoral by any accepted definition, obviously, and since she did not expect me to be faithful to her, it was unlikely that she was faithful to me. Certainly, I could never have introduced her to a friend whose good opinion I valued, such as Jacob. I could not avoid the conclusion that my connexion with this alluring but shameless creature was ultimately contaminating: that it was rendering me unfit for the respectable girl whom I would some day marry.

For more than a year, I told myself repeatedly that I must break with Nora. It is doubtful whether I should ever have had the strength of mind to do so, for I missed her acutely in my solitary room at Craig-derw. But, arriving at Barmouth as usual one Friday evening, I found a different girl behind the bar. The hotel manager told me that he had dismissed Nora after catching her going upstairs with a man. 'I can't have that, you know, Mr Hughes-Talbot. I've got my licence to think of.' I should have been relieved, my task accomplished for me; instead, my heart sank. I did not dare to ask where Nora had gone. I hoped for a letter from her, but never received one.

My next visit to London was due not long afterwards. As I wandered through the streets, I felt desperately lonely – more lonely among the crowds than ever on the empty hills of Wales. I created a fantasy of bumping into Nora, for it seemed reasonable that she might have gone to London, and caught myself staring at girls who looked something like her. Desire for her gripped me like a physical pain: or was it, I wondered, merely desire for a woman? I was surrounded by women, of whom thousands in the big city were doubtless as blithely immoral as Nora, but I was doomed to watch them getting into taxis or entering late restaurants with other men. I still knew not a soul in London except Jacob. Eventually, one of the women who vaguely resembled Nora met my glance with an inviting smile. I went to her flat with a feeling that nothing made any difference now. She complimented me in almost Nora's tone of voice: 'My, my, you know how to make a girl happy, don't you, love?'

I must confess that recourse to the services of a prostitute became a regular feature of my visits to London, generally on my last night in the capital. I always hoped, and half-intended, to go home without it, and yet with part of my mind I looked forward to it. In any case, it was so easy. In those days, they stood thickly on the pavements of certain streets and one had to make a deliberate effort to evade them. They must have recognized me as a lonely provincial youth, an obvious prey. The blatantly mercenary nature of the transaction was repugnant, and so was the absence of any personal relationship. No matter how much the woman pretended to like me, or perhaps actually did like me, I knew that she would have forgotten me in a couple of days. Yet this also gave me a sense of freedom, for I could forget her too, and the problem of how to break with her did not exist. I was ashamed, and disgusted with myself, but I tried to assure myself that I was merely relieving a compelling physical demand. As Nora had said, God should have made me differently.

On one of my visits to London, I found that the second room in Jacob's little flat was occupied by his youngest sister, Martha. It was then quite usual for young Welsh girls, as well as men, to migrate to the cities in order to find employment. Jacob could be trusted to look after Martha, or so it was assumed, and he was naturally glad to have her company and entrust the duties of housekeeping to her. He had found her a job in a branch of Woolworth's.

Martha was then eighteen, and I was twenty-four. I saw her only once, during my customary visit to Jacob for Sunday lunch, and she spoke little. In a sense, she made no impression on me; in another sense, she made a profound impression which had, if I may so express it, a delayed-action effect. She was not what one called a pretty girl, certainly not in an eye-catching manner. I think – perhaps because I did not see her again for over a year – that she became beautiful with the transition from girlhood to womanhood. But an inner beauty was perceptible in the candour of her blue eyes, in her serious and attentive manner as she played the part of hostess, in the music of her soft voice. Thus, the impression implanted in me was one of sweetness, of unaffected good nature, of a purity and innocence so absolute as to be a positive quality. On my last night in London, when I had my usual intimacy with a prostitute, I felt more than ever disgusted with myself. Reproachful faces seemed to hover above the bed: my suffering father, the ghost of my loving mother, my high-principled friend Jacob, and the innocent girl.

It was clear to me at this time that the solution to my problems lay in marriage. I now considered the local girls, not with dreams of seduction, but as possible objects of an honourable courtship. In theory, there should have been no great difficulty. The name of Hughes-Talbot made me the most acceptable match in the neighbourhood, and I could believe without undue vanity that I was a handsome fellow. The insuperable obstacle was my father. He was still the head, and the autocratic head, of the household. I could not subject any young woman to living at close quarters with his perpetual bad temper and his endless reiteration of grievances. His coughing alone would be unbearable to someone not inured to it. Besides, marriage meant children, or ought to mean children – children who would have to be hushed whenever he demanded it, and who would grow up as frightened of him as I had been. There was no way out of the difficulty. Craig-derw was my home and my responsibility; I could not think of leaving it. My father was still only fifty years old, Dr Rees's predictions were not to be relied on, and for all that I could tell he might live another twenty years.

About six months after my first meeting with Martha, I came face to face with Jacob at the door of the Post Office in Bala, where I had gone to cash the money order for my father's pension. I was naturally surprised to see him, since it was term-time. I believe that he had not intended to apprise me of his presence at home, but he was obliged to muster a smile and a greeting. I asked him facetiously whether he had been sacked by the LCC, which did not amuse him. Lowering his voice, he said that he would explain what he was doing in Bala if I would promise to keep what he was about to tell me absolutely secret. I gave the promise. I am now breaking it for the first time, and only because Martha has decided to divulge everything in her past.

Martha, I learned, was to become the mother of an illegitimate child. She had adamantly refused to give the name of her seducer. 'If I knew it,' Jacob said, 'may the Lord forgive me, but I'd kill him.' All she had told him was that the man also worked for Woolworth's, and was married. Jacob, blaming himself bitterly for not having kept a closer watch on her, recognized his duty to help her in any way that was possible. Of course, abortion was then illegal, nor was it a solution that Jacob could have reconciled with his conscience. Advised by the minister of the chapel that he attended, he had got in touch with an institution where young women in Martha's predicament stayed to go through their pregnancies and bear their children, which were then adopted. The cost was considerable; this was why Jacob had been obliged to inform his father of the situation, since it would be necessary to draw on the family savings.

After the birth, it had been decided, Martha was to come home. She still appeared to be fond of the baby's father, and it was essential that she should have no chance of seeing him again. People in Bala would be told that she had spent the intervening months in a tuberculosis sanatorium. This was plausible enough; TB had ceased to be a lethal illness, but a 'patch on the lung', requiring months of treatment, was a fairly common occurrence.

I was appalled by what I heard. I could not help, with my knowledge of the conscienceless sexual voracity of the male, comparing myself with the man accused by Jacob. Often enough, I had meditated on how exciting it would be to trap this or that girl – Gwyneth Williams or Agnes Jones – in a secluded spot and overcome her resistance. But, I hastily reassured myself, it was not what I had done. There was a vast difference between taking one's pleasure with an already corrupted young woman like Nora, and destroying Martha's innocence. That was an act of cynical viciousness, of utterly selfish cruelty. And the man was married, too. As well as making Martha his victim, he had no feeling for his wife either. I was glad that I had never come into contact with such wickedness.

When Martha came home, I heard about it as one hears about everything in a small community, but I did not see her. The next event was that, somewhat to the surprise of those who knew him, Jacob announced that he was getting married. His choice had fallen on a teacher at the same school. I found, on making Margaret's acquaintance, that a pleasant manner compensated for her lack of physical attractions.

The wedding was at Bala. Jacob invited me to act as best man; the bridesmaids were his sisters, Ruth and Martha. Dressed in blue that matched her eyes, Martha somehow looked as sweet and even as pure as she had the year before. But now, I saw that she was beautiful.

From then on, I thought of her continually. There were many questions on which I pondered as I tried to shut my ears to my father's coughing. What marks had her ordeal left on that once trusting spirit? What could be the feelings of a young mother whose child is lost to her? Was it possible that she still felt some affection for the author of her misfortunes? Or was she hoping to turn towards a better future with a man who might offer her an honest love?

I saw her quite often. Indeed, it seemed to me that I saw her whenever I left the solitude of Craig-derw. Of course, it is no great coincidence to meet with any given person in a place as small as Bala. But when one is obsessed with that person, as I was becoming obsessed with Martha, some force other than chance appears to be at work.

I went to the Christmas party given by Sir Richard and

Lady Arbuthnot. Sir Richard, the retired Governor of Bombay (or was it Bengal?), had recently purchased one of the largest houses on the favoured southern shore of the lake. Since the Arbuthnots had a son at Oxford and a daughter at a musical academy, who came home for Christmas, they gave a party intended primarily for the younger generation. I was not eager to accept an invitation from people with whom I had nothing in common, but I did not wish to give offence by a refusal. I was a little surprised to see Ruth and Martha Hughes, the daughters of Hughes the Bread, among the guests. But the Arbuthnots were not snobs, and probably they thought that the attractive sisters would be an ornament to the occasion.

The carpet in the largest room had been rolled up for dancing to the gramophone. I had been chatting with Miss Arbuthnot, and when the music started I felt it polite to ask her to dance – not without trepidation, since I barely knew the steps. I acquitted myself adequately, and after fortifying myself with another glass of mulled wine I ventured to approach Martha. She partnered me for almost every dance. It was wrong of me to monopolize her, no doubt, but I could not bring myself to relinquish her to anyone else, and she seemed to be content. At a rather late hour, certainly by Bala standards, she said with a charming smile that her feet were getting tired in her new shoes. We went to sit down in the library, where a few of the older guests were talking. Soon we were alone; our lowered voices, and Martha's heightened colour when her eyes met mine, must have suggested to the other people that it would be tactful to withdraw. We fell silent, having no need for idle conversation. That silence, far from being uneasy, gave us assurance of the contentment that we found in being together.

I walked home and took no notice of the distance, which was over six miles. It was a beautifully clear, starlit night, and very cold. I felt so warm, nevertheless, that I opened my coat as I climbed the hill from Llanycil. I concluded that the mulled wine must have been stronger than I had imagined.

The truth was, though I did not yet recognize it, that I was in love with Martha.

After this, I could not restrain myself from contriving to see her whenever I was in Bala. I was entitled to a welcome at her home in my capacity as Jacob's friend, and it was soon obvious that I was not calling merely to sample the freshly-baked cakes. Her parents were shrewd enough to see that I was, as the phrase went, 'taking an interest'. They were not likely to discourage me, having two daughters to get off their hands. Once, when I met Mr Hughes out on his delivery-round, he stopped for a chat and mentioned with deliberate casualness that the patch on Martha's lung had completely disappeared. I had to conceal a smile, for Martha was the picture of unsullied good health. Never, even after we were man and wife, did I allow her to suspect that I knew about her misfortunes.

By the spring of 1935, not only was I fully aware of my love for her, but I could think of nothing else. I was confident, too, that she was on the way to loving me in return. I had visions of the perfect happiness, enduring to the end of life, that might be within our reach. In the dull, depressing evenings with my father, I imagined Martha seated in the chair opposite mine – coming through the door with flowers from the garden – filling the neglected house with new life. These were not the only visions. At night, I burned with longing to possess the soft, tender body which I had never seen, but of which I already seemed to know every contour.

Yet what was I to do? The more I loved her gentleness and her sweetness, the more impossible it was to put her to the harsh test of sharing a home with my father. To persuade her into secret, illicit intimacy was equally unthinkable; even at the cost of losing her, I would not treat her as she had been treated by the man I justly despised. I could not even tell her that I loved her, having nothing to propose to her except a restraint that might have become unbearable. I began to keep to the limits of Craig-derw to avoid occasions of meeting her. But, with the coming of unusually fine spring weather, this did not avail. Martha was fond of walking in the hills. A meeting where we were free from observation could offer greater temptations than a chat in the High Street. So, indeed, it turned out.

We met, thus, on an April afternoon so exceptionally warm that I was in shirt-sleeves and she in a summer dress. I had gone to an outlying part of the farm to confirm that the land, swampy in wet weather, had dried out enough to be suitable for sheep. As I was about to return, I saw Martha ascending a path which provided an alternative route from Bala to the higher ground. She waved to me cheerfully. I waited for her to approach; she smiled and said: 'Oh, I'm out of breath.'

'Have a rest,' I said. We sat down on the sloping turf a dozen yards from one of the little streams. The wind gently stirred the new leaves of a young oak tree; the water splashed over the stones; and there was one other sound – Martha's breathing, quickened by her climb and perhaps by an intuitive awareness that the moment was significant. On the delicate curve of her upper lip, I noticed a tiny bead of perspiration.

The sky was cloudless, and the outline of Arenig Fawr was remarkably distinct. Near the summit, there was still a small patch of snow, gleaming in the sunlight. I pointed this out. She gazed at the mountain for a few minutes; then she said, so quietly that she almost breathed the words: 'It's so lovely.' We looked at each other. We were both moved by the beauty of the scene; we both felt, I am sure, a sense of wonderment at what life had to offer. We moved closer together, not urgently but solemnly, and kissed.

By degrees, our kisses became more passionate. I do not know – or rather, I know well – what might have happened. But Martha moved in my embrace and said: 'There's somebody coming.' I released her and looked round. One of the farm labourers was hurrying toward us. I stood up and tried to look as though Martha's presence had nothing to do with me.

When the man was within shouting distance, he called: 'Mr David! Will you come down to the house, quick. It's the Major.'

I gave Martha a glance and a shrug, and ran. Dr Rees had been summoned and was already at the house. He soon told me that my father's life was nearing its end.

Unfortunate to the last, my poor father did not die easily. He gasped, choked and struggled, sometimes losing consciousness and then reviving to confront his agony, through the long afternoon and the longer night. Nowadays he would have been taken to hospital by ambulance, but I do not suppose that it would have made much difference. He tried to speak, but uttered nothing coherent. I caught the word 'Bloody . . . '; I was not to know at whom the imprecation was aimed. I sat beside him on the bed, attempting to comfort him as best I could. Dawn was ushering in another fine day when his convulsively shaking body seemed to crumple under my hand, and his miseries were over.

That day, I was conscious of the guiding hand of destiny. I grieved for my father – not for his death, which was surely a release, but for his sufferings – and yet I carried about with me a serene knowledge that life was just beginning for me. I sent Martha a note to give her the news and to say that I hoped for an opportunity to speak to her soon, but not until after the funeral. The day after my father was laid to rest in the graveyard of St Beuno's Church, my beloved entered Craig-derw for the first time. Apart from servants, no other woman had seen the inside of the house since the departure of my aunt sixteen years before. It seemed already to belong to Martha, to be waiting for her. I told her that I loved her deeply, explained what had prevented me from making this declaration earlier, and asked her to marry me. She gave her consent with a single, quietly spoken word, and it was sealed with kisses.

We agreed to keep our pledge to ourselves, for the sake of propriety, until a month had passed. It was then announced to her gratified family. Allowing Mrs Hughes the time she needed to make the wedding arrangements, we were married on the 24th of July, 1935. We had to leave the church under umbrellas, sheltering from what the Arbuthnots called 'the Welsh monsoon', but that could not mar our happiness. The honeymoon was spent at Llandudno. Martha had suggested Barmouth, but I dissuaded her from that choice. As it was the height of the season, Llandudno was crowded. Strolling one day along the front, Martha remarked that it was as lively as London.

That was forty-five years ago. Martha and I should now be within sight of our golden wedding. I could not know that our life together would last only a little more than four years. But, before I lost her through my own wicked madness, I knew the happiness of which I had dreamed since I began to love her – the only period of happiness, except for earliest childhood, that I have been granted. Every day seemed to bring a deepening and an enrichment of love. I sought, with constant affection and trust, to erase for Martha the memory of earlier events. If neither of us had come to the altar in the state of literal purity demanded by the strictest religious canons, what mattered was that our first experience of sincere love was in marriage.

Martha's marriage had a sobering effect on her sister Ruth, who was two years the elder. She was a flirtatious young lady, with a record of encouraging and disappointing a sequence of suitors. Making a wise decision, she married John Probert, a young doctor who had come to Bala as assistant to Dr Rees and was soon to take over the practice.

If, within an almost complete harmony of outlook, there was a point of difference between Martha and myself, it was that her disposition was more sociable. The guarded attitude formed by a friendless youth was too much a part of my nature to be discarded, whereas Martha had always been popular and sought-after. I regarded attendance at parties or dances as a duty, not a pleasure. Though I liked to keep on friendly terms with people I had known all my life, I saw no need to make new acquaintanceships. Especially, I wanted nothing to do with the strangers whose incursion I deplored, less furiously than my father but none the less emphatically. I did not mind the Arbuthnots, who had the good manners and the social tact that could have been expected from their background, but I could not welcome the assortment of retired accountants, stockbrokers, and people who had made quick profits in some dubious line of business. Most of these intruders settled on the sheltered shores of the lake, but a few appeared on the plateau. One Londoner acquired a cottage not far from the western boundary of my land – the cottage which he was to rent to Estelle Mavros.

The outsiders, in a tactless effort to make themselves acceptable, issued invitations far more freely than had hitherto been normal. The term 'cocktail party' entered our vocabulary. The conversation at these gatherings was loud, frivolous, and to my mind devoid of interest. Martha, however, did not share my views, or what she called my prejudices. She would declare, on the contrary, that someone I preferred to avoid was 'a really interesting person'. The disagreement was generally resolved by her going to the party without me. We bought a car soon after our marriage (my father had refused to have anything to do with motor transport) and Martha had no difficulty in passing the driving test. She invented excuses, when necessary, for my absence, but I am sure that she was more welcome alone than with her stiff, awkward husband.

The next event of importance to us, and the crown to our happiness, was the birth of our daughter on the 8th of December, 1936. From the time of our marriage, I was impatient for signs of a pregnancy and (in the light of what I knew) surprised that these were not apparent as soon as they might have been. Martha, though she looked forward to having a family, pointed out that at our age there was plenty of time, and said that she would not mind a couple of years in which our little world belonged to 'just us'. She believed that conception was more likely to result from an isolated act of intercourse than from 'keeping it up every night', a pleasure from which we could not have refrained. Whether there is any basis for this traditional belief, I do not know. In any case, we did not have to wait so long as to be overtaken by Ruth, a possibility of which Martha was jestingly warned by her mother.

I had my anxieties about the actual birth, like any loving husband; moreover, I could not banish the memory of my mother's fate from my thoughts. I reminded myself that Martha was strong and in unfailing good health. Also, she was to have the assistance of John Probert, Ruth's young and efficient husband, since Dr Rees now limited himself to his surgery. This was just as well; the baby decided to arrive during a wild snowstorm and the old doctor might have run more of a risk than Martha. The birth was as easy as it could possibly have been. John, who naturally supposed that it was Martha's first, expressed his astonishment that it was so quick.

We named the child Ann, adding Rachel as a middle name to conform to the Biblical tradition of the Hughes family. It was soon clear that she had inherited both her mother's beauty and her sweetness of nature. She was that rarity, a baby who never cried. Even my father would have softened toward her. As she grew, she was ahead of all expectations in talking and in dexterity with her toys, and we were able to rejoice in her intelligence too. She is now a professor of sociology – how strange it seems to a father who can envisage her only as a curly-haired toddler!

Picture me, then, endowed with every blessing that a man could desire: a beautiful and devoted wife, a delightful child, a much-loved home, an untarnished reputation. With all my heart, I wish that I could end my story there.

MARTHA

It starts here: I'm standing outside the boys' entrance to the school in Bala. Ruth is with me. We're little girls – I'm six, probably, and Ruth is eight. We're watching the boys.

It was a craze, for a year or so, to hang about near the boys' entrance until a teacher hustled us inside. For Ruth, at any age, boys were fascinating. But I think it was mainly that we wanted to go where we weren't supposed to be and stare at what, the teachers said, was none of our business.

The fun was that the boys were embarrassed, even the big boys. They had to pass a sort of picket-line, a dozen or so girls strung out along the pavement. Some of them got cross and told us we were being a nuisance; some grinned and tried to make a joke of it; some pretended not to notice, but unsuccessfully. There was just one boy who really took no notice. He moved steadily on as though he was alone on a country road – as though the girls didn't exist.

'He's stupid,' Ruth says.

I protest hotly: 'He's not! He's not!'

'He's the stupidest person in the whole wide world,' Ruth declares with eight-year-old superiority.

'He's not!' I don't understand why it's necessary for me to defend David Hughes-Talbot, who won't thank me, has no need of me, and has gone into school anyway. But I throw myself into the battle all the same.

'No,' Ruth concedes, 'there might be just one person who's stupider.'

Falling into her trap, as usual, I ask: 'Who?'

Ruth ponders, as though searching her memory, and says: 'You know, it must be Martha Hughes.' And runs off, screeching.

She was – is – twenty months older than me. We always shared a bedroom until we grew up and got married. When we were young, the house was crowded and we had no choice. Later, when two of our brothers left home, we could have asked to have rooms of our own. But we didn't.

We went through phases that bewildered our parents. For a time, we quarrelled incessantly, got on each other's nerves, went for days without speaking. Then we plunged into loving intimacy, talking past midnight, telling each other everything. Then, abruptly, we couldn't stand each other again. Only one thing didn't vary: Ruth was prettier, cleverer and luckier than me. I was the one who got found out, got into trouble. Then Ruth put on a shocked face, as though she couldn't possibly have done what I'd done – but I knew she had.

When I was six, David must have been twelve. But I didn't ever think of him as a boy, even a big boy. Not a boy who kicked stones along the High Street and pulled girls' pigtails. Sometimes, though not often, he came into our bakery after school, because he was friends with my brother Jacob. He accepted one of the Welsh cakes that our Mam offered, and no more; he wouldn't be drawn into talk; he didn't smile. I couldn't connect a boy with such silence and such gravity.

Certain things about him puzzled me. One was his name. I grasped that you had a surname, such as Hughes, and a Christian name to make you different from all the other people called Hughes. You might have two Christian names, like our Dad who was Abraham John Hughes. But I didn't see how you could have two surnames – Hughes-Talbot. When I asked our Mam about it, she laughed and said: 'They're special, that's what it is.'

What did this mean? It meant that they lived in a big house and had miles of land. David's father had a mysterious title, 'the Major'; that was certainly special. But once, when David had just left the bakery, my Dad said to my Mam:

'Poor boy, he calls for our pity.' (This sounds more solemn in Welsh, enhanced by Dad's pulpit manner, than it does in English.) How was it possible that we were to pity David Hughes-Talbot?

I had the answer, or an important part of the answer, when I realized that David had no family except for his father, the Major. For me, this was almost inconceivable. Everybody I knew had so many relations that you had trouble remembering them all and where they fitted in. I was the youngest of a family of six. My sister Esther, the eldest, had been married as far back as I could remember; so, while I was still a child, I had nephews and neices as well as having uncles and aunts and cousins. Then there were my three brothers, Adam, Jacob and Gideon, and then Ruth. I took it as a law of life that rooms were always full, I was lucky to get near the fire, I had to press for attention if I wanted to be listened to, and at meal-times I was tormented by the aroma from the other plates before I was served.

The pivot of the family was our Mam, whom I recall only as a solid, matriarchal figure – naturally, considering that she was forty-three when I was born. I knew children who had no fathers, on account of the war or of some disastrous accident, but I could scarcely imagine having no mother. David had no mother. When I got to know this, it fully explained why he called for our pity. There would have been nobody to bandage him when he cut himself, or make him a hot drink when he'd been out in the rain, or cuddle him if he woke up with a bad dream, because fathers didn't do that kind of thing. I loved my Dad, but it was clear to me – as it was then clear to all children, in rural Wales anyway – that fathers stood for authority and mothers for reassurance. I began to understand the sources of David's silence. When I was a bit older, and had picked up some gossip about what a grim old tyrant the Major was, I understood still better.

I was still a little girl when David was sent away to a boarding-school in England. In our part of the world it was most unusual for a boy to go to a public school, even if his parents could afford it. Gideon, who was the comic of the family, used to put on a posh accent like the man who read the news on the wireless and ask Jacob: 'Seen your jolly old pal Hughes-Talbot lately, what?' Jacob hated being teased, and must have hated the implication that he kept up his friendship with David out of snobbery.

Without David, however, he'd have had few or no friends, for almost everybody disliked him. He walked in a lop-sided way which, while of course it wasn't his fault – he'd broken his right leg and it was permanently shorter than his left – seemed to give accurate warning of his warped character; he had a coldness of the heart that didn't belong to our family. Why David was friendly with Jacob is more of a puzzle. He must have wanted a friend who, like himself, was apart from the herd.

Once at least in every school holiday, David came to our house. Jacob couldn't have walked up to Craig-derw because of his bad leg, and I doubt if the Major would have let him in. I gazed at David with a curiosity that didn't diminish. I saw a young man who looked less than ever like a boy. In his teens, he was already tall and, with his serious manner, impressively grown-up. What he saw, of course, was a child. I might as well say that he didn't see me at all.

Then David finished school and was at Craig-derw all the time. This didn't mean that I saw him more often, because Jacob was away at teachers' training college. I have a memory from that time. I was fourteen years old, and in a phase of adolescent despair. My body seemed to be growing out of control. I was suddenly covered with rolls of fat, and I was embarrassed by the appearance of breasts which felt like flabby, clumsy appendages. Ruth was slender and the right shape everywhere, as I observed enviously when we undressed at night. Boys were interested in her – I was sure they would never be interested in me. We were on bad terms, the worst ever. The effect of all this was a need to be alone, which was something new for me. I used to go for long walks on the hills. The family thought I was insane; country people don't walk unless they have to go somewhere.

On one of these walks, I noticed a flock of sheep dashing about in a panic. A dog was trying to round them up, and a man was whistling to the dog. It was David. I was on his land, though I hadn't realized it. The dog was obviously young and at an early stage of training. It didn't circle round the sheep but dashed into the midst of them, which is just what a dog shouldn't do. But David didn't get annoyed or impatient. He made the dog settle on the ground and gave it a lecture on the principles of sheep-herding. This, as David was able to prove to me in later years, isn't as silly as it sounds. The dog doesn't literally understand what you say, but you instil a reflex of attentiveness. It may be, also, that the Welsh are so fond of talking that they'd rather talk to dogs than to nobody. But this wouldn't apply to David.

I walked over and said: 'He's got a lot to learn, hasn't he?' David said: 'Yes.' That was all he said. I stood around for a few minutes, hopping awkwardly from one foot to the other, waiting for him to ask what was the news from Jacob, or something, but he didn't. So I said goodbye and went on with my walk. I was furious, and then miserable. I now realize that David had simply failed to recognize me. This plump girl with floppy breasts must have looked utterly different from the child who formed his picture of Jacob's little sister. But what I thought at the time was that he didn't consider me worth talking to – I was less worthy of his interest than a dog.

I brooded on this for days. I'm not sure, looking back, whether I was beginning to be in love with David. I know that he was important to me. He represented the adult world, in which I yearned to be accepted. My family didn't treat me seriously; that's normally the fate of the youngest, and I was behaving foolishly a lot of the time. But I thought that David ought to treat me seriously, because he was an immensely serious person. I couldn't get over being dismissed by him as utterly insignificant.

Years later, after we were married, I spoke to David about

this incident. He was completely unable to remember it.

I didn't speak to David again for four years. If he came to our house while Jacob was at home, I skipped up to the bedroom. If I saw him in the street, I crossed to the opposite pavement. What this meant, I must have known in moments of honesty, was that I never ceased to be conscious of him, but I'd have been indignant if anybody had pointed this out.

Around sixteen, I was managing to cope with the world more successfully. Ruth and I had another phase of being on warm, close terms – the last, as it turned out. Boys were interested in me, too, so we could happily compare notes instead of being divided by my jealousy. I had come to terms with my appearance, which helped. I was resigned to never being slender, as Ruth was slender, but most of my puppy-fat had melted away and I could count on what was called a well-developed figure.

We had one absorbing interest and one inexhaustible subject of conversation – boys. In those days one didn't 'talk about sex'; one 'talked about boys'. This didn't mean that we were innocent, still less ignorant. More than one friend, not much older than Ruth, had gone to the altar from necessity, and if we blamed the young men who were responsible it was for a failure to be careful. But physical facts were transmuted in our talk into emotional states. If one of us described being kissed by a certain boy, the other might ask: 'Did he get passionate?' This was well understood to mean 'Did he have an erection?', but such a choice of words would have been felt as, shall I say, a misplaced emphasis. I still think, despite the change of style to which my daughters have accustomed me, that there was much to be said for our conventions.

So we talked about boys: thrilling boys, nice-but-dull boys, amusing boys, repulsive boys, ridiculous boys. . . . It's extraordinary that there should have been such a variety of boys in a place the size of Bala, but so it was, or so we persuaded ourselves. Anyway, the material for our midnight chats never ran out.

We would never have talked like this about David. The

boys whose kisses we relished – or yearned for, or evaded – were all roughly our own age, and so familiar from years at the local school that we could like them or even love them, but not admire them. They were *boys*; David was a man.

On the other hand, I shouldn't have been astonished by the forecast that I might ultimately be married to David. Barring accidents, a girl expected to nave her fun with the boys and then marry a man older than herself by the significant margin of, roughly, five years. Bala hadn't abandoned the nineteenth-century idea that a husband was a sort of guardian, taking over from the girl's father. When I did marry David it was, in Bala terms, the most normal kind of marriage, assumed to be sensible and secure. But my sister and I, at the time I'm describing, weren't thinking about husbands, just about boys.

These patterns admitted of one variation: the long engagement. A young man and a girl might get engaged in order to make it clear that they were going steady. Once the announcement was made, he wasn't supposed to go out with other girls nor she with other boys. It might also be suspected that they were 'not waiting' (a typically Welsh code-phrase). This was sinful, in principle, but the engagement made it more pardonable. Marriage was deferred to the vague future, ostensibly because they were still young or they hadn't the money to set up a home, actually because they weren't entirely certain about it, or at least the girl wasn't. There was no stigma attached to breaking off the engagement, though a girl who broke off two or three engagements was considered to be overdoing it.

Ruth got engaged to a young man called Gwilym Jones. This caused some annoyance in the family, because it had been decided that she was going to London to keep house for Jacob, who was teaching there by this time. Ruth had suggested this plan herself and it was agreed to be a good idea; our Mam didn't need the help of two daughters at home. Then she said that she wouldn't go after all, because of

Gwilym. Dad took the line that a promise was a promise and she was letting Jacob down. He could guess, too, that the engagement wasn't serious and she would never marry Gwilym (indeed, she didn't). Just for once, Ruth had made a false step and I was the good girl.

Mam produced a solution: 'Martha can go instead.' She was always inclined to regard us as interchangeable. Normally, Dad wouldn't have permitted me to leave home at such an early age – I wasn't quite eighteen. But he had put so much stress on the obligation to Jacob that he had to agree. Without having expected it, or particularly wanted it, I found myself heading for London.

Jacob lived, and also taught, in Camden Town. It was far from being a classy neighbourhood; nowadays, I can hardly believe the prices asked for houses in streets that Jacob warned me to avoid. He had a basement flat – the euphemism 'garden flat' hadn't been invented. My room opened off a corridor, in which a stove and sink had been placed, and had one small window giving on to a yard. This yard was surrounded by brick walls and got practically no sun even at the height of summer, but a few straggly plants had dug themselves into cracks between the flagstones. The main room, where Jacob slept and carried on his minimal social life, was in the front of the house, below the street. You could stand by the window and see legs going past in various types of trousers or skirts, and I played the game of guessing what sort of people the legs belonged to. I could only play this game when Jacob was out, because he kept the curtains drawn. People could look in on us, he said. They would have had to kneel down, but there was no arguing with Jacob.

Years later, when I came to live in London with Alex, I learned how to manage in a big city. You have friends all over the place, and you don't mind travelling miles to see them; these expeditions give a sense of occasion. But when I was dumped in that basement flat, I badly missed the casual contacts of a small town. I thought it very strange and sad that Jacob didn't know the neighbours, or even the people upstairs. I also thought that it was a peculiarity of Jacob's. It was his natural impulse to draw curtains and lock doors.

But in London, it seemed, most people were afraid of somebody or other. Some were afraid of burglars, others were more afraid of the police. A girl of my age was supposed to be afraid of nearly everybody. It was a new experience for me to have to worry about going out alone. Fear was in the air – or, if not exactly fear, a distrustful wariness that hung about like fog.

Life didn't open out for me when I came to London, then, but narrowed in. I missed being surrounded by friends, I missed gossipy chat, and of course I missed boys. I had been used to spending a little time with a boy – a bit of joking and teasing, a few kisses more likely than not – practically every day of the week. It meant nothing serious, but it gave me a certain warmth, a certain tenderness, which grew in importance when I lost them. Back at home, Ruth had everything that I didn't have. She had more, indeed, for I was sure that Ruth and Gwilym were 'not waiting'. I felt that I had been checked in a natural progress which my sister was pursuing. Jacob treated me like a child, insisted on my being home at a fixed time, and was always telling me what to do and what not to do. I thought it was unfair – surely, if I was working for my living and in charge of the flat, I must be more grown-up and trustworthy, not less. So I was ready for a gesture of rebellion.

Jacob had found me a job in Woolworth's, or rather he'd found it for Ruth and I took it on. I stood behind a counter from Monday morning to Saturday evening (Thursday afternoons off) and sold pencils, pencil-sharpeners and india-rubbers. Ballpoint pens didn't yet exist. I didn't mind working in a shop; it was what a girl of my age would be doing in Bala if she worked at all. But in Bala I'd have overcome the tedium by chatting to the customers. A shop assistant's day consisted, you might say, of a series of visits. At Woolworth's in Camden Town, the customers were total strangers and the only possible chatting was with the other girls. The girls did chat incessantly, clustering together and ignoring customers for as long as possible – a tradition which, I notice when I go into a Woolworth's nowadays, has been handed down from generation to generation.

I tried to chat with these London girls, but I couldn't get into the way of it. They talked about boys, of course; but they were talking about boys in general, not about known and named boys of flesh and blood, so it wasn't very interesting. I couldn't understand their London slang, or pick the words out of their slovenly mumbling and gabbling, while they couldn't understand my Welsh accent, or claimed that they couldn't. Besides, I was disgusted by their grovelling humility toward the manager and the supervisors, whom they actually hated. I was brought up in a more independent spirit. On the other hand, they thought that I was currying favour by attending to customers without the traditional delay. In short, there was no understanding between me and the London girls, and therefore no friendship.

One of the staff was a young man called Mr Morshead. He used to walk round the store several times a day, examine the goods on the counters, and make notes on a clipboard which he carried. I never discovered the point of this activity. When I started going out with Mr Morshead – Peter – the last thing we wanted to talk about was our place of work. But the girls had decided that he was a snooper, so they were as rude to him as they dared. If he addressed a friendly word to one of them, she either pretended that she hadn't heard or snapped back with a bad-tempered 'Whassay?'. Derisive giggles followed him as he went on his way. He was a shy, worried-looking young man, and obviously he couldn't think what he'd done to become unpopular.

I decided to be nice to Mr Morshead. I knew that my breach of the united front would make me as unpopular as he was, but I didn't care. To begin with, it didn't occur to me to think of him as I thought of the boys in Bala. My masculine ideal was tall and strong; he was scarcely any taller than me and looked distinctly soft. He had very fair hair, a rather absurd little moustache, and a weak chin. He was older than me (so I assumed, since he had this relatively responsible job) but I didn't think he was much older. I was astonished, later, when he told me that he was twenty-four. It was his pale colouring and smooth cheeks that misled me, but also his timid, ineffectual personality.

Still, there were no other boys on the horizon and – ridiculously, in this huge city – no prospect of finding any. I was under strict orders from Jacob to be at home in the evenings. Once, when I went on my own to see a film I was keen on, he refused to believe that there'd been nobody with me and we had a nasty scene. According to Jacob, I wasn't forbidden to go out with young men, but any young man who asked me was to be invited to Sunday tea and subjected to scrutiny. It was only reasonable, he said, that he should be able to assure our parents that I was keeping the right sort of company. I felt that if a boy had to be inspected by Jacob – and, still more, if the boy was approved of by Jacob – the whole thing was spoilt from the start.

I discovered, by trial and error, that I could do what I liked in the early evening: that is, from five-thirty when I finished work to seven-thirty, when Jacob had done his marking for school and was ready for supper. If I said that I'd been with the other girls from work, he believed me. Actually, I was with Peter – in the tea-shop near Woolworth's, or in the cinema, or in the park if it was fine. Once I'd started on my policy of being nice to him, it soon followed that we were friends outside. I could always, at this stage and at later stages, get Peter to do what I wanted. Most of the attraction, to begin with, was that I was fooling Jacob.

It seemed silly to be with a boy without being kissed, so I got Peter into this habit too. We kissed as boys and girls do in London, in shop doorways or in the back row of the cinema. There was always that feeling of wariness about it, as though somebody might snatch your handbag or cosh you on the back of the head if you got too absorbed. Peter kissed in a somewhat tentative manner, not at all like the boys in Bala. I sensed that he wasn't sure what we meant to each other, and it worried him. I found his gentleness touching, if it wasn't exciting. The best phrase for what we'd slipped into would be, I think, a sentimental friendship. Maybe there was more friendship than sentiment; we certainly weren't in love. Like me, Peter didn't find London a friendly place (he came from Dorset). We were consoling each other.

'We're never alone,' I complained once after two chattering middle-aged women had invaded our corner table at the tea-shop. Then I had an idea. There was nobody in the flat on Thursday afternoons; it was a half-day at Woolworth's, but Jacob was teaching. And the flat was only ten minutes' walk from Woolworth's. Peter, I knew, lived in Hornsey and had a long bus journey to work.

Lying on the bed in my cosy room, I felt that we had secured for ourselves a little zone of liberated territory. I don't know that I was any more excited by Peter's kisses than before, but I was excited by the opportunity I'd created. I whispered to him that he could do whatever he liked. He said: 'Well, Martha . . . ' It was typical of Peter that he hadn't equipped himself, though he'd had plenty of time since I'd explained my idea to him. I said: 'Well, mind you see to that by next Thursday.'

Next Thursday, Peter duly became my lover. I use this word in a technical sense, since there was no change in the terms of our sentimental friendship. I never imagined that my future would be bound up with his – this was something we didn't talk about – but I counted with confidence on an indefinite sequence of Thursday afternoons, the high-point of my otherwise boring life. There seemed to be no risk of Jacob finding out, since neither Peter nor I got so ecstatic as to forget the time.

While I was carrying on with Peter, I saw David again. He used to go to London once or twice a year, apparently, and he came to the flat for Sunday dinner. It was the first time that I'd ever been with him for more than a few minutes, and yet it seemed perfectly obvious that he always had been and always would be the most important person in my life. I was filled, as much as ever, by my awareness of him as someone special. And this was all mixed up with an intense awareness of him as a man. He was tall and strong and (the old photos, which I've never thrown away, confirm my memories) tremendously good-looking. Sitting across the small gate-leg table from him, I was assailed by wave after wave of what Jacob would have called lustful thoughts. If going to bed with Peter was satisfying, which it was, whatever could it be like with David? Just imagining it brought me out in a hot flush.

I prayed that he wouldn't look at me too closely and guess what I was thinking. But what was happening was worse: he took practically no notice of me. I was still a nobody to him – still merely Jacob's little sister. I racked my brains to find something intelligent and grown-up to say, but nothing came. Then, as I was asking him to have some more potatoes or something, I realized that, without thinking about it, I was speaking in Welsh. Jacob frowned, and David checked a smile; we'd been talking English. After that, I didn't trust myself to open my mouth, and avoided David's eyes if he glanced in my direction. As soon as he left, I dashed into my room, lay down on the bed, and sobbed and sobbed.

I thought about David incessantly as I stood behind my counter at Woolworth's, but I soon had something else to think about, because I missed my period. I was puzzled by this, rather than alarmed. Peter and I had been careful right along, so I couldn't possibly be pregnant. I supposed that there must be something wrong with my system, probably due to London food. However, when I missed another period I decided to see a doctor. This, luckily, didn't present any problem. Woolworth's had an arrangement with a local doctor, a woman, and I had been sent to see her when I fell on the stairs in the stockroom and sprained my wrist. She had a brisk but kindly manner, and I thought that she would soon find out what was the matter with me and put me onto the right kind of tonic.

When she told me that I was pregnant, I stared at her and said: 'I can't be.' She explained that no form of birth control was more than ninety per cent effective, and I'd been unlucky. Still in a state of shock, because it was so utterly unfair, I said: 'We've only done it about six times, too – we've only got Thursday afternoons.' This made her laugh, of course, but then she warned me earnestly not to do anything silly, because time was getting along and it could be dangerous. Considering how abortions were performed in those days (at least, within the price-range of Woolworth's employees) I've no doubt that this was good advice. But it didn't tell me what I could do.

I walked round the park and tried to reconcile myself to marrying Peter. He was the sort who would undoubtedly 'do the right thing'. I wasn't in love with him, I knew that I'd be bored with him after a few months under the same roof, I didn't want to spend my life in London, and it was hard to renounce all dreams of capturing a man like David Hughes-Talbot. I persuaded myself to look on the bright side – Peter had no vices, indeed he was good and kind, it would work out as well as most marriages. Besides, I'd be getting away from Jacob. I needn't have bothered with these reflections. When I got a chance to talk to Peter, he told me with an air of some embarrassment that he was already married. In fact, he had two children.

I said: 'Well, it's a week of surprises all right.' But I saw no reason for blaming Peter. I had been the eager one right along, so he wasn't obliged to mention this inconvenient fact, and he might reasonably suppose that I could guess at it. Always carefully watching the clock because of Jacob, I had never wondered why Peter was equally concerned to get on his bus home at a respectable hour. He had no affection for his wife, a sharp-tongued bitch by his account, but he was devoted to his kids. Incidentally, he had married her because she was pregnant. I had been right in expecting him to fulfil that obligation, but obviously he couldn't do so twice. I was much bemused by the potency of Peter's seed. It seemed incredible in a man who was so unimpressive in every other way. I still find it fantastic that my first lover, and the father of my first child, should have been a person whom I never took seriously. He must be over seventy now, but I envisage him eternally plodding around Woolworth's with his clipboard. I'm sure they never made him a manager.

Now I had the unpleasant task of telling Jacob. It wouldn't be long before I started to show, so I faced up to it. He was shocked, and he was also extremely annoyed. He stood to be blamed by our Dad for letting it happen. What he most wanted to know was how I'd managed to elude his control. I said: 'Well, Jacob, it was Thursday afternoons.' At this he looked so astonished, and so furious with himself for failing to provide for this loophole, that I couldn't help laughing. I thought he was going to hit me, but he managed to restrain himself.

It didn't seem impossible, though, that he would attack Peter if he could get on his trail. (Because of his limp, Jacob went about with a wicked-looking oak stick.) Nor was this the only danger for my poor lover. He would catch hell, doubtless, from his wife. He had borrowed money from her parents. It was quite possible that he would get the sack from Woolworth's, and that was no joke in the depths of the Depression. So I was determined not to give Peter away. Jacob bullied me into admitting that the villain of the melodrama worked for Woolworth's – where else could I have met a man? – but I refused to name him. I pretended that Peter and I had fallen irresistibly in love; and, curiously, I did feel more nearly in love with him now that I had to protect him than when I'd been cheerfully getting into bed with him once a week. Anyway, I was more anxious about Peter than I was about myself, and this must have helped to carry me through.

I was ordered to hand in my notice at Woolworth's at once, but the idea that I might slink off and meet Peter worried Jacob badly. I pointed out that I was already pregnant and couldn't be double-pregnant, but this didn't amuse him. He had to get me out of circulation, and he soon found a way to achieve this.

There was an institution called Saxby House (inevitably, it became Sexby House) where girls in my predicament were housed and fed until they became unmarried mothers. The babies were then removed, as Saxby House was linked to an adoption society. It was subsidized by pious donations but it wasn't free, and Jacob impressed on me that he was making a sacrifice for my sake. Later, however, I discovered that after dumping me at Saxby he went on to Bala to tap the family savings, so it was Dad who made the sacrifice.

Saxby was in Lincolnshire, a part of England which had no associations for me. There were twelve or fourteen girls in the house at any given time. For the birth, you went by ambulance to a private maternity hospital in a town a few miles away. These departures were the big emotional dramas of Saxby life, because a mother would go straight back to the outside world from the hospital and the rest of us wouldn't see her again.

The house was a Victorian building, something like Craig-derw, my future home, but bigger. It had enormous stairways and landings, so it was the sort of house that's always cold no matter what efforts are made; there was central heating, a novelty for me, but we shivered nevertheless. England is rich in houses like this, and nobody knows what to do with them. Not quite ten years after my spell at Saxby, I found myself in Lincolnshire again. By then I was married to Alex, and he was stationed at one of the big bomber bases. I went one afternoon, taking Ann for the ride, to have a look at Saxby. It had become an RAF officers' mess. I wondered if the pilots called it Sexby, and if the scores of unwise or unlucky girls who had put in time here had left any trace in the atmosphere. I wondered, too, whether I would ever see Gladys or Angela or Doris again, or recognize them if I did. But the whole point of Saxby was that one wouldn't have to admit to it. One thing's sure: there is no Saxby Old Girls' Association.

Coming from the mountains, I felt the strangeness of a landscape in which there were no views, because no heights, and also no hiding-places. Where space was infinite and featureless, time tended to become like that too. What I was waiting for could be neither avoided nor hastened, hadn't been desired, could bring relief but no joy. I arrived in autumn. Rain made wide, shallow ponds in the fields; when the rain stopped, the ponds didn't go away because water in Lincolnshire didn't flow as it did in Wales. For a time, snow covered all distinctions of shape and colour. It melted, the ponds reappeared, it rained again. The sky was seldom blue, seldom dark; in my memory it's always a flat, unvarying expanse of off-white. I left in what should have been summer, but didn't look like it or feel like it.

Alex, when I described Saxby to him, said that it must have been devised by some moral sadist. You might think, indeed, that the girls who were consigned there – without the men who had given them pleasure and in some cases love, without the diversions of ordinary life, without the pride or the hopes that ought to go with motherhood, and with nothing to think about except to wish that it hadn't happened – would be intensely miserable. Somehow, it wasn't like that. Mrs Potter, the Warden, never delivered any moral lectures (as perhaps her predecessors had) but conveyed unsentimentally that she wasn't sorry for us and we could gain nothing by being sorry for ourselves. She had earned her living since her husband was killed in the war; she had scrubbed floors, she let us know, and she couldn't stand a skimper or a grouser. The floors of Saxby House were scrubbed by the girls who could still kneel down without undue difficulty. Girls in the later stages cooked and washed dishes. The activity, obviously, was good for us. We took pride in producing tasty meals, making the common-room look nice, getting everything done without rush or muddle. In some measure, Saxby was a substitute for the family home that we didn't have.

A girl who had just arrived would, as likely as not, sit

huddled in a cold corner of the common-room, break into sudden fits of weeping, live only for the sight of the postman. But, by degrees, the vision would dwindle and become indistinct, like the vision of a man left standing on a platform when a train moves off. You would see the girl skim hastily through a letter and leave it lying around. By this time, she had made friends with someone who had been at Saxby longer, and was talking freely about what had seemed incommunicable. She would say, surprising herself: 'You know, I don't think I care if I see him again.'

In the common-room, we had a way of talking about men that helped us to simplify our feelings. 'They don't care, do they?' . . . 'Just want one thing' . . . 'Selfish pigs!'. But this was a ritual of feminine solidarity. We knew that some men, at least, did care; I'm sure that Peter missed me more than I missed him. It was more honest to be sorry for them. The girl was left with something – something undesired, even calamitous, yet significant and absorbing – while the man was left with nothing. And even if the man had indeed been absolutely selfish and callous, he had responded all the same to a natural urge in which we secretly rejoiced. In any case, to hate men because they were like that was like hating bulls because they were dangerous; it was at your own risk that you crossed the field.

There wasn't much room at Saxby for self-pity. There was always someone who was worse off than you were yourself. Gladys, for instance, wanted to marry her young man and keep the child, and he was prepared to marry her, but her parents wouldn't allow it and, since Gladys was a minor, that was that. 'He'll have taken up with somebody else before I get out of here, I know he will,' she said hopelessly.

Angela, who came from an upper-class family, had been engaged to an officer in the Navy. While he was with his ship in Malta, she became pregnant. Something had happened, or in view of the consequence it must have happened, at a country-house dance. She was still bewildered, incredulous, and literally unable to remember. 'We were drinking champagne, he was kissing me on the stairs, after that it's a sort of blur.' She had forgotten the man's name; could have traced him, but saw no purpose. Her fiancé had written her a cold, unanswerable letter.

Doris, on the other hand, knew quite well who had pushed her down on the couch one afternoon while her parents were at the café they owned in New Cross. It was her uncle, but since he was the most impressively respectable member of the family and didn't even smoke or drink, nobody could be expected to believe her if she accused him.

We all made a pet of Doris; she was only fourteen and it seemed intolerably unjust for a girl to become pregnant before receiving any affection from boys, before being kissed. We all befriended Angela because the transition to Saxby was so drastic a break for her. She made willing efforts, but she was lost with the domestic chores that she had never needed to attempt. Despite the continual arrivals and departures, Saxby was a real community: everybody had to help and comfort everybody else and nobody could afford to put on airs. It was like a school in which there were no lessons, since the one lesson that mattered had already been learned.

The making of a child, as it progressed, seemed to have nothing to do with the way it had started. The part played by the man, the hasty thrusts, the passing excitement – all that was casual, almost trivial. We had left the men behind to embark on a great, slow, solemn process of transformation and creation. So Saxby couldn't be all loss, it couldn't be a waste of time. We arrived angry or wretched or scared, and we became calm and confident – even little Doris. I used to go into the common-room and gaze at the heavy, rounded bodies, resting and passive but ceaselessly at work on their silent task, clumsy and devoid of the grace that caught men's eyes, yet beautiful in a way they couldn't have been before. They were like loaded ships swaying at anchor, like ruminative cows at pasture. I loved them all.

We were constantly touching and feeling one another,

tracing the movement within the womb, guessing how long there was to go. Because we would be just girls again when the pregnancy was over, it was an experience with a value in itself. This didn't mean that our babies were merely burdens to get rid of. We knew, as a fact, that they would vanish, but emotionally we didn't accept it. The loss of a child, as much as the death of a child perhaps, is something for which one can't prepare. Every one of us made up her mind, guided by bits of folk-wisdom, whether she was carrying a boy or a girl. There was endless discussion about names; we chose to forget that the unknown adopters would have the decision. My baby was to be a boy and I called him Danny, for no reason that I can remember now.

The system then was that adopted children were never told that they were adopted, let alone who their natural parents were. Maybe that was right – I can't decide. Anyway, I don't kid myself that Danny knows anything about me. He's forty-six now, a fine age for a man. I'm convinced, since I can think what I please, that he has achieved something outstanding. This means that I must have seen him on television, a tantalizing thought. Just what he's achieved, I change my mind about every time I think of him. The only thing I really know about him is that, at one day old, he was healthy and taking well to the bottle.

Dad came to collect me, driving the van which had replaced the old pony-trap a few years before, and took me home across the broad waist of England. On the way, he informed me that I'd been in a TB sanatorium with a patch on my lung. I don't suppose he expected anybody in Bala to believe this – I'm sure I didn't – but it conformed to Welsh conventions. If you produce a suitable cover-story, you can get practically anything erased from the public record. Only the public avowal of misconduct is unforgivable, as I was later to learn.

'London must be full of TB,' Ruth said. 'You never know who you're safe with, do you? It's a pity you weren't more careful.'

'Things can happen anywhere,' I gave back to her. 'Are you still engaged to Gwilym?'

'We decided we don't suit each other,' she said smoothly. 'It's best to find that out before you've cause to be sorry, don't you think?'

To balance the trials our parents had to endure, Jacob got himself engaged. We younger ones couldn't imagine who would have him. 'Prepare for a hideous sight,' Gideon said. She wasn't that, but she was one of those women who infallibly dress wrong, do their hair wrong, and seem to be working hard to put men off. So, although she deserved better, it was no wonder she'd finished up with Jacob. He disapproved of women who made efforts to attract men, so she had at last found someone for whom her helpless appearance was a positive recommendation.

Jacob and Margaret were married in Bala. Her home was in South Wales, but her parents were dead and our Mam took charge. Ruth and I were the bridesmaids. The best man was David Hughes-Talbot.

As we got ourselves ready, I was ten times as nervous as Margaret. If David didn't take notice of me now, I thought, he never would. There's a tradition that the best man and the bridesmaid make an impression on each other. The trouble was that Ruth was a bridesmaid too. She looked smashing in her form-fitting dress, and she had no black marks on her record. Jacob was a sanctimonious sneak, so it was prudent to assume that he'd told David all about me.

At the reception, which was in the big lounge at the White Lion, I was suddenly aware that David was staring at me. We were at opposite ends of the room. I felt as though, standing in darkness on the bare ridge of a mountain, I had been picked out by a searchlight.

From then on, whenever I saw David, I sensed the extraordinary force by which he was possessed and driven. This force wasn't simply sexual, though it went into sexual channels. It was a compelling demand to do what he had to do, and to have what he had to have. He was a man of desires, not of choices.

But because this force could take him beyond all control or calculation, he struggled to hold it down. So long as he could, he guarded himself even against reaching for what he wanted. The calmness and the self-discipline were more than a disguise, but they were maintained by an act of will. There was always the risk of an explosion.

I remembered my childish question and thought: no wonder he needs two names. You sensed the pulsating, volcanic force of Hughes, while all you saw was Talbot.

Did a girl of nineteen achieve this understanding of a man with whom she'd never had an intimate talk? Or is a woman of sixty-five recreating a man long unseen? I don't know. I'm recording, I hope, what became slowly clear to me – part of it before we were married, part of it through living with him, part of it only four years on, because of Estelle.

At first, I understood very little. He wanted me – I didn't think I could be wrong about that. But he seemed to be pulling away from me, trying to thwart what could easily and naturally develop. I spent miserable hours pondering on whether he was in love with me, without knowing exactly what I meant by that. Nobody had ever been in love with me yet.

Then I wondered what sort of girl he liked, and if there was something he needed that I would never be able to give him. He was twenty-five, so it was silly to imagine that I was the first to be drawn into the powerful magnetic force of his desires. I used to look at the Bala girls, or those who had a bit of a reputation, and think to myself: 'Was it her?' But this was something I never found it possible to ask him about, even when we were married.

Then, of course, it occurred to me that he was put off by my record of shame. I could count on Jacob to make the story as black as he could. I'd appear as the sort of shallow little slut who would open her legs for a greasy, middle-aged Woolworth's manager and take payment in silk stockings. David wasn't a chapel-going humbug, but I reckoned him capable of a grave, stiff moral fastidiousness. It could certainly rule me out as a possible wife.

I saw, or I think I saw, that it could work the other way. A man like David might be drawn to a victim of seduction, an outraged innocent to be consoled and restored. He would have the credit of generously forgiving me or, yet more generously, pretending not to know.

This was, indeed, how I did become David's wife. But there was a cost, which in time we paid heavily. David and I never built up the capacity of speaking frankly to each other. Reticence and evasion came naturally to him, I suppose, because of his years of enforced self-reliance; and I was willing to take the easy way if it was of advantage to me. After we married, he still pretended to believe that I'd been in a TB sanatorium. Perhaps, had I supposed that he really believed it, I might have said: 'Look, I want to tell you the truth.' As it was, there didn't seem to be any point.

There was one other solution to the problem. The stories that went round about old Major Hughes-Talbot (not that he was really old, but I was only nineteen) made it clear that he was difficult to live with. Perhaps David would be asking me to marry him at any moment, if it weren't for the nasty old Major. This idea drove me into a frenzy of anger and frustration. I was sure that I could coax the Major into liking me; and even if I couldn't, putting up with him was a price I was entirely ready to pay. But we were boxed in, David and I, by not speaking to each other frankly. There was no way of saying: 'If you'd like to marry me, I don't mind about your father.' In any case, maybe I was inventing this explanation because David wasn't so keen on me as I wanted to believe.

At Christmas, Ruth and I went to a party at Sir Roger Arbuthnot's house. Sir Roger was an old Englishman who had been Governor of Kenya. He had bought a big house beside the lake which had been empty for a number of years. The house isn't there now, I've heard from Ruth; Sir Roger didn't grasp that it had termites in the woodwork, you may be sure that no Welsh solicitor was going to tell him, and after much wasteful expenditure it ultimately had to be demolished. At that time, however, Sir Roger and Lady Arbuthnot were extremely pleased with it.

During the summer, Ruth had been picked up – literally, with a sports car – by the Arbuthnot son and heir, Cecil. He was at Oxford, and the long vacation gave them plenty of time to get well acquainted. 'If you get engaged this time you're going through with it, girl,' our Mam said. Ruth knew perfectly well that Cecil hadn't the least intention of proposing to her. A family link with the local baker would have horrified the Governor and his lady, who were outrageous snobs. Nor, to be fair to Ruth, would she have married an English upper-class twit like Cecil. But she enjoyed dashing about the countryside in the sports car and drinking gin and it in fancy pubs. Her view, doubtless, was that it made sense to get as much value as possible out of Cecil while the going was good. She got a weekend at Oxford in the autumn, staying at the best hotel, and naturally she got an invitation to the Arbuthnots' Christmas party.

'Who'll be there?' I asked casually.

'The nobs, such as they are,' Ruth replied. Then she gave me a sharp look and added: 'David Hughes-Talbot, I expect.'

'I see.'

'I could get you invited too, you know.'

'I'm sure I don't care.'

'Well, it's no trouble to me.'

The guests at the party were mostly young, or youngish people, whom Cecil had met while exploring North Wales. English accents predominated. There were also friends from Oxford who were staying in the house. Ruth knew a lot of people, but I didn't. David was standing by himself, looking bored. I saw that he knew hardly anybody, just like me.

He asked me to dance. He was a perfectly atrocious dancer, and from the set expression on his face it was evident that he didn't enjoy it, but he wasn't prepared to give up and I wasn't prepared to give him up. Eventually, I pleaded for a rest. We went and sat down in the library. There were some other people there – older people – and they cleared off with the sort of smiles that older people put on when they leave a young couple alone. The idea that David and I were a young couple filled me with joy.

We talked for a while. It was pretty halting, and soon it petered out. David and I were never much good at talking to each other, though we improved somewhat after we were actually married. When we did communicate, it wasn't through words.

Part of the trouble was that we talked English. In our family, we were completely at ease with English and didn't think of it as a foreign language, but it was Welsh that came to our tongues when we wanted to express our feelings. It was the same for most people in Bala. I'd always used Welsh with Ruth, whether we were sharing secrets or quarrelling. The boys who kissed me always spoke Welsh, which is a good language for sweet talk. (It was English with Peter, of course, but that underlined the coolness of our sentimental friendship.) I would have liked to talk Welsh with David. But the Hughes-Talbots had always spoken English – I suppose ever since they became Hughes-Talbots, and had more land than anybody else around, and built a big house. So English became the language of our marriage, even in bed. All along, and although we seldom thought about it consciously – nor, of course, talked about it frankly – this made it harder for us to open to each other.

So there we sat in the Arbuthnots' library, silent. Yet we were alone, there surely couldn't be much doubt of our feelings, and I thought he was bound to kiss me. There was even a mistletoe branch hanging from the chandelier, right before our eyes. But nothing happened. We sat side by side on the couch like two strangers on a bench in a railway waiting-room, until it was too late. The music stopped and we heard people in the hall saying goodnight. I went to find Ruth.

Cecil drove us home. It was a miserable winter night, cold

and foggy. Ruth was snuggling up to Cecil and it was obvious that they hadn't overlooked the mistletoe. I wished I'd never gone to the party.

From that Christmas to Easter was – so I believed, not knowing what else I'd have to face – the worst time in my life. I saw David quite often, and although we didn't so much as hold hands I was sure that the Bala gossips had their eyes on us. I became tense and snappy, and had a few really vicious spats with Ruth. Gideon teased me. Mam, now reluctantly convinced that there was nothing serious between Ruth and Cecil, was watching me with, I was well aware, crossed fingers. I felt that David was treating me badly, but I had nothing to accuse him of. In any case, I couldn't hope to steer him into doing what I wanted, like Peter.

By the spring, which really does put a twitch in the nerves, I was ticking like a time-bomb. So was David, though I didn't know it. I went for long walks in the hope of cooling myself down. Sometimes I went up to the rough grazing that belonged to Craig-derw. I didn't admit to myself that I was hoping to meet David. I was in such a state that I was walking blindly, scarcely knowing where I was.

Then I did meet him. It was almost on the same spot – this flashed through my mind – where he had so cruelly ignored me when I was a clumsy, self-conscious girl of fourteen. Now he was happy to see me; that was progress, at least. I said I was out of breath with the climb, which wasn't true. I sat down on a shelf of turf and he sat down reasonably close to me. He made some fatuous remark about the view. The English words sounded dry and flat, like a sentence in a school textbook. I didn't answer. I knew that I would burst into tears if he didn't kiss me. He must have known that too. He kissed me.

It was the explosion. It was as though we had to pack into a few minutes all the kisses we had denied ourselves for months. We clung together, twisting and writhing, rolling on the grass.

And then I felt him pulling away from me – literally so. He was gone, with a few muttered words of which I caught only 'See you later'. I sat up and stared at the clouds massed above Arenig Fawr. It had all gone sour. He hadn't meant to kiss me, hadn't intended to commit himself, and now he regretted the impulse and was angry at his loss of control.

I spent the evening in my room, alternately weeping and assuring myself that I didn't care. Ruth came in late and hummed dreamily while she undressed. I said: 'Have you had Cecil up you?' She was shocked; we'd yelled at each other often enough, but we didn't use language like that.

The next day, I had a note from David telling me that his father was dead. I hadn't realized that the Major was even ill, more than his chronic condition. I saw now that David must have gone out to take a breather from the misery. The thought of what his father was going through while he was enjoying himself with a girl must have jumped suddenly into his mind and horrified him. But, being David, he couldn't explain.

Still – we were alive and we were young. The note said that he looked forward to seeing me after the funeral. That sounded hopeful.

I went up to Craig-derw without any delay. A maid answered the bell, and ushered me into the front room. Her manner was polite, even deferential. I suppose she had her ear to the ground and reckoned that she'd be out of a job if I didn't approve of her.

While I waited for David, I felt cold. It was a late, chilly spring and the fire hadn't been lit. But it was more than that; the room was dead, as I had never known any other room to be dead. At that time, all houses except those of really poor people had a front room which was used only on special occasions. But at Craig-derw there were no occasions. The room, meticulously swept and dusted, was waiting for nothing. I guessed (rightly) that all the things in it had been acquired and set in their places many years ago, and nothing ever changed. I tried to imagine what it must have been like to grow up here, and shivered.

David came in and made a prepared speech, which culminated in a proposal of marriage. I said 'yes', of course. But now that my happiness was complete, as the cliché goes, it seemed to be mysteriously seeping away. When we kissed, it wasn't like the way we'd kissed a few days before; it was too heavy with meaning. I found myself thinking of how little I really knew of David. The whole idea of marriage – of two people promising a lifetime of devotion – suddenly struck me as unnatural, a claim to impossible certainties, wildly dangerous.

I make too much of this, perhaps. Panic seizes most young women, and young men too, at the moment of commitment – quite often, at the altar. Later, if all goes well, we laugh at it. But we laugh out of relief; the warning is a true one.

David told me that his father had been the obstacle, and the only obstacle. It wasn't so simple as that, I thought. Something within David – something 'Talbot' – had been holding him back. And the obstacle, assuming its reality, didn't consist solely of the Major's ill-health and ill-temper; what was crucial was his authority. So long as he was alive, David was still taking orders, accepting rebuffs, being treated as a boy. It was just tolerable to endure that, but it wouldn't have been tolerable to let me witness it. Only when he became the master could he allow me into Craig-derw.

We didn't tell anybody for a month. David didn't want it to look as if he'd just been waiting for his father to vanish. But when I gave the news to my family they weren't surprised; they had noticed me being less snappy. 'Well, you've got what you wanted,' Ruth said. I didn't feel like that. I felt that I was only at the beginning.

I was going up to Craig-derw practically every day, to get used to the idea of living there. It wouldn't be like the High Street in Bala. There, I could always hear people talking as they stood outside our windows, and kids playing hopscotch, and trains whistling in the station. Craig-derw was so quiet that you could hear the grass growing – or rather, you couldn't. I wondered how much of David's habit of silence came from the silence around him. And I wondered, anxiously, how I'd take to it.

It occurred to me that the house had been built deliberately to turn its back on Bala; and so on a world of broadening valleys, roads and railways, towns and villages. The Hughes-Talbots wanted nothing but their view of Arenig Fawr. Or, I sometimes thought, their view of their own land. I detected in David a tendency to behave as though he were the Earl of Shrewsbury, or someone of that order; his vision transformed what was, after all, a sheep-farm into a grandiose estate, and the house into a castle. I didn't see how I was to come to terms with this, but I didn't think it ridiculous. He was a natural aristocrat, and it wasn't his fault that our corner of Wales had no place for anyone of that dignity.

For me, the house would be what mattered. I had to persuade it, or challenge it, to accept me. Its size wasn't the trouble; Saxby had been bigger. The trouble was that there was no room for me, a newcomer. The house was much too full of objects, of which few were beautiful and many were useless. For instance, there were massive candlesticks in all the rooms although electric light had been installed. The furniture tended to be too large for the space it occupied; you were always squeezing between a carved-oak chair or table and the wall. I laid schemes to get rid of things, but I saw that I would have to proceed very cautiously. In fact, I got rid of only a few small items in the four years before events got rid of me. In the forty years since that, I'm sure that not a candlestick or a warming-pan has left the house. However, there was one formidable object which I attacked right away, before we were married; I forced David to sell and replace the bed in the main bedroom. I was damned if I was going to make love with him in the bed where both his parents had died.

I never tried, during our engagement, to tempt David into

'not waiting'. On warm summer evenings, we ached for each other so that we hardly dared to kiss. But I knew that our marriage had to be made, partly, out of that aching.

It rained on our wedding day, steadily from morning to night. We went to Llandudno for our honeymoon. I'd have preferred to go up to Craig-derw and lock the doors, but a honeymoon was the proper thing. The journey was slow, with a boring wait where we changed trains. There was nothing to see but drifting clouds which swallowed the smoke from the engine, and flooded fields which reminded me of Saxby. We didn't talk. I thought about the night and then – as if we weren't married – hoped that David didn't guess what I was thinking.

I had never been in a hotel before. David clearly knew the procedure, and it occurred to me while he was signing the register that he must have stayed in hotels with girls. There were jokes in Wales about Llandudno, like the London jokes about Brighton. The desk clerk gave me a funny look, and so did the man who carried our suitcases upstairs. I imagined it, I suppose. I couldn't very well pipe up and assert that I really was David's wife. And was I, anyway? All I'd done so far was to say that I would be. I hadn't yet made a start.

We unpacked and changed our clothes. It was the third time I'd dressed that day, in my wedding dress and my going-away dress and now in a long dress for dinner. I wasn't hungry, and I didn't want to be stared at by other people in the dining-room. I'd have liked to get into bed right away, but I didn't dare suggest it to David.

We went down for dinner. David ordered wine, which cheered me up; the reception had been dry, under Baptist auspices. But I found, to my embarrassment, that the wine was making me sleepy. The dining-room was crowded, as it was peak holiday time, and the service was terribly slow. When David asked if I would like coffee, I said: 'Please let's go to bed.'

After we'd been in bed for a while, I grasped what David was doing. He was being gentle with me. It wasn't at all what

I wanted. I wondered how long it would take, and hoped that I wouldn't yawn. My mind drifted into questions. Had he actually convinced himself that his bride was a virgin, or did he just want me to believe that he believed it? Would we ever be frank with each other?

So we started off wrong, although David clearly didn't think so. He was soon asleep. But now, infuriatingly, I was wide awake; it seemed that we couldn't get into the same rhythm. I thought about all the things that had gone wrong in my life, and then I thought about Danny. He'd had his first birthday by now. Perhaps he was walking, perhaps he could say a few words – 'Mummy', at least. I cried, very quietly so that I wouldn't disturb David. But if he woke up, he wouldn't know what I was crying for, and of course I wouldn't tell him.

I was depressed right through the fortnight, though I think I succeeded in hiding it. As in all honeymoons, we had to pretend to be enjoying every minute. The only thing I really enjoyed was standing on the cliffs and watching the waves crashing and breaking; it was rough, windy weather all the time, and I was glad. In the town, we were always queuing for this or that, or battling for a drink in a crowded bar, or pushing into a café and finding that there wasn't a table. We were constantly up against strangers, to whom our wishes and feelings didn't matter – it brought back my memories of living in London. It was better in our room, but of course the room wasn't really ours. Not being used to hotels, I kept thinking of the other people who had slept in the bed. I wanted to be at home – Craig-derw. And I knew that David wanted that too. He talked mostly about changes he intended to make on the farm now that it was his, about the dogs he was training, and so forth. If we'd been honest, we'd have packed up and gone home early. But we were committed to our pretence.

When we got home, we began to reach out to each other. David stopped being gentle when we made love. His force pounded me, like crashing waves pounding and reshaping the sea-shore. I loved that, but when it was over I was left with questions that I couldn't ask. Was it really for me, this force? Or was I grasping at what belonged to some imagined idea of a woman, quite different from me? When he said that he loved me, did David know who I was? Did I know who he was? We made love every night in our first year together. It was a search that gave us no rest.

After our honeymoon, we never went away any more. David suggested holidays because he felt that he should, but I wouldn't go. I didn't leave Craig-derw for a night until, in the end, I left it for ever. Everything depended on our staying together, in our own place, learning about each other.

'Happy, darling?' David asked – often, too often. Of course, I answered 'Yes'. That wasn't wholly truthful, but 'No' would have been less truthful; it was the question that was wrong. Happiness was the end of a journey, the resolution of all questions, a point of rest. At some unknown time to come, I believed, we should be able to claim it. But not yet.

ESTELLE

It was raining when I arrived in Bala. I wasn't much surprised; Mr Barker, my landlord, had warned me to expect rain at any time of the year. But as a welcome, it was disappointing.

There was one taxi outside the station, and I took it. I asked the driver if he knew Ty Pellaf. This didn't register with him, so I tried: 'Mr Barker's cottage.'

'Ah – Ty Pellaf.' I made a mental note that it was pronounced like 'tea', not 'tie'. 'We haven't seen Mr Barker lately.'

'He's gone abroad. I'm renting the cottage.'

'Indeed. Will you be staying long?'

'Quite some time, probably.'

'All by yourself, are you?'

I wondered whether I should explain that I had been divorced for some years and had just been two-timed by my most recent lover, a French law professor. It would be unwise to take offence, anyway. I might have need of the Bala taxi.

We drove through the town, which appeared to consist of one wide main street, and then along the shore of a lake. I hadn't heard about the lake and hoped that Ty Pellaf was close to it. But we took a sharp right turn and climbed a steep hill. After that, I couldn't see much; the taxi seemed to be cleaving its way through the rain, as a boat might be plunged into the spray of the waves. I had only a general impression that Wales was very green and very wet.

The last part of the journey was on an unpaved road. The taxi, an old Austin with worn-out springs, lurched from one pothole to the next. By now, I could see practically nothing. It was only the middle of the afternoon, but a combination of rain, mist and the sheer poverty of the light made it seem that darkness had fallen. Unexpectedly, the taxi stopped. 'Here you are,' the driver said.

I clambered out. We were in the yard of what looked like a farmhouse, stone-built and roofed with slate. It was bigger than I had imagined; I remembered that English people who had second homes always referred to them deprecatingly as cottages.

I paid the driver and added a good tip. I couldn't afford extravagance, but it had been a nasty drive, and the twists and turns had caused me to over-guess the distance. The man thanked me, said goodbye, and then asked: 'You'll be all right, now?'

'Sure I'll be all right,' I said. But when the taxi had disappeared, I didn't feel so cheerful. Rosemary hadn't been kidding when she called the cottage isolated. I was used to living in the countryside, as opposed to town, but always in a village or at least on a moderately well-frequented road. This road, or rather track, ended in the yard of Ty Pellaf. I could see no other houses; there must be some, hidden in the gloom, but there were none at all close. Maybe it wasn't the best possible house for a woman living alone. The thought irritated me, because I didn't like to think of myself as subject to fears, but it wasn't easy to dismiss.

I put the key into the lock. It was stiff, and for a panicky half-minute I wondered if I'd be spending the night outside, but I managed to get it to turn. I lugged my things inside – two suitcases, a cardboard box full of books, and another cardboard box with a stock of basic food. Naturally, the house was dark. I knew from Mr Barker that it wasn't reached by the electric grid, but I had lived without electricity before. I explored with my flashlight, found the oil-lamp, and lit it. Next, with rather more difficulty, I started up the stove, a massive affair of black ironwork. Having eaten nothing on the train, I cooked a meal. It was early for dinner by French standards, but that was irrelevant. In the darkness and the silence that enclosed the house, it could have been the middle of the night.

Ty Pellaf, I made out by exploring, had two good-sized rooms downstairs and two upstairs. The inner downstairs room – the living-room, it might be called, since it contained armchairs – had a large fireplace, but I didn't have the energy to light a fire that evening. The kitchen was still cold despite the stove, so I decided to go to bed. Upstairs, it was colder still. I slept covered by all the blankets I could find and with my toes on a hot-water bottle, a piece of equipment which nobody then would have dreamed of being without, especially in the country. The winter was ahead of me, I reflected anxiously. But by that time I would have the fire going strong. Old stone-built houses, I knew from experience, became as cold and damp as caverns if they were left empty, but kept the heat once they were warmed.

In the morning, I had to make a great moral effort to crawl out from under my blankets. If it had still been grey and rainy, I don't know how I'd have managed it. But the square window over the bed showed me a clear blue sky and the blaze of the sun. I dressed, made some coffee, and ventured outside. It was a beautiful October day, with the calmness and gentleness that sometimes come like a blessing between storm and storm.

I stood in the yard and gasped. Right in front of me there was a great mountain, for which I'd been utterly unprepared. It had been invisible when I arrived, and it was often to be invisible while I lived at Ty Pellaf; now, it was as though by a majestic act of will it had thrown the clouds aside to astonish me. I call Arenig Fawr a great mountain, knowing that the Alps around Grenoble rise to three or four times its height. But I had never lived so close to a mountain, and I felt very small in relation to it.

Besides, Arenig Fawr had a magnificence that couldn't be measured in feet or metres. A wide stretch of moorland prepared the way to it, like the spacious courtyard in front of a palace. Then the mountain rose in overlapping folds, all a rich shade of green, as though it had been created by some lavish god who'd decided to add more, and then more, and then more again. Pleased with his work, he'd decorated it with streams that made glittering streaks on the green and emphasized the mountain's height. Away on the north flank, to the right as I looked from Ty Pellaf, there was a long, forbidding cliff of grey rock. The peak, a perfect and noble cone, made me feel that I'd never have the daring to scale it. Some mountains – not many – suggest the thought that in primeval times they must have been worshipped by the people who dwelt below, and Arenig Fawr was certainly one of these.

I could see now why the road didn't go any farther. There was absolutely nowhere for it to go, except impudently – impiously – up the face of Arenig Fawr. In fact, as Martha explained to me later, Ty Pellaf meant 'the farthest house' or 'the last house'. The farm, when it was a farm, had been the last on the uplands between the lake and Arenig Fawr: the last attempt to subdue to human purposes what was naturally wild and intractable. The soil was thin and broken, the gorse and bracken couldn't be beaten back, the sheep had to range for miles to find any nutriment, and as they wandered up the mountain they were regularly lost and frozen to death in hard winters. The farm had always struggled, and eventually admitted defeat. While the house was snapped up by the astute Mr Barker, the land reverted to its ancient emptiness.

I set out for a walk – going back the way I had come in the taxi, of course, since there was no other direction. In the bright daylight, I could spot four farmhouses, each standing among its fields. One of them, built near the crest of a hill, was larger than the others, suggesting that its owner might be somebody special. There were sheep everywhere, planted on the green fields like counters in a children's game.

On my own stretch of dirt road there was nothing, except a building that might have been a house or might not. Set back across a couple of Ty Pellaf's abandoned fields, it was a rough rectangle of stonework with a wide entry instead of a door, and no windows. It looked like a barn, suitable for keeping farm-carts or for sheltering animals in bad weather, but there was a chimney at one end and smoke was puffing into the air. I stopped for a few minutes and looked for signs of possible neighbours, but I saw nobody, so I walked on.

Soon after the dirt road joined the paved road, I came to a junction which I hadn't noticed the day before. A signpost read: 'To Parc, ½ mile.' Hopefully, I took the road to Parc. It led steeply down into a narrow valley; I came to an old stone bridge across a rushing, foaming little river. The village of Parc was sandwiched between the river and a small forest of oaks and rowans. It consisted of a dozen houses, a two-room school, a shop and – much the largest building – a chapel. In England you can have a pub without a village but you can't have a village without a pub; in Wales, read chapel. This chapel had a big signboard, of golden letters painted on black, which provided my first encounter with the Welsh language.

A bus, which appeared capable of holding the total population of Parc, was standing by the shop. The engine was running, making a fearsome clatter. Motor vehicles in those days had a way of heaving and panting, like great clumsy animals. The driver, assuming that I'd walked into the village to catch the bus, opened his window and called to me: 'Come on, miss, just in time!' I smiled and shook my head. The bus roared into movement, crossed the bridge, and went on its way to Bala.

I went into the shop. It sold practically everything from HP Sauce to wellington boots, and functioned as a post office too. I bought a loaf of bread, a string of sausages and a cabbage, quite enough to put me on a chatty footing with the woman behind the counter. She thought at first that I was on holiday and assured me that the weather would keep fine to the end of the week. I explained that I was living at Ty Pellaf. 'Needs living in,' she said emphatically. She hadn't approved of the Barkers, who were gone almost before you knew they'd come and bought practically nothing in her shop. I made it clear that I had no other home. 'Your luck'll soon change, dear,' she said.

I felt grateful to Rosemary for having sent me here. If I wanted to be undisturbed – and that was what I did want at present – I couldn't have found anywhere better than Ty Pellaf. If my inclinations became more sociable, the Welsh seemed to be the friendliest people in Europe. I saw nothing from my window but wild and beautiful country, but a twenty-minute walk would bring me to the shop in Parc and the bus for Bala. I didn't need any better luck than this.

During the afternoon, I arranged the house as I wanted it. The living-room was spacious but rather bare, with an expanse of floor between the armchairs, placed either side of the fireplace, and a dresser against the far wall. I had a sudden idea: if I kept the fire going in this room it would be beautifully warm by evening, so why not sleep in it, and save the cost and effort of heating a bedroom? I couldn't move the bed unaided, so I brought the mattress downstairs. It wouldn't exactly have been a feature of an elegant drawing-room, but I had nobody to please but myself.

So I settled down to living at Ty Pellaf. It was a peaceful life, with each day, by my own choice, like the day before. I went out to the woodshed every morning and spent an hour or two sawing the logs which Mr Barker had bought in quantity before he was ordered to Singapore. Then I laid the fire and lit it.

English fires, in my opinion – and I can't say 'British' in this context – were at the heart of a way of life. English literature, for that matter, would be the poorer without its fire-words: flickering, blazing, glowing. The wastefulness of the fire, which could easily be proved by scientific measurement, was just the beauty of it; it showed an easy grandeur, a generous disregard of calculation. Maybe it was when the English took to central heating that England lost its true character and its self-confidence. The fire was a living, growing thing; it had the quality, which I had sought and valued since I first came to Europe, of unhurried maturity. The warmth developed across the hours from a thin, pale hope to splendid richness. Sitting before the fire in a deep armchair, I started out with a blanket over my shoulders, then wore a sweater, then only a blouse, and finally came down to my bra.

I sat there for a greater or smaller part of each day, according to the weather, and all the evening until I took the few easy steps to my mattress. I read a good deal, but mostly I let my thoughts wander; a fire encourages that. I was in need of a pause, a space for recovery. I allowed each episode of my life to be consumed, crumbled away, as one log after another was consumed before my eyes. Sometimes I tried to imagine what Georges was doing now, or Arthur, or even Mavros. But it was a relief to me that I didn't really want to know – I honestly didn't care.

I didn't go into Bala for a couple of weeks. It was enough to become recognized, and able to recognize people, in Parc. Mrs Bowen, the shopkeeper-postmistress, introduced me to most of the local women. I could see that they were agog with curiosity about me. I was American, I had the mysterious name of 'Mrs Mavros', there was no sign of a husband, presumably I had private means but I shopped frugally – what did it all mean? I let them figure it out as best they could. One day, the preacher from the chapel engaged me in talk and asked me, very politely but with intense earnestness, what faith I followed. I replied that I was Greek Orthodox. It occurred to me later that he might know something about my alleged religion – I of course knew nothing, beyond distant memories of the wedding ceremony – but if he did, he kept tactfully quiet about it.

I was accustomed to walking along my dirt road as though it had been a private drive. It was a surprise, therefore, when I met someone coming toward me as I was on my way to the village. He was a young man, of average height but a skimpy, narrow-shouldered build. He wore what might once have been a passably respectable suit, but either he was wearing it to death or he had bought it at a cheap second-hand stall. Thought it was a cold day, he had no coat. A curious fact was that his hair was long, reaching to the collar of his jacket. In 1938, only the most extreme Bohemians wore their hair like that. But I was sure that the young man belonged to the neighbourhood. He must have simply omitted to have a haircut.

'Good morning,' I said brightly.

He looked at me – not a glance but a keen, examining look – but didn't answer. I maintained a fatuous smile, as though it were necessary to encourage him, or maybe to placate him. We stood there in the road for two minutes or so, a long time in the circumstances. Then he turned abruptly and made off through the bracken. I watched him until I saw him enter the house without windows.

The idea that I had failed to make contact with my nearest neighbour, after finding the rest of the village so friendly, was disturbing. But a simple explanation occurred to me: he didn't speak English. Once, in the shop, an old woman had nodded to me and walked out with speaking, and Mrs Bowen had explained that she spoke only Welsh. I didn't grasp then that the vast majority of people around Bala were bilingual; I imagined that they were divided into English-speakers and Welsh-speakers.

I consulted Mrs Bowen. She asked me to describe the man.

'Quite young. Kind of skinny. With long hair.'

'Oh, that's Sam Pritchard.' Mrs Bowen laughed. 'You don't need to worry about him, Mrs Mavros. He's a bit touched, that's all.'

'Touched?'

Still laughing, Mrs Bowen tapped her forehead. 'A tile loose, you know. Not bad enough to shut him away, just a bit lacking. They couldn't do anything with him at the school, I remember.'

'I thought perhaps he couldn't speak English.'

'Oh, he can spout away when he wants to. English, Welsh, either.'

'What does he do for a living?'

'Odd jobs, when anybody'll have him. Selling bits and pieces. Scrounging.'

'He lives in that house on the way to Ty Pellaf, doesn't he?'

'It's not a proper house, mind,' Mrs Bowen said. 'It used to be the barn for Ty Pellaf when there was the farm. But when the Lewises sold up and left, Mr Barker only bought the house and the land was nobody's, in law if you follow me. So Sam Pritchard moved into the barn. It wasn't his to take, but it's his now by squatter's rights. He made it fit to keep out the weather and put in the fireplace. They're good with their hands, you'll often find, those that are a bit touched.'

What Mrs Bowen told me wasn't so surprising as it would be today. Social workers and psychiatrists hadn't penetrated the rural parts of Europe, nor was it considered wrong to leave the Sam Pritchards to shift for themselves. I decided that I wouldn't try to speak to my neighbour again.

The incident reminded me, however, that I had thought of learning Welsh. I took the bus to Bala and found the public library. It was a good library for a small town, although a bias toward theology limited its appeal to me. After a bit of browsing, I went up to the librarian's desk and asked what he could give me for learning Welsh.

The request evidently astonished him. He didn't speak Welsh himself, he said, though he was a hundred per cent Welshman, and he could assure me that I wouldn't find it necessary. In his eyes, I gathered, Welsh was all right for the peasants but of no interest to educated people. This attitude was old-fashioned even then – the librarian was an elderly man – and Martha tells me that nowadays professors and television executives down in Cardiff pride themselves on their fluent Welsh. We tried speaking Welsh together, sitting in a bar in Crescent City, California, though I was groping for lost words and Martha confessed that she was rusty after thirty-odd years of living in England. While we chuckled at the barman's mystification, we were near to sentimental tears from thoughts of Craig-derw and Ty Pellaf. When we got back to my house I tried to find the book I'd learned from, but of course it hadn't clung to me through three marriages and many homes.

It was a solid grammar, designed for serious students, and I daresay the librarian expected that it would extinguish my absurd whim. However, I had always learned languages from books like this, despising simple short cuts to puncture repairs and rooms with a bath. Welsh had peculiar ways of its own, unknown to any of the four other languages I had tackled; it wasn't easy, but I persevered.

Autumn was fading into winter. It rained a lot of the time, but I was coming to terms with Welsh rain and even growing quite fond of it. It wasn't like the harsh, stinging rain I had known in some other places; it didn't seem to fall so much as to drift about in clouds, and since the Welsh ignored it as they walked steadfastly along or even stood in the open chatting, I tried to do the same. I was ready now to make more expeditions to Bala. It might not be so easy, once the real winter set in. Mrs Bowen warned me that Parc was sometimes cut off, with neither delivery trucks nor the bus able to make the climb from the lake on an icy road, and advised me to keep a stock of canned food.

I found Bala friendly, like Parc; it was a compact town, easy to get to know, in effect another Parc on a not much larger scale. Because of its summer visitors, it had a surprising choice of good shops and of inns that just made the grade as hotels. In winter, the excess of supply over demand endowed Bala with an air of generosity and – added to the Welsh friendliness – made you feel that the place had been kept open just for you. On a second visit to any shop or pub, I could count on being remembered. Between the eleven o'clock bus from Parc and the five-thirty bus going back, I could make the round of the shops, read the magazines in the library, eat lunch at one place and tea at another. If it was a Saturday, I could go to a movie. It was likely to be a movie that I'd seen a couple of years before in London, but I didn't mind that.

My favourite haunt was the saloon bar of the Red Lion, which had an enormous fireplace and offered a settled, accumulated warmth even before lunch. Here, one rain-soaked day, I was jolted from tranquil thoughts by a loud voice, female but far from softly feminine, announcing: 'Ghastly weather.' I had spent enough time in England to recognize the authentic accent of the upper class; it rang like a battle-trumpet now that I was accustomed to the subtler Welsh rhythms. I turned from the fire to confront Lady Arbuthnot, who looked like her voice. There was no one else in the bar, so it was up to me to respond. I agreed that it was ghastly weather.

'You must be American,' she said, in what I might have taken as an accusing tone if experience hadn't taught me that this was not the intention. 'Staying in the hotel?'

I explained that I was living near Bala.

'Oh, we must see something of you.'

'That's very kind of you.'

'Not a bit of it. Exiles must stick together.'

So I was invited to tea one day in the following week. Lord and Lady Arbuthnot lived three miles the other side of Bala; I went by taxi and left the problem of getting home to luck. Everything was very correct, in a style that I recalled from my training as Lady Hitherleigh's companion: silver teapot, eggshell cups, a maid in a starched apron handing round tiny cucumber sandwiches. Half a dozen ladies had been gathered. Most were exiles, and this determined adherence to convention made it seem that Wales was on another continent from England. I believe that Lady Arbuthnot genuinely liked the Welsh, but years of living in places where the English were dominant but outnumbered (Lord Arbuthnot had governed Burma) had made her cautious and selective in admitting natives to terms of equality.

'Mrs Mavros – meet Mrs Hughes-Talbot.'

Martha arrived late, when tea was already in progress.

She brought with her, as she always did, an air of directness and candour. It was as though the windows were opened to let in a gust of fresh air.

She also looked very young, especially among Lady Arbuthnot's other guests who were all middle-aged or elderly. I wanted to talk to her because she was of my generation and because her accent was Welsh; I was wary of aligning myself with the English club. But I was the newcomer, so all the ladies were testing me with probing questions under the guise of making me feel at home. I told them that I disliked cities and loved mountain country, and my last home had been in the French Alps. This went down well enough, but I could see them noting for later discussion: 'She hasn't mentioned a husband.' For the present they would do me the favour of assuming me to be a young widow, but they would soon pin me down as a divorcee.

When I said that I must leave, or else I'd miss my bus, it caused mild dismay. One was expected to have a car, or to have made effective arrangements.

'Aren't you at Ty Pellaf, Mrs Mavros?' Martha asked.

'That's right.'

'I'm at Craig-derw. You come with me.'

She smiled at me, and I smiled back. The message was that we would talk later, and surely we could be friends.

I told her that she could drop me at the end of my road, but it was raining and she dismissed the idea. So I asked her in for a drink. I had a bottle of Chartreuse, one of my few tangible reminders of Grenoble. It was getting low, but it would do well to celebrate the start of a friendship.

'This is marvellous,' she said. 'What is it?'

'Chartreuse. You get it in the part of France where I was living. It's made by monks.'

'Monks? Roman Catholic monks? Are they allowed to drink?'

'Yes, they can drink.'

'Well, that's something for them, anyway.'

Then she asked me how long I had lived in France. Years,

I said, off and on.

'You must have liked it.'

I was about to say that it depended on the company, but I didn't yet know her well enough. I said: 'Yes, on the whole. Have you been there?'

'No, I've never travelled. I've lost my chance now, I suppose. I've got a little girl, two years old. Farthest I've been is London, and I don't think I saw London properly.'

'You've always lived here?'

'Bala born and bred. Bread is right – my father's Hughes the baker, in the High Street. You might have noticed.'

A little later, she said: 'Excuse my asking – is that where you sleep?'

'On the mattress? Yes. I decided it was pointless lighting another fire, just to undress by.'

'I see. It's sensible, that. All the same, I'd feel funny. I mean, a bedroom's a bedroom. But if I'd travelled, like you, I wouldn't be so set in my ways. Arabs sleep in tents, don't they?'

We talked until we forgot the time, but it wasn't enough, and she asked me to tea a few days ahead. Then she rushed, to be home before her little girl's bedtime. She hadn't told me where Craig-derw was, but I found out from Mrs Bowen.

It turned out to be the big house which had struck me as different from the other farms. Martha spotted me walking up the drive and opened the door as I reached it. 'You've got a lovely house,' I said. This wasn't an honest statement; Craig-derw was built in a style that might have been acceptable in a prosperous London suburb, but was an offence on a Welsh hillside. I meant that I wanted to know more about the house and its owners, and Martha understood this.

'The family built it to put themselves up a notch,' she said. 'It still works. It gets me on Lady Arbuthnot's list. But this is a sheep farm, just the same.'

'Somebody's done fairly well out of sheep farming,' I suggested.

'You mean, all these things?' The room into which she'd led me was like an antique shop. 'I wish I could make a clean sweep of them. But my husband wouldn't ever let me.'

She was using the tone of humorous tolerance in which wives often spoke of their husbands. It didn't tell me much; that tone could conceal anything from ardent love to misery. I vaguely wondered what Mr Hughes-Talbot was like, but I reckoned that Mrs Hughes-Talbot would be my friend.

I couldn't pursue the subject, in any case, because a couple of other guests arrived. One was the wife of the Bala police sergeant, the other was the wife of the garage-owner. Tea got under way. It was distinctly less formal than at Lady Arbuthnot's and more abundant materially, with an array of cakes and scones which I guessed to be the products of the Hughes bakery.

From then on, I was drawn firmly into the social life of Bala and its neighbourhood. Whether because I was sponsored by Martha, or because I had been admitted to the presence of Lady Arbuthnot, invitations arrived two or three times a week. The postman, who had appeared at Ty Pellaf only to bring a loyal screed from my parents, steered his bicycle regularly through the potholes. Since we were getting near Christmas, it was an exceptionally lively time. As well as the afternoon tea gatherings, there were evening parties which were often quite elaborate productions: we played charades, some people sang, some offered recitations, and there was dancing to wind up with. The principle was that everybody invited everybody else, so I always found some familiar faces. Martha, clearly, was very popular. Her contribution was a comic song which sent everybody into shocked but delighted laughter. Unfortunately for me, it was in Welsh. My Welsh was progressing, but was far short of a grasp of sly double meanings.

These parties were for both men and women, of course, and mainly for young married couples; but Martha's husband was never there. Once, another young woman asked: 'How's David, Martha? – if you've seen him lately.'

Martha took the crack in good part, but I could catch her expressions well enough by now to see that she was upset. It was her sister, the wife of the local doctor, who had flung the question. Martha and Ruth had one of those prickly relationships, close enough to know what would hurt.

When Martha knew that we were asked to the same party, she used to fetch me from my cottage and drive me home at the end of the evening. Then she would come in for a final drink; the Chartreuse ran out, but I replaced it with brandy. Our friendship was drawn tighter, more by the fact of being together in that end-of-the-road house than by anything that was said. Generally, Martha left after ten or fifteen minutes. Ann was teething and troublesome at night, she explained; the living-in maid was fully trustworthy and devoted to the child, but it wasn't fair to keep her on duty late at night. In Bala, eleven was late and midnight was very late indeed.

After the peaks of Christmas and New Year, the parties dwindled. Instead of two or three invitations a week I was lucky to get one, and then it was a tame afternoon tea-party. Correspondingly, I saw less of Martha. The weather became unpleasant, even forbidding. It was unsettled and unsettling, raining one day and snowing another, but almost always with fierce winds carrying dark clouds low over the hills, closing out the light. I kept the warmth up in Ty Pellaf, or at least the downstairs of Ty Pellaf, but it was chilling outside. So I fought shy of the walk to Parc, let alone an expedition to Bala. For days together I stayed in and saw no one; and I could sense each of the scattered houses drawing into itself, dourly standing the siege of the winter. When I first came to Ty Pellaf, I had been quite contented with the intermittent contact of the village shop, and glad otherwise to be alone. But now I had been spoiled by the parties, by my surprising inclusion in a generous community, above all by the friendship with Martha. Being left alone again was depressing. My lover from last winter's ski slopes, to whom I'd given scarcely a thought since putting the Channel between us, slipped into the emptiness. Annoyingly, humiliatingly, I missed him.

Instead of reading my collection of solid, worthy books or doing my Welsh grammar exercises, I gazed into the fire and brooded. With the turn of the year, all my uncertainties piled up. I had a feeling that 1939 would force change and decision on me, but still couldn't make up my mind whether it would see me back across the Atlantic. Sometimes I thought that I might commit myself lastingly to Bala. The country was beautiful, the people were kind and pleasant . . . why not? But then I reflected that I had no roots here, I would always be a stranger; Bala might tolerate me, but had no need of me. It had been the same, though, everywhere else through this decade of my wasting youth, from Hitherleigh to Grenoble. In Martha's eyes, it might appear marvellous to have chalked up so many journeys, so many homes and (as she doubtless guessed) so many men. But at the end of it all – if this was the end, and on cold January nights it felt like it – I possessed nothing unchallengeably valid or durable. It was useless, then, to ask Bala to give me what I had been unable to create for myself.

During this spell of wintry discouragement, two strange incidents added to my sense of uneasiness. One day, as I was sitting at the table and working on my Welsh, I heard the crack of a gun-shot. Less than a minute later there was another, then two or three more from a different direction. I went outside and crossed to the far side of the road, where I could get a view all round. But it was one of those gloomy days when, quite early in the afternoon, the light was failing. I could see nothing except the familiar thickets of gorse and bracken, soon losing their colour and fading into grey mists. The guns, however, kept firing.

Except in the movies, I had heard guns only a few times in my life. In the Camargue, poachers occasionally invaded the nature reserve and killed birds. I never caught sight of them, but I made a note of the number of the shots and where they seemed to come from, and informed the wardens. Presumably, what I heard now was shooting of that kind – pheasant shooting would be the most likely. It was legal here, since Arenig Fawr wasn't a nature reserve so far as I knew.

Strange, all the same, that the hunters were out in this foul weather and bad visibility, when there had been no sign of them on milder autumn days. They weren't finding much game, it seemed, for I heard no squawking of frightened birds. For all that I could tell, they were firing at random into the mist. This made me think that standing in the open was a risky thing to do; if I couldn't see the hunters, they couldn't see me. I retreated to my fireside. The incident did nothing to cheer me up; it wasn't only the cold and the rain, now, that were confining me to Ty Pellaf.

Something stranger than this happened about a week later. I was sitting in front of the fire with a book on my knees, of which I had read maybe five pages in the last hour. In the long darkness of winter, measurements of time lost their meaning. It must have been fairly late, though, because the fire had become a roasting furnace and I had stripped down to my slip and bra; I relished the heat on my skin as I relished the sun in summer. Mysteriously – not suddenly, but like a growing call on my attention – I had a feeling that someone was looking at me through the window in the end wall. The Barkers, using the house mainly in the summer, hadn't put up curtains, and I hadn't bothered about it.

I had to make a resolute effort of the will to look up. I believe that, for a split second, I saw a face. Tested on oath, I couldn't have sworn to it. And I believe that I heard footsteps on the muddy gravel of the path that edged the house; but it was a noisy night, with the wind beating at the bushes and rain-water pouring down from the gutter into the butt, so I couldn't have sworn to that either.

I tried to decide whether it was more likely to have been a robber, or a Peeping Tom, or a tramp who thought that the house was empty. But it wasn't easy to imagine any of these making his way to Ty Pellaf on a stormy winter night. 'The guy would have to be nuts,' I said to myself half-aloud. Then it struck me: my nearest neighbour was in fact nuts, or 'touched' as Mrs Bowen said.

The next time I saw Martha, I asked her what she knew about Sam Pritchard.

'Oh, he's one of those misfits,' she said. 'Every place has a few, doesn't it? He's worked on two or three of the farms round about, and at the quarry down at Corwen, but he couldn't stick to anything. Now he doesn't work at all, not properly.'

'Mrs Bowen says he's crackers.'

'Some do say that. I don't think he is. Just lazy and good for nothing. Mind, he's never had much of a chance.'

That, indeed, was true. When Sam was a young child, his father deserted his mother and went off – 'believe it or not,' Martha said – with a girl who had knives thrown at her in a circus. Sam's mother looked after him, on her paltry earnings as cleaner of the Baptist chapel, until he was sixteen. Then she managed to land a job as a cook in a seaside hotel. It was a living-in job and she couldn't take Sam with her. Mother and son, not being the letter-writing sort, were soon out of touch. Sam had been on his own ever since.

Martha thought it quite possible that Sam had been peeping in at my window, and didn't find it alarming. 'He must be soft on you, Estelle,' she said. This seemed to amuse her.

'I don't fancy being jumped on, one of these dark nights,' I said. 'I haven't even bothered to lock my door up to now.'

'Oh, you needn't worry about that. His mother brought him up very religious. He's never tried anything on with a girl, that I ever heard of. Mind you, I don't know what kind of girl would have any time for him' – Martha wrinkled her nose – 'but he'd be scared to do anything, you know, sinful. Peeping, now, that's different. All these Holy Joes have got their funny little habits. When the minister over at Llanuwchllyn died last year, they found boxes full of dirty pictures.'

'I think I'll put up curtains, anyway.'

'Well, it makes a room cosy. You can come over and use my sewing-machine.'

I hadn't been to Craig-derw since the tea-party back in November. This time, Martha's little girl was with us. She watched, enthralled, as the needle of the machine bobbed up and down and the line of stitching magically appeared. She was a very pretty child, as one would expect from knowing her mother, and for a two-year-old she was remarkably quiet and well-behaved. But as the afternoon wore on and it grew dark, she started to ask repeatedly: 'When's Dadda coming? When's Dadda coming?' Finally, Martha rang for the maid and told her to give Ann her supper. To me, she said: 'David's out some evenings. I ought to remember which, but I don't.' This must have been one of the evenings, for he didn't come in before I left.

With the curtains in place, I forgot about faces at the window. It was possible, anyway – and, as time made the memory vaguer, it seemed likely – that the whole thing had been an illusion. And if a glimpse of my flesh did give pleasure to such a deprived, unfortunate fellow as this Sam Pritchard, why should I mind? I felt almost ashamed of my curtains.

The shooting, on the other hand, was getting badly on my nerves. I heard it every few days, or once a week at least. Sometimes it was loud and must surely be close; sometimes distant, barely audible. I couldn't always be sure whether a shot was real or imaginary. Several times, I was misled by the crackling of a twig in the fire. I would rush outside in the hope of confirming my guesses; then, as in some teasing game, the shots would cease. The worst of it was that I was perpetually listening for them, helplessly on the alert. I even seemed to hear them when it was pitch dark, which made no sense at all.

I had never thought of myself as a nervous person, and I gave myself orders to stop bothering. But I had to reckon with the possibility that the hunters, whoever they were –

some kind of sporting club, perhaps not even Bala people – assumed that Ty Pellaf was an empty house and that the whole sweep of countryside rising to Arenig Fawr was deserted. In that case, I could be fired on walking back from Parc.

That was exactly what happened. It was, exceptionally, a crisp, clear day; I had my eyes fixed on the noble crest of the mountain, whose covering of fresh snow evoked wistful memories of last year's ski-ing expeditions. The shots, carried in the dry air, were startling close. I turned instinctively in the direction of the sound, and saw half a dozen men kneeling or crouching in a line amid the bracken. I shouted: 'Stop! Stop!'

One of the men stood up and walked toward me. He was tall, and took long unhurried strides which ignored the broken surface of hummocks, pools and rocks. He wore a khaki tunic, breeches and riding-boots stained with mud, and one of those basin-shaped helmets which recalled old photographs of British soldiers in the war fought in my childhood. While the other men had rifles, he had a revolver in a leather holster.

I asked: 'Are you the Army?'

'Not quite,' he said. 'We're the Territorials.' I hadn't heard this piece of British jargon, but I rightly guessed that it stood for a force of part-time reservists.

'Well, look here,' I said, 'you can't go firing your guns all over the place. It's dangerous.'

'Nonsense. They're firing blanks.'

I felt foolish, of course. For a man, it was the perfect example of a woman's ignorance and a woman's unnecessary alarm. He did nothing to help me over my embarrassment, but stood fingering the lanyard of his revolver with controlled impatience.

'All right,' I said. 'Carry on with your game, please do. I'm sorry I got in your way.'

In the evening, as I was clearing away my supper, there was a knock at the door. I was astonished and, to my shame and annoyance, somewhat fearful. Except for Martha, I'd never had a visitor – certainly not an unexpected visitor after dark. Suppose it was Sam Pritchard, and Martha's assurances about him were not quite trustworthy: what was I to do? But I could only hope for the best.

I opened the door. It was the same man, the leader of the war games. I was relieved, and glad to renew an encounter so badly begun, so absurdly broken off. Somehow, I felt that there was more to be said and more to be known.

He now wore an ordinary jacket and, instead of the tin hat, a tweed cap, but he was still in boots and breeches.

'Mrs Mavros, I believe.'

'Yes,' I said, not surprised. Anyone in the neighbourhood would know about the American woman with the Greek name.

'I came to apologize for the way I spoke to you today. It was inexcusable.'

'I wasn't very polite either,' I said. 'Let's forget it, shall we? Come in.'

'Thank you. Only for a minute.'

He came in, bending his head. No one had yet been here who was tall enough to remind me that my ceilings were low. David, from that first moment, lessened the size of Ty Pellaf and made it a place where we were close together.

He said: 'My name is Hughes-Talbot.'

I might have said: 'Oh, I know your wife.' It would have carried us smoothly from formality into a safe friendship. Why I didn't say it, I can't altogether explain. I may have already glimpsed, below the threshold of conscious thought, the place that David and Martha would hold in my life separately, but not together. And if I had said it, would everything have been different? After more than forty years, I prefer not to examine that question.

David sat down in the chair that, since I'd lived in the house, had been used only by Martha. I offered a drink. He accepted my brandy without enthusiasm; later, on Martha's advice, I kept whisky for him.

Carefully, he explained what the Territorials were.

'It's a question of being prepared. Continental countries have conscription – we don't. It may be too late this time to do the training after the war's started.'

I said: 'I thought the war was off.'

He looked at me, for a measurable silence, gravely and even sadly. I felt rebuked for my flippancy.

'You think so?'

'Well – you know, after Munich.'

'No, Mrs Mavros,' he said with finality. 'The war isn't off.'

'I'm sorry to hear it. I'm afraid I don't know much about politics.'

'It isn't politics.'

He didn't enlarge on this. He meant, I believe, that the issue of war or peace was decided by vaster forces than those of ordinary politics, and was not to be altered by another speech or another conference. The likelihood of war wasn't, for David, a matter for argument or even for informed judgement. It was a glacial movement of history, dwarfing the individual will.

He said no more of this but, after we left the subject, anything else sounded trivial. He asked me whether I had been to Wales before, how I'd heard of the cottage, how I liked it. As I presented the answers that I'd given several times to others, I was aware of a groping, difficult exchange beneath the words. He wasn't, clearly, a man for small talk.

'You don't mind living alone?'

This question, his last, was also a regular around Bala. As in most country districts, a woman didn't live alone unless she was old, or at least at the stage of being called a 'spinster'.

'No, I don't mind,' I said. 'I've lived alone quite a lot. But now we've met, do call in whenever you're this way.'

He stood up and put his empty glass on the mantelpiece, which was the right height for him. I thought: that must be where he puts a glass when he's at home. (It was.) As we shook hands, I saw him glance at the mattress. It was impossible for him to remark, as Martha had remarked, on my sleeping habits. We looked at each other, briefly, with constrained speculation.

I went to the door with him. Outside the circle of the lamp, darkness gave reality to the outer world, the cold night.

'You didn't come by car?'

'No, my wife's using it.'

I wondered where Martha had gone. At a social evening in the town, they would barely be serving supper now. As David's steps crunched on frozen puddles in the road, I was thinking: he could have stayed longer.

February moved into March. The weather, most days, was wild and stormy; spring was breaking through in a confusion of violence and hope. Touches of healing sunshine – when it could be astonishingly warm for half an hour, or just a few minutes – intensified the uncertainty. I became restless, couldn't sit at home, and found excuses to go into Bala, though rain was almost certain to catch me in the street at some time of the day.

I bought a newspaper more often than not. I had never followed the news with any regularity, but now I was more than usually out of touch, having no electricity and therefore no radio. And I had, as a general rule, been kept informed by the man whom I was seeing.

So I learned – and shouldn't have learned unless I'd gone into Bala on the right day – that German troops had marched into Prague. I sat by the fireplace in the Red Lion, staring at the smudged wire-photo pictures. However little one might know about politics, it was easy to grasp that this was the end of the Munich deal. We were back to last autumn's climate of alarm and menace; the war, if it wasn't inevitably on, was by no means off. I thought of the rifle-shots round my house, and of David Hughes-Talbot.

I had been hearing the guns at intervals, and next day I heard them again. It was getting on for evening, but the days were longer and there was still a fine, silver-grey light. I hadn't lit the lamp; I used to put it off as long as I could – as though, by refusing to admit that the day had come to an end, I kept its possibilities open.

The shooting stopped, the greyness took on a deeper shade, but I still did nothing about lighting the lamp or cooking my supper. I had been working on my Welsh and I was trying to remember a word that had escaped me: not actively searching, but waiting for it to fall into the trap of my mind. At times like this, I entrusted myself to the belief that, if I kept still and quiet, some good must come to me. So I remained sitting at the table in the room which served me as kitchen, dining-room and study – my hands, as I picture myself, clasped on the wooden surface and my face turned toward the door. When I heard a knock, I didn't go to open it, but only said: 'Come in.'

David came in and stood outlined against the fading light. He was in uniform, but with an officer's peaked cap instead of the helmet. I couldn't make out his expression, but I felt the intentness of his eyes. For a minute, he didn't move; nor did I. This was the minute, I thought later, in which it became certain that we should be lovers. Then, reaching behind him and still looking at me, he closed the door.

I said: 'I heard the shooting.'

'You know what it is now.'

'Yes.'

'You remember, you said . . . '

'I remember. I knew it was you, this time.'

He took the two long steps to the table and put his cap down on it. Then he unfastened the holster with the revolver and put that down too. I looked at it and said: 'I'm sure you're a good shot.'

'I am, yes. But a pistol's not much use in the open.'

'Why d'you have one, then?'

'I suppose it's a badge of rank.'

I undid the holster and took out the gun. It was larger and heavier than I'd expected; it wouldn't have fitted into a pocket, like the guns used by gangsters in the movies.

'I'd rather you didn't handle it,' David said.

'Why? Is it loaded?'

'Of course not. You never go about with a loaded weapon. It's a good rule not to fiddle with it more than necessary, that's all. It's not even mine, strictly speaking.'

'Whose is it?'

'His Majesty's.'

'And you're the only person who has one? Because of who you are?'

'You could say that.'

I put the gun back and snapped the press-stud again.

'I'm being a very poor hostess,' I said. 'Let's go and sit where it's comfortable.'

We went into the living-room. I was about to light the lamp, but I changed my mind. The fire painted the room with spurts of flame and depths of shadow. Each moment was altered by the next, and I found that good; there were dangers in definition. But I drew the curtains.

'Would you like a drink?' I asked.

'I don't think so, thanks. But if you . . . '

'No, I don't think so either.'

I could see him searching for a way into a conversation. Since he had already asked the obvious questions, he couldn't ask them again. I said: 'You shouldn't feel that you have to talk. It's enough that you're here.'

'I wasn't sure whether to take you at your word.'

'I'm glad you did. I'm very glad.'

Our chairs were just close enough for hands to reach. Then we moved towards each other, as if pressed from behind by a pair of invisible giants, until we were kneeling on the hearth-rug. His arms went over my shoulders, mine over his, in what might have been a curious wrestling lock or test of strength. There we stayed, scarcely moving, swaying a little perhaps, breathing deeply and slowly, welded by the heat of the fire, joined not in any urgent demand but in a reflective recognition, a submission to incontestable truth. It must have been two or three minutes before we even kissed. Still without haste, but also without the smallest imagined possibility of doubt or hesitation, we worked on hooks and buttons until we were naked. We crawled or shuffled to the mattress, and settled to make love.

All this time, not a word was spoken. I must have understood already that, for David, silence was the language of conviction. This silence, this absence of the customary whispers and murmurs, imparted to the act of making love with him a special and mysterious quality. Words, indeed, seem to bear no relation to what I found, that first time and every time, inexplicably magical. His dark weight, not so much pressing on me as enclosing me, was like the weight of night itself. The ceiling, lit by reflections of the fire, was infinitely high above us. I was embraced and carried away by a power as elemental and as hugely irresistible as the wind. We travelled, my lover and I, out of known reality into discovery; it was an ascent, a conquest. We reached – and it was never possible that we should not reach – a true consummation. I was, after I had been so high and so far, laid gently down on my mattress again. When David lifted himself from me, it was as though a cloak were drawn away.

While he dressed, I dreamily watched the patterns on the ceiling. I heard him say, as from a great distance: 'I must go.' I had dropped into a pleasant state of weakness, of the sort that follows a rare but successful exertion, and I was just able to raise my head for a kiss. After he closed the door, I reached out for my watch. I had no notion of the time, having gone where time ceased; but it wasn't even late for supper.

I might have stayed where I was until I fell asleep, but the fire died down and I had to put on more logs. I stayed for a while kneeling in front of it, still naked, drawing the warmth into my body. It was almost possible to believe that I had woken from a vivid and persuasive dream. My scattered clothes, however, were hard evidence.

I lit the lamp. There was no point in getting dressed again, so I put on an elegant kimono which had been a present from Mavros. It had gone round Europe with me, an accomplice in my indulgences. I hadn't worn it since coming to Ty Pellaf; but, now that I was with a man again, it felt right.

In the kitchen, I stared at the place on the table where David had put his cap and his revolver. Now, there was no sign or trace of his presence. I had never given myself to a man of whom I knew so little, and yet I had never given myself with such certainty. It had all happened as in the old myths, when the chosen woman received the god in the shape of a bull, a swan or a shower of gold.

The next morning brought one of those transformations in the weather typical of England, and still more of Wales. I was woken by the sun, sending in an arrow of light even though I hadn't drawn back the curtains. I dressed and went outside, eager to test the truth of this revelation. Though it was still early, it was warm. Incredulous, I found that I was wearing more than I needed and threw my sweater into the dimness of the kitchen. I carried a chair and a small table out to the yard and had breakfast there. Bread from Hughes' bakery, farm butter, Welsh honey: it all tasted fresh and nourishing.

I decided that I must see David. I wanted to share with him this day of confident promise: to be with him in the open, in the sunlight. I had only a vague idea of what a sheep-farmer did all day, but presumably he was out on his land. I walked a little way along the road, then struck out at right angles. Where I could see sheep, I reckoned that the land belonged to Craig-derw and no longer to the derelict farm of Ty Pellaf.

As I came nearer to the sheep, they ran away from me. I thought at first that this was sheer silly fright, but then I saw that they were being herded by a small, nimble black and white dog. The dog, in turn, was controlled by a man who stood by the gate of a field: David.

He gave me a glancing smile as I approached, but his eyes went quickly back to the dog. When I reached him, he took my hand and held it firmly. He was cautioning me to keep quiet and warning me not to claim too much of his attention, but he was also admitting me to companionship. He signalled to the dog by whistling, but surely that wasn't all; I guessed at some kind of telepathy, some link of trust and response. It was an alliance of minds capable of sustained purpose, exerting their command over creatures of no understanding. When the dog crouched vigilantly on the turf, the sheep forgot its existence; when it leapt into action, they obeyed its will; when some of them rushed blindly in the wrong direction, the move was instantly checked – you would have sworn, anticipated. Within less than five minutes, the sheep were all in the field. The dog rested, plainly conscious of its success but asking for no praise or reward.

I had never watched this sheep-herding before, though I knew that Welsh dogs were famous for it. It had the beauty of swiftness and precision, like a goal at ice-hockey or a downhill slalom. I said: 'That's terrific.'

'She's very good,' David said. 'The best I've ever had.'

'She?'

'It's always she. The best ones.'

'What's her name?'

'Nellie.'

'My name's Estelle,' I told him. 'In case Mrs Mavros sounds awkward.'

'Mine is David.'

I almost said: 'I know it is', but checked myself.

He realized that he was still holding my hand, and dropped it. He was gazing at me with an air of seriousness, even solemnity. All along, David considered that I didn't take things seriously enough.

'I suppose I'm in love with you,' he said abruptly.

It was a phrase that some men avoided for weeks or months, because it implied a loyalty beyond their intention. Other men used it too easily, as the small coinage of an affair. It was drawn from David reluctantly, the necessary statement of a stern and demanding honesty.

'Is it painful?' I asked.

'It can't be helped, can it? Not now.'

'I don't know. We could say that you came to pay a social

call, opportunity and the old basic instinct got the better of us, and now we can be sensible and forget about it.'

'Yes. We could. But that wouldn't be true, would it?'

'No, it wouldn't.'

We didn't, either of us, know what to say next. Anything was possible, and yet nothing was needed.

'It was lovely, last night, wasn't it?'

'Yes,' he said, again with that reluctant honesty.

'When can you come again, David? Could it be tonight?'

'No, that's impossible. I must tell you, Estelle, I'm a married man.'

'The best ones are.'

'I'll come whenever I can. It won't be long.' He confirmed this promise with a kiss, but it was a quick one, and I had to take it as a dismissal.

'But I don't think – I hope you'll understand – I don't think we ought to meet in public.'

'All right,' I said. 'I'm sorry. I'm quite a careful person really, you'll find.'

I might have remarked that Nelly, though obviously intelligent, lacked the gift of speech. But I saw that it would never be sensible to argue with David.

Instead of going back to Ty Pellaf, I walked on to the next farm and then the next. Barking dogs, whose enmity dissolved into pretence, met me at each border. I jumped the little streams, still brim-full from the melting of the snow. Arenig Fawr presented new faces as I swung a circuit around it. The sky was blue, but so pale that it might have been made of powdered clouds. The climbing sun spread light like a fire across the bracken. I charted my way through a world remade.

The energy of love carried me sailing through the next couple of weeks. I spring-cleaned the cottage, scrubbed the stone floors, and even swept the upper rooms which I didn't use. I attacked the overgrown kitchen garden, tore out great clumps of weeds, dug the soil over, and then planted whatever the Bala market offered – peas, runner beans, leeks, onions, radishes, lettuce. Some days, on an impulse, I walked miles: into Bala and back, or to the head of the lake, or over Arenig's flank to the lonely Tryweryn valley. On other days, I grudged the time to hurry to the shop in Parc. When I looked at my watch, it was always later than I'd thought.

Time to get ready for David. True, I never knew whether he was coming or not. Ty Pellaf wasn't on the phone, and I don't think Craig-derw was either. He might have sent notes, for the mail was cleared and delivered with a speed that would nowadays seem miraculous, but probably he wouldn't risk having his handwriting recognized. So I hoped to see him every evening, and was mostly disappointed. But I preferred this guesswork, and the sudden joy when I did hear him at the door, to the calculated regularity of other lovers.

So, as the light faded, I applied myself to washing the dirt and sweat from my hard-used body. I had to take the tin tub down from its hook on the wall, carry in bucketfuls of water from the rain-butt, and heat a couple of pans on the stove. The rain-water was good for my skin, maybe, but the process wasn't relaxing. I could sit in the tub only with my legs outside and the underside of my knees pressed to the sharp rim. I was always afraid that David would come in and find me in this ungraceful posture; once or twice, he did. However, I was usually able to get myself dry, the water emptied in the garden, and the tub back on its hook. Then I eased in my diaphragm (I had been reckless the first time, but no harm came of it), dabbed myself with French perfume, and put on the kimono. The perfume was unlikely to last the duration of the affair, but there was no telling what that might be, so I didn't stint it in those brave early weeks. All that remained was to build up the fire. No matter how warm the day, a sharp chill asserted itself when the sun went down. Besides, the dancing firelight on the ceiling was the signature of our love.

David always came on foot; it was less conspicuous than driving, and in any case the opportunity was mostly created by Martha going out. We were sharply conscious of the narrowness of time. We would sit down in our accustomed chairs and begin to talk, for I felt obliged to prove myself capable of a cool and civilized enjoyment of our meeting, and no doubt he felt the same, but it was never long before we dropped into the language of hands. We were still discovering each other, still seized by a marvelling delight.

Early on – perhaps on his third or fourth visit – David asked me what had become of my marriage, and whether I was divorced or merely separated. Fully divorced, I replied, and scarcely likely to recognize my husband in the inconceivable event of his appearing in Bala High Street. Nothing, I made it clear, could be more absolutely over than that brief and misguided episode.

'It's all quite simple for you, then.'

'So far as that goes, yes.'

'I wish it were equally simple for me.'

I waited. As usual, getting out the words wasn't easy for him.

'I love my wife. I don't understand how I can love her and love you too, but so it is. I've searched myself since . . . since this started, and I don't find myself loving her less. It's fair for you to know that.'

I said: 'Maybe it's simpler than you imagine. The human heart's very elastic. Please believe, anyway, that I'm not out to take anything from your wife. Your marriage is, strictly, none of my business.'

I saw that he had indeed searched himself, tramping alone across the fields. Then he had resolved on his statement. Prepared statements were distinctly in David's line; but with him the preparation was a sign of honesty, not of deceit as with most people. It wouldn't have occurred to him to pretend, for the sake of pleasing me and justifying himself, that there was no love between him and Martha.

When he left me that evening, I stood at the door and watched him on his way to Craig-derw until the darkness enclosed him and the wind silenced his steps. I was thinking that it was good to have a lover whom I could believe and respect.

There was some irony, certainly, in my having a lover at all. Rosemary's comment, if she knew, would be easy to imagine. I had genuinely rented Mr Barker's isolated cottage in order to be alone, to retreat and reflect; but I couldn't claim now that the intention had been profound or durable, since it had vanished from my mind when the first man knocked on the door. It seemed that the mere act of installing myself in the farthest house, coupled with the impression that a cosmopolitan divorcee was bound to make on all around, amounted to hanging out my shingle. Things had panned out, it could be said, nicely. My lover and I were freed from the wearisome bus or train journeys which had been governing factors in earlier affairs; he could be with me at the end of an easy walk, half of it on his own land. Well, I pleaded to the invisible Rosemary, I guess I'm just lucky.

On one of these April mornings – in my memory, they were all sunny – the postman brought me an invitation to tea with Mrs Craddock, the police-sergeant's wife. I was about to accept, pleased that social life was stirring again after the stillness of winter, when it occurred to me that Martha would be there. I hadn't seen her since plunging into love with her husband. But I had thought about her – I put this the best way I can – persistently and evasively. Persistently, because her importance to me was not to be denied: evasively, because even in my thoughts I could do nothing but hide from her.

Always, I had played this game of blind man's buff with my lover's wife. I had composed letters in my head to Madame Lecourbe, explaining just what I meant to Georges and Georges to me, begging her not to be angry and not to be hurt. But Madame Lecourbe was, after all, a shadowy figure the other side of France. Even if she knew that Georges had someone else, the name or face of Estelle Mavros could mean nothing to her. Martha was at Craig-derw, as close to me as David. She was my best friend in Bala. Indeed, since for years I had been dropping friendships on the roadside of my life, she was my best friend in the world. We had fastened to each other on impulses of warmth and trust – a case of falling into friendship, with the same enthusiasm and certainty as falling in love. I loathed the thought of betraying that friendship by deceit. I loathed, almost as much, the thought of dodging Martha. That wasn't practicable, in any case. I was as likely as not to come face to face with her the next time I shopped in Bala or changed books at the library. I could decline Mrs Craddock's invitation, but I couldn't decline many more. If I pretended to be sick, Martha would quickly appear at Ty Pellaf.

More than this: I figured that Martha was sure to find out. She was observant, as some of her remarks about local people proved, and perceptive. David, secretive though he might be, probably wasn't skilled in dissimulation. And Bala wasn't London or Paris, nor even Grenoble; there was a narrow limit to the places where a man could be when he wasn't at home. The evening drills and lectures connected with the Territorials were, I gathered, practically David's only engagements. He was lucky that Martha didn't remember which nights he was due to be out, but a slip-up sooner or later was close to inevitable.

It was even possible that Martha had found out already. I had no way of knowing and no proof to the contrary. It was possible that Mrs Craddock – advised by her husband, perhaps – had asked me to tea so that, confronted with Martha, I'd convict myself by nervousness. This was far-fetched, I told myself – I was slipping into paranoia. But how could I avoid paranoia, when I could be sure of nothing?

If Martha knew, meeting her could only be a humiliation for me; I was condemned to appear as a deceiver and a fool at the same time. If she didn't know, I was committed to a dishonesty that became baser from day to day, and from day to day it was at the mercy of chance. Either way, the outlook was intolerable.

So, on another of those sunny April mornings, I made my

way to Craig-derw like a penitent to confession. I was fearfully anxious, rehearsing in my mind words that nevertheless seemed impossible to utter, and shielding myself in advance from what Martha might say. Halfway up the drive, within observation from Craig-derw's windows, I decided that I must be crazy. In half an hour, I'd have lost my friend and probably my lover too. But it was too late to turn back. And indeed I had no option; I was doing what I had to do.

Martha was sorting through the household linen, a domestic rite of spring. An antique oak chest, which normally looked as though it were never opened, now had its lid thrown back and gave out a powerful smell of camphor. Sheets, pillow-cases, table-cloths and napkins were stacked all over the landing.

'Isn't this mad?' she greeted me. 'There's been no use for this stuff, most of it, since David's grandfather's time. But we're keeping it because we've got it. Come up, Estelle, you can chat to me while I'm doing the mending.'

We went to the room where I had made my curtains. Martha sighed as she showed me the frayed edges of the linen. How the edges became frayed, in the peaceful depths of the chest, wasn't easy to understand. Martha called it natural decay.

'How have you been, then?'

I didn't answer. She pressed the treadle of the sewing-machine, started a line of stitching, then stopped. The machine faded into silence.

'Something's the matter, Estelle.'

'Yes.'

'Tell me.'

'That's what I came here to do.' But, now I'd reached the point, it seemed theatrical, even unconvincing. I had the wild thought: suppose Martha doesn't believe me?

I gripped the edge of the table to steady myself and said: 'I'm having an affair with David.'

We looked at each other over the top of the sewing-machine. The word SINGER, in ornate gold lettering, is still what I see when I remember that moment. Then Martha said, in a tone not so much questioning as reflective: 'An affair?'

'Yes. You know.'

'Are you actually . . . ?'

'Yes. About twice a week.'

'On that mattress?'

'Exactly.'

I was tempted, I suppose by this allusion, to yield to wild, panicky laughter. Clearly, that would be most unsuitable. Imitating Martha, I maintained a decent solemnity.

'I thought there was something,' she said. 'He's been behaving strangely, just lately. He's been worrying, I could see that. But it shouldn't be worrying, should it?'

'It depends. It's just a spot of fun for some men. But David isn't like that.'

'No, he's not. He's a strange man altogether. Don't you think so, Estelle?'

'I can't say. I'm in love with him.'

'Oh, you're in love with him too?'

I wasn't sure – and I'm not sure now, recalling it – whether this meant 'as well as having an affair' or 'as well as me'. I nodded, and wondered what could possibly come next. I had imagined anything from Martha, from grief to fury, but not this degree of calmness. It indicated, I saw, a supreme self-confidence. That she was at all threatened, as David's wife, didn't seem to occur to her as a possibility.

'I'll just finish this hem if you don't mind,' she said after a minute. The machine whirred. I contemplated her steady hands, the precise downward-glancing angle of her head, the regulated pressure of her foot on the treadle. If there was a contest, she was the clear winner.

I said: 'I think I'd better go now.'

'I'll come down with you.'

On the stairs, she took my arm. It was as though I was the one in need of strengthening. Perhaps I was.

'We must have another talk, Estelle. After I've had time to think this over.'

'Right.'

'Are you going to Mrs Craddock's on Saturday?'

'I'm not sure.'

'Why not? There's no need to hide away. I'll come and pick you up, shall I?'

'Thanks very much.'

We went outside. The sun was still shining, but the wind was strong and dark clouds were taking up positions like battleships on the sea. As so often in Wales, anything was possible.

'Well . . . ' Martha said.

'Well . . . '

We managed to smile, struck both together by the element of comedy in the situation.

'I must say, Estelle – if it had to be anybody, I'm glad it's you.'

I couldn't find a worthy answer. We shook hands, and lingered over a few seconds of reassuring pressure. I looked into her eyes, but the wind was blowing her hair across them and I couldn't be certain of their expression. It did seem that we were still friends.

MARTHA

Count on nothing: that was what I learned in 1939. I began the year as Mrs Hughes-Talbot of Craig-derw. My marriage crackled with unresolved questions, but they seemed to do no more harm than to keep me on the alert. Marriage itself, like the solid walls of the house, was the frame within which answers were to be sought. I was in my own country, close to my family and among many friends. When Mrs Mavros from goodness-knows-where came to our neighbourhood, solitary and a stranger, I found a patronizing pleasure in helping her to settle.

By the end of the year I was husbandless, friendless, homeless and poor. I lived in lodgings in the dreary city of Manchester. I worked in the rationing office, and raced home every blacked-out evening to see how Ann had survived in the care of our slatternly landlady. Nobody knew who I was; I called myself Mrs Hughes. It wasn't the conditions of life that ground me down, except for Ann's sake. Jacob's basement flat, and working at Woolworth's, had been much the same. But I was older now, and the sense of loss was bewildering. I didn't want to believe that it had all been inevitable.

Looking back, I remembered that I had begun to worry in the restless spring. Messages from David came, as they always did, without words. Deep in the night, I woke to find him clutching me. We clung together while we made love, as we might have clung together in a place of danger – a ledge above a precipice, a raft on swirling seas. It must have been then that we began to say goodbye to each other. With yearning, with pity, with undiminished love; nevertheless, goodbye.

'When your husband makes passionate love to you, you can bet he's got another woman.' So I was told by new friends years later, when the knowledge was useless to me. There's truth in it, in more than the obvious cynical way. Estelle must have put a new charge in the force by which David was driven, so that desire for her renewed and sharpened his desire for me. But I understood that only slowly.

I never asked her exactly when they became lovers. They were 'having an affair', she informed me in the middle of April. I gathered that it was something quite established, with its own routine. Her statement, offered in a clear and level voice, took me completely by surprise. I hadn't been aware that she had met David at all, or that she would even know that David was my husband's name. As a matter of fact, I had been careful not to tell David that I'd made friends with an American divorcee called Estelle Mavros, because this was just the sort of person he would disapprove of. Then, the word 'affair', which wasn't in the Bala vocabulary, didn't at first convey anything to me. When I grasped the meaning, I saw it as an activity carried on in places where Estelle was at home, such as the Riviera, by people whose style and skill were far beyond me.

I asked a string of silly, naïve questions. I really wasn't certain whether an affair included anything so crude and straightforward as fornication, to use the traditional Welsh word. Estelle assured me that it did. I even asked whether they made use of the mattress in front of the fire. The idea of sinking to the floor instead of leaping into bed struck me as comical, and I was on the verge of bursting into a hysterical giggle. In the face of Estelle's perfect calmness, I restrained myself.

Luckily, I was seated at the sewing-machine. This gave me something to hold on to – literally – and then I had the inspiration of pretending to be a compulsive hem-stitcher, which won me a few precious minutes to regain a semblance of self-control and collect my thoughts. I was, in truth, very frightened. It's true that I didn't apprehend, then or later, a 'threat to my marriage' in the usual sense. An affair didn't presumably, mean that David would replace domesticity with me by domesticity with Estelle, and I saw right away that this wasn't her purpose. Anyway, he was immutably attached to Craig-derw; at the simplest level, how would a displaced sheep farmer look for a job? No, no, that wasn't it. But I was being repaid for my failure to achieve the true understanding with David to which our marriage was a claim. And if I had been unsuccessful before Estelle set up another pole of attraction, what hope could I have now?

One thing that absolutely threw me was that Estelle gave me this information of her own accord. I had always assumed that adultery was cunningly concealed. But of course I knew practically nothing about it, whereas Estelle must be assumed to know plenty. Perhaps she was doing precisely what the modern mistress . . . 'mistress?' was that the right word? . . . did do, on the Riviera for instance. It certainly put a wife on the defensive and deprived her of the weapon of indignation.

I saw that the great, the irretrievable mistake would be to make an enemy of Estelle. I needed all the clues to David, all the tapped lines and broken codes, that I could get; if Estelle would share what she had, I ought to be grateful. We were friends – was that something to be thrown away? Suppose that David were having this affair with a woman who owed me nothing and didn't like me: how much worse that would be!

Before we were married, I was astonished that other girls didn't see David with fascinated eyes. Ruth, notably, was quite unimpressed. While this was a relief to me – Ruth would have been a mean competitor – I was also close enough to my sister to be puzzled and upset by the divergence of our tastes. Now, when Estelle said that she was in love with David, I was able in the midst of my alarm to salute a validation of my own love. Well, I said to myself, as we shook hands at the door, she's a tremendously attractive woman; she's had her pick of Europe and discarded a Greek millionaire; I ought to be proud.

That evening, I stayed at my sewing-machine until it grew dark. Ann demanded: 'Where's Daddy?' She connected his return to the house with darkness, in winter or summer, and – in the nature of farm work – she was generally right. To take her mind off it, I let her do the sewing: that is, hold the material while I pressed the treadle. Outside the windows, the silver-grey light of spring dissolved and it was completely dark. David was with Estelle. It was something I would have to get used to.

He came in when I had just finished giving Ann her supper. I went out to meet him in the hall. He kissed me on the cheek, in his usual way. I had been wondering if it would feel any different; it didn't.

He carried Ann up to bed and told her a story. Ann didn't really like his stories, which were flat and unimaginative, while mine were more fanciful. No one had told David stories when he was a child, so he had no recollections to draw on. But Ann would never have let him see what she thought. We're born, I suppose, knowing how to deal with men.

He came downstairs again. He moved with a slight weariness, unlike the weariness of a day out of doors. Or so I thought; perhaps I imagined it. I went and stood by his chair, and rested my hand on his head. After a minute, he reached up and held my hand. We kept the contact, the renewal of all our days and nights, but we didn't say anything and we didn't look at each other. I saw that the way we lived together would need more care, more artifice.

On the Saturday, I fetched Estelle to take her to tea at Mrs Craddock's She heard the car coming, and opened the door before I pulled on the handbrake. She must have decided that I wouldn't want to go into the house, with the mattress and all that. Actually, this piece of tact worked the wrong way – I found it sad to be excluded. But we would understand each other better in time, Estelle and I. She got briskly into the car. I turned and drove off.

'You were marvellous, the other day,' she said.

'What did you expect me to do? Slap your face?'

'Why not?'

'Because you'd have told David, for one thing. How would I look, slapping faces?'

'No, I wouldn't have told him. I mean, that would have meant telling him I'd gone to see you.'

'Haven't you told him that?'

'Good God, no. It's the last thing . . .'

The car crashed into a pothole. I was driving too fast for the road, as I always did when my mind was elsewhere. Estelle hit her head on the roof.

'I'm terribly sorry.'

'Not at all. Help yourself.'

I got the car onto level ground and we proceeded more cautiously.

'I'm still wondering why you did come to me.'

'We had to see each other again, Martha. If not at Mrs Craddock's, then somewhere. I hated the thought of not being able to look you in the eyes.'

'I see.'

'Don't you believe me?'

'Of course I believe you. Where d'you think we'll end up, if we start not believing each other?

'Well, can I ask you . . . I don't have any right, but . . . can I ask you what you're going to do now?'

'I don't know,' I said. 'I can't think of anything. Can you?'

She meant, of course: did I intend to assert myself as a wife and demand that David should stop seeing her? My mother, or any other sound member of the wives' trade union, would have told me that this was not only my right but my duty. But, when I imagined myself doing it, I didn't see how to achieve the required conviction. Strangely, I should have felt ashamed. 'I possessed nothing that I could offer to David as recompense for that deprivation. And Estelle? For her candour, she deserved a better return.

'Oh, Martha . . .' she said, and broke off. I looked at her as I stopped the car at the corner of the paved road. Her face was flushed, burning with relief and gratitude. She loved him, sure enough.

During April and May, we saw each other often. It was a good time of the year, when each fine day was a gift. We used to meet in Parc, sometimes by chance and sometimes by arrangement. We sat on the bridge, dropping words like twigs into the clear racing water. We ambled along the road, stopping to pick primroses from the crevices of the moss-covered stones. We met in Bala, too, and shopped or window-shopped the length of the High Street. Rain, or any other excuse, took us to the saloon bar of the White Lion. It wasn't strictly proper for women without men to buy drinks, but I had a name for being careless about the conventions, and of course an American would know no better.

'I'm seeing more of you than I do of David,' Estelle said once.

'Is that bad?'

'No, it's not bad at all. I'm friends with you, more than with him.'

'You know, that sounds funny.'

'Does it? But when you get down to it, a lover can't be exactly a friend.'

'A man could be a friend, though, don't you think? Or only a woman?'

'Maybe a man could be, if you could really forget about him being a man. You could be friends with a homosexual.'

I stared at her. 'Friends with a queer?'

'D'you think that's impossible?'

'I've never thought about it. We don't have them in Bala. I expect you know about them, though. What are they like?'

'They're human beings.'

'Well, yes. I'd keep thinking about what they do.'

'They don't want to do anything to you, that's the point.'

It may have been a little later in this conversation, or in another, that Estelle said: 'Friendship lasts, that's the great thing. Or it can, it has a chance. These love affairs never do. That's why it's so intense, why there's so much packed into every minute, because right from the start you feel the clock ticking away to the time when it'll be all over.'

I tried to console her. 'Don't think about that, Estelle. Not yet, anyway.'

'It's better not to have any illusion, I've found. And I want you to know, too. He wants to stop it, Martha. It's not something he ever planned to do, or imagined himself doing before it happened, and that worries him. I've seen that from the first time he put on his clothes and walked out of the house. So, sooner or later, he will manage to stop it. You've only got to wait. I know that's easy to say. But at least it's a certainty. You've only got to wait. And then, you'll always be his wife.'

'I hope we'll always be friends, too. Even when we're old ladies with white hair. D'you think we will?'

'I hope so.'

'But if this does come to an end – you and David, I mean – won't you go back to America?'

'Maybe I will. I've thought about it.'

'You ought to. There's going to be a war.'

'I don't believe there is,' Estelle said. 'They haven't got the guts.'

'Who haven't?'

'Men. European men. It's all yelling and screaming and boasting, like the monkeys in the *Jungle Book*. That's what they're like, the whole lot of them. Hitler, too. They couldn't go through with a real war. David could, because he's a real man. That's why we love him, isn't it? But he's just about the last one left.'

And she said, then or another time: 'What I call a real man, you see, is a man who carries the weight of his responsibilities. Loving me as well as you is one hell of a responsibility for him.'

This seemed strange to me. 'Don't you think he's enjoying it?'

'I think there's joy in it. There's always joy in love. But it's painful, too. It could tear him apart, and he knows that. So he'll be most sincerely relieved when it's over. And yet, being the man he is, he'll go through with it.'

'Like the war?'

'Yes, like the war.'

I thought, after talks like this, that Estelle understood David better than I did. That came from her experience of men; she had told me by now about some of her others. Measured by David, she said, most of them were simply not serious. My own experience was limited to Peter Morshead, but she was certainly right if he was anything to go by.

It was four years, that spring, since David had agreed to marry me. It cost me an effort to put it like that, even in my own mind, for it was plainly on the record that he had asked me to marry him. But the truth was that I had devoted all my young life to pursuing him. If he now asserted his freedom, I had no one to blame but myself. It wasn't fair, surely, to blame Estelle; she hadn't pursued, she had simply been there at the right moment. Wrenching him away from her could prove, fatally, the shakiness of my title. Whether she knew it or not, she was doing me a good turn when she advised me to wait for the affair to run its course. Otherwise, I risked a victory for which I might never be forgiven.

And I found that, as the weeks passed and I got used to it, honestly it wasn't as bad as I had expected. Knowing about it helped enormously; I couldn't have lived with suspicion and uncertainty. I could always guess when he had been with Estelle. I checked with her when I next saw her, and I was hardly ever wrong. After he came home from her, I behaved toward him with a sweetness that wasn't exactly in my nature. I was testing my power to love without jealousy; on the whole, I was satisfied with my success.

Toward Estelle, I felt a kind of mystified tenderness. In most respects, I looked up to her. I was four years younger than she was, which wasn't usual, I presumed, for the wife in a triangle. Since I hadn't managed to meet anyone like her in

London, clearly I was lucky to do so in Bala. Some of the things she said, though not at all intended to put me down, were quite beyond me. When I listened to her I was often aware of a glittering cleverness, and not seldom of what I humbly took to be wisdom.

Yet there wasn't much wisdom in her life, I couldn't help thinking when I heard about it. There was immense bravery – I gasped at the vision of making one's way alone, in strange countries, a strange continent indeed, from the age of twenty – but that wasn't the same. Her marriage, though she told the story amusingly, had been a grotesque blunder. Her affairs had given her pleasure and she stoutly denied regretting any of them, but all the men – until David – had disappointed her. My Mam would have said: 'She needs looking after.' Certainly she needed a friend. I didn't think it fair to refuse my friendship to her, just because she had a few hours a week on that mattress with David.

One day, I met Estelle in Mrs Bowen's shop in Parc. The shop was crowded with the village women, and one of them was telling how a certain Mrs Lloyd had been pursued across two fields by a ram in the flush of the season. Mrs Lloyd, it was agreed, might have enjoyed a thrill that hadn't come her way since her schooldays, being well beyond the estimated capacity of Mr Lloyd. All this was in Welsh, naturally. Welsh was the language of easy intimacies; what might have sounded improper or even nastily obscene in English was no more than pleasantly comical in our vernacular. Besides, there may have been a feeling that the subject wasn't for the ears of the stranger among us.

Estelle and I did our shopping and went to sit on the bridge, our place for chatting on fine days. I embarked on a translation.

She said in Welsh: 'Yes, I thought that was what they were saying.'

I nearly toppled into the river. I hadn't been so surprised since she told me that she was having an affair with David. In fact, this was in some ways more surprising. I must explain.

Forty years ago, more people in Wales spoke the language than they do now – one-third of the population has dwindled to one-sixth, I believe – but it had an entirely unofficial character. No one, for instance, was ever asked if he knew it when applying for a job. Legal documents, like a contract or the deeds of a house, were always in English. So were the signs that said 'Drive Slowly' or 'No Smoking'. A visitor, staying in hotels and entering no homes, might never have discovered that any other language existed. Welsh was the private code of the Welsh people, and had nothing to do with anybody else. So the idea of learning Welsh, as it might be learning French, was close to inconceivable. Even a Welshman wouldn't learn Welsh if he came from a district where it wasn't spoken, let alone an Englishman, and still less a foreigner.

Equally hard to accept, it follows, was the idea of somebody speaking Welsh imperfectly and with an accent. The American accent in English was familiar to us from the films; it was odd, but millions of people did talk like that. An American accent in Welsh sounded like an imitation – like one of my brother Gideon's comic turns. Estelle had been teaching herself Welsh from an old-fashioned book, and her mode of expression tended to resemble my Dad's pulpit style. This was flavoured with colloquialisms picked up from the humorous column in the weekly paper, a sprinkling of grammatical errors and wrong genders, and the American accent as the final weird touch. It's safe to say that nobody else ever spoke Welsh like Estelle. I broke down, occasionally, into helpless giggles. She took that in good part, but I don't think she ever quite saw what was funny.

Still, when I found that she was learning Welsh – or rather had learned Welsh, for she brought her usual cleverness to it and could say pretty well anything she wanted – I was touched, indeed moved. I saw in it a wistful hope of belonging to this country into which she had been carried by a wave of chance, even if it could be only for a while – to be accepted, not to be a stranger. And, although it couldn't literally be true, I liked to fancy that she had learned Welsh to talk to me. We did speak Welsh, by a tacit impulse, whenever we said things that belonged to ourselves alone. Already close, we were wrapped closer by the language. But each of us spoke English, the language of the outer world, with David.

I had been cautious about going to Estelle's house after I knew that it was also (to use a newspaper word of the period) David's love-nest. But we had reached, by the time I'm now describing, a friendship so honest and frank that nothing could embarrass us. One morning, impatient because a spell of rain had prevented us from meeting, I got in the car and drove to Ty Pellaf. Estelle was delighted; she had been hoping she could ask me, but uncertain about it. As I came in, she jumped up and kissed me. The kiss as a social formality was a couple of decades away, so this was a true welcome.

From then on, I took the potholed road to the farthest house about as often as David did. Sometimes I went by car, either because I had Ann with me or because it was raining or simply to lengthen our time together. But I preferred to walk; the distance was just right for a pleasant stretching of the legs. David, I knew, always walked.

'He reckons it's safer,' Estelle explained. 'A car would attract attention, with the noise and the lights. People would soon start wondering whose car it was.'

'Yes.' Welsh people certainly would. 'But if they couldn't see inside the car, they'd think it was me. Everybody round here knows we're friends.'

'Everybody except David,' Estelle said. We laughed. We often seemed to be laughing, these days. The tension between us had died away.

Since it was in daylight that I went to Ty Pellaf, I did occasionally meet somebody. It might be the postman, or the police sergeant, or Sam Pritchard. The postman, rarely; Estelle got few letters. The police sergeant, Evan Craddock, was sure to get off his bicycle for a chat with me. I knew him well; he was the same age as my eldest brother, Adam, and they were close friends. Unlike most sergeants, he wasn't fond of lounging about in the police station. Whenever he could, he left the constables in charge and took to the road. You would see him pedalling methodically along at slightly more than walking pace, apparently day-dreaming but actually, you felt sure, noticing if a blackbird took an unauthorized worm. Evan made a deliberate effort to pass himself off as a fumbling, thick-headed country copper, then a standard figure in detective stories and films. Those who knew him weren't fooled; he was as sharp as they come. I wondered what he was doing on the dead-end road. Perhaps he considered it his duty to keep a protective eye on a woman living alone. More likely, he was checking on what Sam Pritchard was up to.

As a squatter and scrounger, Sam was viewed with disfavour by the police. A year ago, he had killed one of our sheep, cooked it over the fire in the old barn where he lived, and eaten it. So David believed, as did Evan, though the one solid fact was that the sheep was missing when David made his count. I had annoyed David by suggesting that Sam was hungry. In a hard winter, with no odd jobs going, he probably was. There was no social security then, and if there had been, Sam would have been one of those people who don't know how to apply for it.

My own attitude to Sam, like that of most Bala people, veered between contempt and pity. He didn't have much of a life, surely – chopping wood here, carrying stones to mend a wall there, and going from house to house trying to sell his pictures. The last-named device was generally regarded as an absurdity. People said accurately enough that, when you took into account the work of producing the pictures –that is, painting and framing them – and the cost of the materials, they couldn't bring in enough money to live on even if he'd sold them all. In fact, I was one of the few people who ever bought one. I didn't dare to tell David, and disguised the expenditure of three pounds in the household accounts as 'new parts for sewing-machine'. This meant that I couldn't hang the picture (not that I could have displaced an item of the Hughes-Talbot heritage, anyway). But I was content to shove it into the loft, having bought it on an impulse of charity and not because I liked it. I unwisely told Ruth, who said, 'Just the sort of soft thing you would do.' It was a large painting of the Resurrection, with souls shooting out of the Llanycil graveyard as a shaft of light struck the lake. The day after David was arrested, I ripped it out of the frame and burned it. I didn't want any risk of David finding it if in the course of time he was released and came home. I might have had it kept by the bank, but no such thought occurred to me; I was pleased with my prudence in saving the frame, which went to a second-hand shop for ten bob. Alex estimates that, if the painting could itself be resurrected, it would fetch fifty thousand at Sotheby's.

Interviewers have asked me, all these years later, whether there wasn't anybody around Bala capable of discerning the quality of Sam Pritchard's work. Well, it was the 1930s; conventional taste had just about advanced to the acceptance of Van Gogh. Besides, what the Welsh know about is chiefly music and poetry, to the neglect of the visual arts. Imagine Sam as a bard, and it could have been a different story. As for the English settlers, they weren't the cultured types who gathered at a place like Penrhyndeudraeth. They had come to Wales to be left alone, by Modern Art as well as other disturbances. Lady Arbuthnot would barely have accepted Van Gogh. On canvas, perhaps: definitely not in person.

In fact – though I couldn't say this to the interviewers – it was mainly because we knew Sam that we could confer no value on his pictures. By the time the Pritchard boom got under way, I had been married to an artist for twenty years, and the infinite diversity of art was a truth he'd hammered into me. Yet I couldn't bring myself to place Sam in the ranks of those people of talent and achievement who were now my friends. To see anything in the Pritchard paintings, I had to disconnect them from the despised, pleading figure of the man who offered them at the kitchen door for three quid, or I found myself protesting: it can't be true, it's all a big con.

Some people maintained that Sam was cracked. I rejected the notion for Estelle's benefit; nobody, however courageous, wants a nut as her sole neighbour on a deserted road. For the Pritchard public of later years, such a reputation has put him grandly in the Van Gogh class and proved his title to genius beyond all doubt. In his lifetime, the effect was just the contrary. It made his paintings pathetic, indeed ridiculous, along with everything else about him: his inability to keep a job, his begging and scrounging, and his religious ravings.

On certain striking occasions, denunciations of sinfulness and appeals to repentance would burst from Sam's mouth like screams from a scalded child. The rhetoric wasn't, I daresay, very different from that of famous revivalists whom older people in Bala could remember. What was ridiculous was for Sam to imagine that he had a right to it. The Welsh view of religion is, I still think, a sensible one. It is believed, firstly, that if a moral code is to be effective it must be combined with realism and an understanding of human desires. It is believed, secondly, that religion, being a serious matter, should be the concern of serious persons, such as my Dad. Sam's ravings – that was the usual word – offended against both these principles. And they were the clinching factor in making it impossible to look favourably on his paintings: those fervid visions of such subjects as the Massacre of the Innocents (acquired by White Lion, 1938; Tate Gallery, 1965), the Crucifixion (stored by Bala Council, 1939; Chicago, 1970). or the Resurrection (destroyed by M. Hughes-Talbot, 1939). If he didn't deserve attention when he talked religion, why should he when he painted it? Indeed, the critics who put Pritchard on the map and revered the compelling intensity of his faith were of course agnostics, like the rest of our friends when Alex and I lived in Hampstead.

On Whit Monday (now secularized as Spring Bank

Holiday) Estelle and I adjourned, as we sometimes did, from a tea-party to the lounge of the White Lion. Here we were surprised, but less than astonished, to see Sam Pritchard. He didn't drink, for reasons both of principle and penury, but he was doubtless in the place for a talk with Mr Stanley, the manager. Hotels and restaurants in Wales, or those that are any good, are generally managed by Englishmen; I suppose that catering to the tastes of strangers contradicts Welsh inclinations. Mr Stanley, who hadn't been long in Bala, was under the totally erroneous impression that he would earn approval by patronizing the local artist. He had therefore bought four or five of Sam's paintings; one of them hung above the staircase until later events caused its removal. In retirement, and interviewed by Melvyn Bragg, Mr Stanley claimed to have been the first to recognize Pritchard as a great painter. This wasn't true, but he'd certainly made a great investment.

Sitting in the corner of the lounge were a boy and a girl, probably just old enough to buy drinks, whom I'd noticed mooching along the High Street earlier in the day. They belonged to a group of campers, from Birmingham to judge by the accent. For urban youth, a trip to Bala must have been boring to the point of distraction. It had rained or at least drizzled all through the weekend. The town, with its closed shops and empty streets, was chilling to strangers. Only the pubs – when they opened, which they didn't on Sunday – offered a refuge. All they asked for, this boy and girl, was a place where they could be together, dry and unobserved. Having found this, as they believed, they were absorbed in each other, and reaching for physical contact as a solace for the world's coldness. I knew the feeling, from Thursday afternoons with Peter. What they were doing was beyond the publicly permissible for Bala in 1939, yet it was discreet and certainly not defiant. To be exact, the boy's hand was up the girl's skirt.

Sam Pritchard, coming from Mr Stanley's office, halted abruptly in the middle of the lounge like a dog catching a scent. He raised his right arm and extended it in the direction of the Birmingham couple. The movement recalled the accusing dignity of an Old Testament prophet, as depicted in the coloured prints I'd grown up with; the resemblance made it absurd, since this was no prophet or even latter-day preacher but only silly Sam. Then he spoke.

'Be gone from this place! Be gone from among us, for you are an offence to our sight. In your shame you shall be known, and your evil ways shall not be hidden.' And more of this, plenty more. The rhetoric is self-renewing.

The boy gaped. This was an onslaught, clearly, for which nothing in his whole life had prepared him. The language that Sam used has little meaning except in its tradition; he might almost as well have been speaking Welsh. The girl shrilled a nervous giggle, not likely to improve matters.

'Now then,' the boy said, getting to his feet. 'Now then. What's all this about?'

Sam raved on. He had a singularly flexible voice, mild and soft in ordinary speech, loud and full of resonance when it was powered with this kind of charge. Or, you could say, he had two voices.

'I've got a right. I've got a right,' the boy said. He must have felt obscurely that some kind of right was under threat, whether it was the right to his affections or simply the right to be in the White Lion. I noticed that he had, automatically, grasped the nearest thing to a weapon, which was a heavy ashtray.

There were eight or ten people in the lounge, but most of them were Whitsun visitors and no one felt called upon to intervene. The scene continued for three or four minutes, which can seem a long time. Eventually, Sam's voice drew the attention of the barman, who held the job because of his natural authority and physical strength. He summed up the situation with a glance and ordered: 'Out, the lot of you.' Sam obeyed; probably it never surprised him to be brushed aside and denied recognition, whether as prophet or as artist. The young people from Birmingham obeyed too, still bewildered and doubtless resolving never to come to Wales again.

'Fantastic,' Estelle said. 'Just fantastic.'

I said: 'Didn't I tell you? He's highly moral, is Sam.'

'It's called moral, is it? The hatred was what scared me. He really hated those kids, Martha.'

She was shaken enough to need another drink quickly. Like other outsiders, she had formed an idea of Wales as a haven of friendliness and tolerance; glimpses of a different Wales were bound to remind her of her own vulnerability.

From Whitsun to July we had, as usual in Wales, the best weather of the year. The whole month of June was lazily warm, a time when it was easy not to worry. In the long evenings, without fires and without drawn curtains, night fell so gently that a tinge of light always remained in the darkness. Midsummer Day came within this time. It was a day of which Bala people took some note, if it wasn't exactly celebrated. It was the year's meridian, the point of balance, the moment to count blessings. After it, the days would become shorter; time would close in, instead of opening out. Besides, there was still a vague memory of Midsummer as a high holiday, the outdoor counterpart to Christmas. And perhaps the stirring of a remoter memory, when the sun's ascendancy was the sacred core of the old religion.

Near the ending of this longest day, I went out of the house – leaving the front door open, a careless pleasure that was seldom possible – and walked the short distance to the place that had given our home its name, the rock among the oaks. By that ancient belief, it was hallowed at the solstice. David and I had once, on our first Midsummer day, got up and dressed before dawn to see if the sun's first rays did actually strike on the rock; they did.

Now, the sun was setting over the fine-etched shoulder of Arenig Fawr. We had many dramatic sunsets, with clouds torn to shreds and daubed every shade of pink red and gold. This sunset, without clouds, wasn't dramatic although it was beautiful. The sky did, for once, represent infinite distances, not the tangible roof we mostly imagine. The sun was about to disappear in the most absolute sense: to drop out of somewhere into nowhere. It would leave behind nothing but stillness and empty space.

Ann had been put to bed, protesting because it wasn't dark. David was with Estelle, I supposed. These midsummer evenings obliged him to walk to Ty Pellaf in daylight, a possible risk, but he wouldn't return until well after sunset. I should have preferred him to take the car and save time, but I couldn't very well make the suggestion.

Then, just as the sun departed, I saw him walking up from the house. He must have gone in, since he wasn't wearing his cap as he did all day. He couldn't have been with Estelle after all. Though I had conquered jealousy, I was relieved; the evenings when he'd been with her were still difficult for me. He was likely to behave more normally than usual (that should be clear, if not quite logical) and the falsity grated on me. I wished that he would stay with Estelle all night – another suggestion that I couldn't make.

'I wondered where you were,' he said.

'It's a lovely evening. Look, the sun's only this moment gone. You just missed it.'

'I'm sorry.'

'Well, it was special. The longest day. Have you said goodnight to Ann?'

'Yes, but I don't think she'll go to sleep yet.'

'Never mind. Let her enjoy the longest evening. It's hers too.'

The oaks formed a circle round the rock, open only to the east. David took my arm, and we began to walk inside this circle, under the branches of one old tree after another. Our slow pacing had the solemnity of ritual, though I wasn't sure what it affirmed.

He said, in a voice pitched barely above the silence: 'I don't know how many more evenings like this we'll have.'

He might have been thinking of the strain that he had placed on the trust between us; or the danger of war, which

154

oppressed his mind more and more as we approached the customary season for crisis; or simply of the weather, unsafe in Wales any time after the solstice. I chose the last of these meanings.

'There'll be another year,' I said. 'Many more years.'

'Yes,' he said with an uncertainty that was disturbingly unlike him. Then, suddenly: 'Will you believe – whatever happens – believe I'll always love you?'

He let my arm go; we faced each other. Our walking came to a halt, just at the break in the circle of trees. Here was the highest point of our land, the crest impending above the fall to the lake. The sky was the colour of no colour, of daylight's vanishing. David's eyes shone like black stars.

I answered steadily: 'I believe that. Now and always.'

But I felt myself balancing on a pinnacle of risk, unsupported, exposed to unknown threats. I went hurrying into the shelter of the trees, to rest on the smooth bulk of the rock.

Sharply, David called: 'Come back, Martha!'

I caught myself and swung round, almost falling. I remembered what must have been at the back of my mind, but barred from consciousness. The grove was, in the faith of our ancestors, more that a place of prayer and ceremony; it was the place of sacrifice. The old gods were all around us, in the trees and the streams. The victim chosen to appease their just anger, once led to the rock, was beyond rescue and beyond pity. And I remembered too that, although we had walked here often, I had never seen David sit or tread on the rock.

'I'm here,' I said. 'But the day's over, David. It's dark. It's starting to be cold. Let's go indoors.'

Through these serene and cloudless days of June and early July, the balance held. David was very loving to me, and I was sure that it wasn't from cunning pretence, for that was never in his nature. At the same time, I knew that his love for Estelle hadn't begun to wear out. She was amazed, she told me, by its rooted intensity. I had been afraid that, if he loved her more, he would – helplessly, against his will – love me less. Now I saw that there was no such crude logic. Love was a stock that renewed itself as it was spent. Love was a fire that warmed everyone within its reach.

One afternoon, when I had driven Estelle home from a tea-party in Bala, she said: 'I won't ask you in, Martha. I've a hunch David may be coming.'

It was comical enough, picturing David's face if he walked in and found us together. We discussed whether I should 'make an excuse and leave' or whether I ought to hide upstairs, and had a good laugh over it. Then I said: 'But seriously, Estelle – he must have guessed I know all about it by this time.'

'Oh, no! Absolutely not! He hasn't any idea. He's always telling me how disastrous it would be if you found out.'

'Hasn't it occurred to him I might wonder why he comes in late?'

'He's got answers. A farm isn't like an office job, he says. There's been the busy season – sheep-shearing, is that right? And his war games; you're not to know how late they go on. But the truth is, he can't bear to think of your finding out. He believes it would destroy you.'

'I'm tougher than he thinks.'

'Well, aren't women always tougher than men think? It would destroy him if you lost faith in him, that's more likely.'

'Do you think we're being fair to him? We know everything, don't we? And he doesn't.'

Standing beside the car, Estelle looked at me anxiously. 'Look, Martha,' she said, 'you can pull the trigger any time, you know that. It's your full right. This has gone on longer than anyone could have believed. If you can't stand it any more, I'll understand. But if you can, then please let David work his own way through. Let him set himself free. I promise I won't try to hold him, when the time comes.'

'You don't have to appeal to me, Estelle.'

'I wouldn't ever appeal to you for myself. Only for him. If we love him, we have to help him. We have to sustain him.'

'Yes, that's right,' I said, although I was glad that David couldn't hear us. She looked, once again, relieved. But the strain was telling on her, as she lived from day to day.

As it happened, I found David at home. Estelle's hunches were sometimes wrong, and evidently he hadn't thought of going to Ty Pellaf that evening. We went to bed early, before it was dark, and made love with caressing tenderness, as though we were consoling each other for the deceptions of which we couldn't speak. Afterwards, I wondered how long Estelle waited before she reconciled herself to disappointment: wondered if she was now lying on her mattress and trying to sleep, or fortifying herself with coffee or maybe whisky, or immersing herself resolutely in one of her heavy books. David asked what I was thinking of. I yawned and said: 'Oh, somebody I saw this afternoon.' It was true, but a poor truth. I had an uneasy feeling that, of the three of us, I was the most dishonest.

The next time I saw Estelle, she said: 'I've been thinking over that talk we had the other day, Martha. I want you to forget it.'

'Forget it?'

'Cancel it. I was asking too much. You've been wonderfully patient, but this whole business can't go on any longer. I see that now.'

I stared at her. She looked strained and tired, and I could guess that she hadn't slept much. Though it was the morning of a July day, the light in the kitchen of Ty Pellaf was weak. It was the kind of day we seldom had in our fresh, lively climate – hot and still, probably the hottest day of the year, but without sun. The sky was obscured, not by clouds as we normally saw them, but by a dense, humid layer of stale air. The weather was near to breaking up. I had thought as I left Craig-derw that there was rain somewhere in the mountains, and that it would be a healthy relief when it reached us.

I started to say: 'If you think I ought to tell David I know. . . ' As I spoke, I realized that it was the last thing I wanted to do. It could bring us nothing but ugly scenes, abasement and humiliation; it would not reunite us, but divide us.

'No, that's not what I mean.'

'What do you mean, then?'

'I'm going away,' Estelle said. She was speaking English, not Welsh, beginning already to mark out a distance.

'Estelle . . . why?'

'Oh, Martha, I must. Nobody's been hurt yet, but somebody will be if we go on walking this tightrope. You can't go away from here, David can't – I'm the only one who can. I've done it before. I'll survive. I'll go back to America, that's the sensible thing. I guess I'm wrong about the war, it's really coming. David says so.'

'Have you told him?'

'No, I don't want to. OK, I can't. I'll write to him later. But I couldn't go without saying goodbye to you, Martha.'

I continued to stare at her, as though she might fade away before my eyes. The light seemed to dwindle every moment; it could have been evening instead of morning.

'It might as well be today,' she said in a flat, tired voice. 'I don't take long to pack. You could drive me to the station.'

All I had to do then was to say: 'All right.' What happened, just a few weeks later, wouldn't have happened. David and I would still be living in Craig-derw, untroubled by distant memories, cherishing our home for our children and grandchildren. Or . . . I don't know. Alex says that what's in store for us is bound to happen, if not in one way, then in another. For instance, David could easily have been killed in the war. Reality is hard enough, without devising variations on it.

What I said was: 'No, Estelle, don't go.' I didn't stop to think; I was astonished by my own words. I went on speaking in Welsh, without thinking about that either. I said: 'It'll come out right, truly it will. We'll manage somehow. But I can't manage without you, Estelle. I don't want to lose you.'

A little smile, which she tried to hide, twitched at the

corners of her mouth. She said, in Welsh too: 'I'll stay. I want to , that's the truth. Remember, I did ask you. I shan't ask you again.'

I took full account, for the first time, of what I had valued and what I should have missed: Estelles's loyal courage, and the secrets we had together, and her wise or clever sayings, and even her funny Welsh. But we knew that, if we needed each other, it was because dangers were gathering.

She made an impulsive, stumbling movement toward me, and we embraced. Women then didn't embrace, even less than they kissed. It would have been thought grotesque rather than suspicious. But, after the crisis we had passed, we needed to give each other more than words. So we gave each other the awareness of our bodies, which by differing made a complement: mine solidly rounded, hers taut and delicate. In that close and silent minute, I knew Estelle as David knew her, and she knew me as he did.

When we drew apart, we looked steadily at each other and knew that we had been thinking the same. We shouldn't have known how to speak of it. But there was no need.

'I'll see you soon,' I said.

'Yes. Soon.'

I went outside. A rising west wind was breaking up the hot, stale air. Before I had gone far, the rain started.

DAVID

From the beginning of the year 1939, a sense of doom descended upon me. I have never been superstitious in the commonplace manner, but I believe that a strong conviction of this kind can validly be taken as a warning. There are modes of knowledge that transcend the accepted rules of logic and evidence; when we feel an apprehension, it is because we apprehend. If we were wiser, we could discern patterns and cycles in the life of a man, a family or a nation, and we should then be able at least to prepare ourselves for the inevitable.

I was close to my thirtieth birthday, a sobering point in any man's life in that it marks the end of youth. At the same age, my father had witnessed the sudden eclipse both of his personal happiness and of the universal peace which so many had taken for granted. Once, in my boyhood, he had said to me – I remember it because he very rarely brought himself to take me into his confidence, or to recall the vanished past – 'It was all too perfect to last.' These words came back into my mind in the fullness of time.

I knew all too well that I did not deserve the boundless love, or the absolute trust, that I received from Martha. I valued, more than I could ever express, her open and candid nature, her spontaneous readiness for smiles and laughter, her gift for spreading good feeling and happiness wherever she went. Far from equalling these qualities, I could not adequately respond to them. The truth was that I had tempted fate by venturing to marry her, and surely fate would bring the lesson home to me. The apprehension grew in me that, somehow or other, I should lose Martha. I watched vigilantly over her health, excellent though it was. I fretted anxiously when she went out by car, especially when the precipitous descent to the lake was coated with ice. But I feared, most of all, the disaster whose seeds were already present. She might at any time open her eyes to my unworthiness, and then she would cease to love me. Perhaps she would leave me, although her natural compassion and the conventions in which she had brought up argued against such a step. Perhaps she would remain with me for the sake of our child, and of the other children we might expect to have, but increasingly embittered by the consciousness of having been lured into a irreparable mistake. Living out our lives in the grim hollowness of such a union was scarcely the more inviting prospect. I could do nothing to avert these horrors, nor could I speak of my fears to Martha herself, for she still loved me with all the innocent generosity with which she was so richly endowed. Yet I had begun to live with the agonizing thought that our happiness could not endure.

On a less personal level, my forebodings were just as keen. I was certain that the nation was being drawn inexorably into another war. I did not care to argue with those who took an optimistic view, for my expectation did not depend on any precise political knowledge, of which I had no more than my neighbours. Rather, I was aware of an immense and tragic drama which had been interrupted but not carried to completion. My father had repeatedly complained that the victory of 1918 had been cast away and the sacrifices of his generation betrayed. Whatever his sourness and his prejudices, the charge was just; the wisdom of the politicians in the post-war (or, it must now be said, inter-war) years was pitifully inadequate to eradicate the causes of war and construct a stable international order. We who had inherited the failure had no option but to atone for it. In this sombre perspective, efforts to avert the catastrophe by the so-called policy of appeasement, which occasioned much heated controversy at the time, appeared to me neither right nor wrong but merely futile. In 1939, I did not read the newspapers or listen to the wireless any more sedulously than in earlier, more carefree years; but I never deviated from my anticipation that the war would begin in the season indicated by precedent – that is, in August or September.

Much more than my father in 1914, I knew what to expect. It was obvious that the age of limited wars, in which the combatants were professional soldiers or volunteers with a zest for adventure, was gone for ever. The impending conflict would reach its tentacles into every home in the belligerent nations. Weapons which had been experimental novelties in 1914-18 would attain devastating power. Tanks, advancing in massed formation, would shatter the stability of the front line and rove throught the defenceless countryside. Bombing aeroplanes would inflict appalling destruction on towns and cities. Poison gas, in uncontrollable clouds, would bring an agonizing death to civilians as well as soldiers. Only the last of these predictions was, in the event, unfulfilled, but I was by no means alone in making it.

Despite this knowledge, available to any intelligent person, Britain was shockingly unprepared for war. I recognized that it was dishonest to deplore this state of affairs without efforts to remedy it, and I decided to enrol myself in the Territorial Army. It never occurred to me that I should not be involved in the ferocious battles of 1939 or, at latest, 1940. I felt myself to be pursued by the same cruel fatality as my father, and I could do no other than to accept my inheritance.

In late 1938, the Territorial unit covering our district consisted of little more than a locked arsenal and short list of names, mostly those of veterans of the previous war. I had only to volunteer to be appointed company commander. This was indeed a measure of the general unpreparedness and the amateurish atmosphere of the period. However, I was young and enthusiastic, I had earned commendation in the OTC at school, I could claim to be a first-class shot, and of course my social position made me acceptable as an officer.

I went from house to house asking men of suitable age to

join my company. A sufficient number responded; if I was not always liked in the neighbourhood, I was respected. My argument that, when war came, those with the greatest skill would have the best chances of survival proved effective. It was decided that the winter months, with their inclement weather and early darkness, would be devoted to indoor training sessions, designed to instruct the recruits in the handling and maintenance of weapons and in the rudiments of infantry tactics. As soon as possible, the theoretical knowledge would be applied in vigorous field exercises, for which the rugged country on the slopes of Arenig Fawr provided an ideal terrain.

All in all, I was entering upon a year full of dangers. I was like a soldier who, advancing into strange territory, senses peril in the air but cannot tell from what direction he may come under fire. Soon, however, I found myself threatened by a force to which my own weaknesses made me fatally vulnerable: the magnetic attraction of an unscrupulous woman.

It was from Mr Stanhope, the manager of the White Lion, that I first heard mention of Estelle Mavros. Perhaps because he was himself a newcomer (as his name indicated, he was not Welsh), he adopted a reserved and sometimes critical attitude to those whose arrival was more recent than his own. His tone was one of glum disapproval as he informed me of the presence of a more than usually dubious stranger. To judge by her accent, she was American. She had a married name but was living alone, and Stanhope was positive that she was a divorcee. She had moved into the cottage belonging to Mr and Mrs Barker and was presumably a friend of theirs; this did not commend her to Stanhope, who (for reasons of no relevance here) already viewed the Barkers with disfavour. He described Mrs Mavros as an extremely attractive woman, conscious of her charms and practised in enhancing them. He said that she dressed in a style more suited to a metropolitan cocktail party than to our sober environment, that she made up like a

Hollywood star, and that she was drenched in French perfume. I was to find the word 'drenched' an exaggeration; Estelle was capable of subtlety.

'I know that sort,' Stanhope confided to me. 'You've got to, in my job.' He defined her, using a word then much in vogue, as a siren. He cited her practice of entering the saloon bar without a companion and striking up a conversation with anyone, of either sex, who happened to be there. I understand that such conduct is regarded as normal in the Continental countries where Estelle had lived, so it may be said that Stanhope was displaying an insular prejudice. Nevertheless, he was not far wrong in noting her indifference to accepted standards of feminine modesty, and in inferring her moral laxity. He suspected – and he was right – that she had involved herself, since leaving her husband, in a sequence of transient sexual liaisons in various parts of Europe. He also advanced the theory that she had been compelled by embarrassing circumstances to 'do the vanishing trick' and execute a rapid withdrawal from the scene of certain imprudent activities. It was not likely, he argued, that a woman of her type would voluntarily embrace the seclusion and monotony of a winter in rural Wales. What concerned him was that she took advantage of his premises to exert her attractions.

It was not unusual, and was then considered perfectly legitimate, for a landlord to refuse admission to unaccompanied females, or even to all females. But Stanhope could not do this because the White Lion was a residential hotel. The guests sometimes included ladies who arrived alone, taking a holiday which their husbands were too busy to share. Since they appeared in the bar, it was not obvious on what grounds Mrs Mavros could be excluded. Stanhope had to concede that in social terms she must be classed as a lady – insofar, he added, as any American could be a lady. Not long after her arrival, Lady Arbuthnot had conversed with her affably and invited her to tea. Stanhope considered Lady Arbuthnot excessively tolerant, but it was not for him to correct her. Nor was it possible to maintain that anyone could be eligible for admission to Sir Richard Arbuthnot's home but not to the saloon bar of the White Lion.

While Stanhope was telling me all this, my imagination leaped ahead of his words. I had the strange feeling that I already knew this Mrs Mavros whom I had never seen; that I knew more of her than I should ever disclose to Stanhope. I almost smiled as I gravely sympathized with his problems. Indeed, I presented to him the same hypocritical face that I had once presented to another hotel manager in Barmouth, when he explained the dismissal of a loose-living barmaid.

The warning was as clear as it could well have been. But if we could avoid dangers as soon as they confront us, they would not be dangers. I quickly assured myself that the idea of my being tempted by an over-painted American siren was ludicrous. After all, when I followed Nora to the attic room I was a callow youth excited by pent-up urges, and there was nothing to restrain me except a shaky loyalty to the prevailing moral code. I was now a mature man, a husband and father. My marriage, grounded in sincere and durable love, gave me entire contentment – in the physical sense, for that matter, as well as in the emotional.

I decided – such was the extent of my self-delusion – that it would be quite interesting to take a look at Mrs Mavros, as a human type seldom encountered in Bala. I made it a point to stroll into the White Lion whenever I was in town, but I saw no one answering to the manager's description. When I put a casual question to him, he said with some relief that Mrs Mavros' appearances had become rarer. She had no car, and the cold weather since the turn of the year must be a deterrent to 'gadding about'.

Perhaps, I thought, I might catch a glimpse of her in the vicinity of her residence. Ty Pellaf, as the cottage was called, was within easy walking distance of Craig-derw. The land, now that the farm had been abandoned, was common grazing; my own sheep frequently wandered across it. If my steps took me in that direction, it could not appear abnormal. I looked for Mrs Mavros repeatedly, indeed persistently. But she had no reason to go out in the cold except for occasional shopping expeditions, and then I must have missed her.

My desire to see the woman – simply, literally to see her – became an obsession. It led me into an action which is peculiarly humiliating to recall; I have steeled myself, however, to omit no stage in my descent. Gazing at Ty Pellaf when I was out after dark, I had observed that the curtains were not drawn. One winter night, after a Territorial training session in the Bala drill hall, I returned from the town on foot; I forget whether Martha had taken the car or whether it was under repair. I followed a path which skirted the hillside of Gwastadras, making a shorter route than the road via Llanycil. At a certain point, this path (symbolically enough) divided; one branch led to my home, the other to Ty Pellaf. I paused and made my choice. It was late, but not so late that Martha would be concerned about me. The night was impenetrably black. I walked steadily toward the two squares of light which revealed that Estelle was in her downstairs room. When I reached the cottage, I made my way to one of these windows and peered in. I moved stealthily, but the wind was blowing in strong gusts and there was little risk of my steps being audible.

I could see Estelle clearly from a distance of no more than ten feet. She sat in an armchair close to the fire; she had been reading, but some reverie had distracted her from the book. She wore nothing but her underclothes. Huddling in the bitter wind, I could scarcely imagine that she was warm enough for comfort; however, our old farmhouses are strongly built and a blazing fire amply suffices to heat a room of moderate size. She was twisting a strand of her long hair in her fingers. I came to know, later, that movements indicative of half-conscious pleasure in her own attractions – toying with her hair, smooting her thighs, lifting her arms to reveal her armpits – were characteristic of Estelle. With or without design, such movements can be intensely provocative in their effect on a man. Her assumption that she was unobserved, together with her *déshabille*, gave me the illusion of an intimacy achieved without resistance. Yet the solid wall between us, and the fact that I lacked the slenderest acquaintance with her, frustrated the impulses aroused by this contemplation. In short, I had never found a woman so maddeningly desirable.

Thus, before we had even met, we were impelled toward each other. For me, Estelle's reputation was part of her attraction. I have admitted that, while I was capable of loving Martha for her purity, I was also lured by women of a very different stamp. On the other side, it would not be immodest on my part to suggest that Estelle's interest was aroused by what she could easily have heard about me. It was in the winter, she told me later, that she became aware of feeling lonely. This word, I remembered from Nora's use of it, did not imply a merely social deprivation. Living in her immediate neighbourhood there was a man who had been married long enough to be, perhaps, open to the temptation of variety; who was free from the routine of paid employment; and who commanded a respect that placed him above suspicion. Since the position of Estelle's lover was vacant, these were fair qualifications for a candidate.

With the first signs of spring, I commenced field training with my Territorial company. The best area for it, as I have said, was the uncultivated moorland to the west of Parc. The land was common, so there could be no question of trespass, and the only habitations were Ty Pellaf and the barn of which Samuel Pritchard had taken unauthorized possession. It was here that Estelle chose to accost me with a complaint about our rifle-fire. She pretended not to know who I was, and even affected not to realize that a responsible military unit would be using blank ammunition, which certainly would have occurred to a person – even a woman – of ordinary intelligence. In point of fact, at that stage of their proficiency my recruits would probably have killed one another had they been equipped with live rounds.

I reacted with considerable irritation. I had little patience with anyone who did not take the necessity for military preparedness as seriously as I did myself, particularly a citizen of a nation that might well be safely neutral in the coming conflict. But later, when my temper had cooled, I felt that I owed Mrs Mavros an apology. I had been brusque to the point of rudeness, and no one likes to leave the impression of being a boor, if it can be erased. In a confused manner, I saw that I was devising a justification that covered a wholly different motive; I saw that I was falling, or indeed steppping, into a trap. I convinced myself, however, that I should be able to keep the interview reasonably brief and confine it to its stated purpose. In that, indeed, I was successful.

Naturally, Estelle was as affable and charming as she knew how to be – and the charm of a woman who had devoted her life to attracting men was quite a revelation to me. She accepted my apology gracefully and, although she referred to the Territorial exercises as my 'war games', she did so in a lightly teasing tone at which one could not take offence. But there was danger, I kept reminding myself, in this very charm, as well as in her powerful appeal to my senses now that we were face to face, and in the opportunity provided by this isolated dwelling. In the room into which she ushered me, there was a mattress on the floor. Estelle always claimed to have adopted this extraordinary arrangement for the sake of warmth, and this may possibly have been true (although the mattress was never taken upstairs in the summer). Be that as it may, it presented a vivid image to any male visitor; one could neither look at it nor look away from it.

When I took my leave, Estelle invited me to repeat my visit at my convenience. I evaded a positive response, and decided that I would do nothing of the kind. For about three weeks, I adhered to this resolution. It was a painful period, though not so painful as others to which it was the precursor.

Visions of a lascivious nature seized me and tormented me, by day and by wakeful night, as they had not for years. Greatly to my dismay, my love for Martha and even its satisfying expression seemed to make no difference. At the same time, I was ashamed to have to admit that I was afraid of being alone with the siren: unable to trust myself, unable to control myself. So I conceived the idea that the only cure was, in medical parlance, to acquire an immunity. I would visit her as she had suggested, preferably after a Territorial exercise, engage in a little small talk, and make my way home. After an interval, I might do so again. The first time would be difficult; others, progressively less so. Ultimately, I should have regained my balance, while she would have renounced her designs on me.

I still believe that the scheme gave me a chance, or at least that it was a reasonable strategy for a man in a desperate position. Perhaps, however, I was once again deluding myself and merely finding an excuse for following the course charted by my desires. As to this, speculation is as useless as regret. What happened may be briefly described.

Estelle drew the curtains, contrary to what I knew to be her custom, but did not light the lamp. With the fire as the only source of illumination, the scene was powerfully suggestive. I realized – too late – that she was in entire control of the situation. I stupidly declined a drink, which might have helped me; I found it impossible to produce any small talk, and she remarked on my silence with cool amusement. Her chair, facing mine, was close enough for me to be aware of her slightest movement – her breathing, indeed – beneath a dress of some almost transparent material. When she touched me, reaching out and resting a hand on my knee, it was as though she had pressed a spring. I embraced her with a curious sensation of relief. There was no longer a choice, but only an acceptance of the inevitable.

I walked home in a daze, stumbling on the unpaved road and stepping into puddles left by the spring rains. It was pitch dark, and I had no notion how long I had been with

Estelle. The memory of what we had done together was at the same time intensely vivid and strangely unreal, like a dream which recedes as one emerges from it.

Reaching Craig-derw, I walked up and down for a while before I could nerve myself to enter the house. Everything was normal, so normal as to create another kind of unreality. Martha placed our supper on the table and asked whether I was as hungry as she was; I found that I was. She made only a perfunctory inquiry about the Territorial training, a subject that never interested her. Had I told her that I had rounded off my evening by committing adultery, she would have thought that I was raving.

In the morning, I rose early and left the house after a quick breakfast. I told Martha that I should have a busy day, wretchedly conscious that it was my first lie to her; the truth was that I needed to think over a situation for which nothing in my experience prepared me. I took my favourite bitch for company, and gave her some herding to keep her in trim, or perhaps to reassure myself of an element of continuity in a life that could never be truly the same again.

Irrevocably, I was now an unfaithful husband. Less irrevocably, I was involved in what people like Estelle Mavros called 'an affair'. It was still possible for me to break off the association, simply by never going to Ty Pellaf again; or it was possible if I could muster the fortitude, an assumption scarcely warranted by my recent record. Yet I felt that, if I hoped to retain any shred of self-respect, it depended on the acceptance of responsibility. What I had done was no wild aberration, to be dismissed as out of character. It was, sadly but truly, the act of David Hughes-Talbot. It was the eruption of a part of my nature which, though I had suppressed it for years, I could not honestly disclaim.

I reflected, too, that it would be disgracefully callous and selfish to turn my back on Estelle as soon as I had gratified my curiosity and indulged my lust. She was a woman of easy virtue and of transient attachments, no doubt, but she was not a prostitute. If she had set herself to attract me, it was in the hope not merely of arousing my passions but of securing my affection. And, remembering certain moments of tenderness, I could not deny that we had exchanged a tacit pledge.

I was thus led to examine, as honestly as I could, the nature of my feelings toward Estelle. They were neither so crude (which was a consolation) nor so superficial (which was more disturbing) as I had supposed. At this very moment, I was anxiously concerned to know what she was doing and what she was thinking. I longed to see her, to hear her voice, to catch the moods that enlivened her mobile and expressive features. It dawned on me that I had been falling in love with Estelle through the weeks since our first meeting, or perhaps ever since I had gazed at her through the window. Certainly, if an intense and incessant preoccupation was proof of love, that conclusion was undeniable.

I had hitherto believed that, even if I were to be guilty of some sexual transgression, I could never love anyone but Martha. Loving Estelle, I argued against myself, was doubly impossible: firstly, because I could in no way esteem or respect her, and I was free from the illusions traditionally cherished by lovers; secondly, because I could not, however ruthlessly I searched myself, detect a particle of dimunition in my love for Martha. But the heart (there is some such saying, once quoted to me by Estelle) has its own reasoning which reason cannot interpret.

My train of thought was interrupted when I saw Estelle herself making her way toward me across the fields. She was losing no time, evidently, in consolidating her conquest. Yet the coolest or even the most cynical appraisal of her motives could not eclipse a surge of delight at her approach. We talked, for the first time, with an assumption of intimacy and with absolute candour. I made it clear to her that I was a married man – though I did not imagine that she was in any doubt on the point – and enjoined on her the necessity for discretion. We permitted ourselves a kiss, since there was no one within sight. More surely than the ecstasies of the night before, that calm and deliberate kiss in the open air nailed me to a commitment.

I promised Estelle that I would visit her again at the first opportunity, and so I did. It was four nights later, on an occasion when Martha was attending some social gathering in Bala. Estelle's bare arms were round my neck, and her warm lips pressed to mine, before I was through the door of the cottage. She wore nothing but an exotic silk gown (the correct word, I believe, is 'kimono') which had doubtless been a gift from one of my predecessors. She told me with a laugh that she had dressed herself – or rather undressed herself – in this fashion every evening, 'on the offchance'. Already, our affair was so firmly established as to create an atmosphere of familiarity. The sexual act, this time, gave a sense of renewal rather than of adventure, but this may well have been an effect achieved by the skill and confidence of my experienced mistress.

I need not give a detailed account of my relations with Estelle over the ensuing four months. A situation which would have appalled me, had it been predicted a year before, became an integral part of my life. I made my way to Ty Pellaf once or twice a week, either taking advantage of favourable circumstances or simply impelled by an impatience that I could not restrain. To succumb to the temptation was, for practical reasons, as easy as it had been the first time. The cottage was near. Estelle was almost sure to be there, so that there was no need for advance arrangements or assignations. The door was always unlocked, an apt symbol of the standing invitation extended to me.

I could say that, during these spring and summer months, I was carried away by my infatuation. The truth was that I knew very well what I was doing. The consciousness of my shameful surrender, of my betrayal of standards and loyalties whose authority I fully recognized – in short, of my guilt – was acute and relentless. It attacked me in times of brooding solitude, when I was with men (such as my employees or my Territorial volunteers) who trusted and respected me, and of course most painfully when I was with my dear, loving wife. I could forget my guilt only when I was utterly and helplessly immersed in it: that is, when I was with Estelle. This apparent paradox had a clear explanation. Estelle, like Nora before her, was in the strict sense of the word shameless. Such concepts as moral principle, self-control and fidelity held no meaning for her. Thus, she created an atmosphere in which they were not even denied, so much as dissolved. A step across that threshold brought me into a world hermetically insulated from what, elsewhere, was deemed to be proper and normal.

It was for this reason that Ty Pellaf became, by degrees, a second home for me. This may seem extraordinary, considering that the duration of each of my visits was about two hours and, of course, I never stayed the night. But Estelle had a remarkable talent – it is, I suppose, among the accomplishments of such women – for building up a spurious domesticity. As I settled into what soon became my habitual chair, she was ready with a drink for me. She even provided, as though by instinct, the brand of whisky that I preferred. She sometimes persuaded me to join her in a meal, and I was obliged to recognize that her cooking was better, or at least more varied and interesting, than Martha's. Although our physical desires never lessened in intensity, she taught me that there was a kind of pleasure in delaying their indulgence. Thus, part at least of our time together was spent in talking. Estelle talked with obvious enjoyment and unbounded fluency, and I was quite content to listen, or indeed to gaze at her without listening very attentively. However, when she chose to employ her charm and her cunning in loosening my tongue, my customary reserve deserted me. To questions about my previous amatory experiences, I responded frankly with an account of assignations with a hotel barmaid, which Estelle found highly diverting. Uneasily, I reflected that my mistress had prised from me a secret never divulged to my wife; was this not the most lamentable aspect of my infidelity? But then, I had always been concerned to retain Martha's respect as well as her love.

On her side, Estelle was nonchalantly and disarmingly frank about her record of promiscuity. I observed, nevertheless, that to be frank was not the same as being truthful; she was as indifferent to truth as to other moral values. It was easy to guess, for instance, that she had married the unfortunate Mr Mavros for the sake of his money, and had deserted him as soon as she had established a claim to a substantial slice of it, on which she was still living. But, to justify her conduct, she gave me an unpleasantly malicious picture of Mavros' character and his alleged defects. Her descriptions of her various lovers were also, to a greater or lesser degree, tainted by slander and denigration. As her current choice I belonged, needless to say, in a different class. She often declared, with every appearance of conviction, that she loved me as she had never loved any man before and that I possessed all the admirable qualities generally lacking in 'European men' (Estelle had an absurd habit of including the British in this 'European' category). I took her flattery with a generous pinch of salt, and I sometimes wondered how she would compose the discreditable portrait of David Hughes-Talbot that would be purveyed to my successor. Fortunately, I could regard the prospect with indifference. The scene of Estelle's next affair would doubtless be far from Bala; very likely, in the view of the approaching war, it would be across the Atlantic.

When I was alone, I asked myself how I could possibly love a woman with such patent bad qualities. I loved Martha because she was true and loyal, radiantly sincere, unselfish and uncalculating, utterly free from malice or unkindness, eternally innocent in spirit. Meanwhile, helplessly and miserably, I loved Estelle. There was only one answer to the question. I had always known that I was unworthy of Martha, and since the beginning of this fatal year I had become more sharply aware of it. Now I knew that, while I did not deserve Martha, I deserved Estelle. I might form a realistic view of her character, but I had no right to despise her or even to blame her. When I gazed into her dark eyes, they showed me the mirror of myself.

Yet it was precisely this chilling insight that gave me tenuous grounds for hope. I began to see my involvement with Estelle as a bitter lesson, from which it was my duty to profit. Now that I understood its significance, I could guard against a repetition; besides, few women as temptingly desirable as Estelle were likely to place themselves in my path. My love for Martha, however tarnished, was still real and deep. She, poor darling, believed in my integrity. Provided that the catastrophe which I feared could be averted, we might look forward to many years together. My task was to redeem myself by a life of unfailing devotion – to strive to become worthy of Martha. But the sooner I set my foot on the road, the better.

Estelle, I could see, was well aware of my wish to extricate myself from my enslavement to her. As might be expected, she played her hand with consummate skill. She assured me earnestly that she had never yet broken up a marriage and hoped that she never would.

'You love your wife, don't you, David?'

'Indeed I do,' I replied.

'I'm glad, honestly I am. I wouldn't stop you loving her, even if I could.'

I daresay that she was sincere (or as sincere as she ever was) in disclaiming any intention of breaking up my marriage, for she can have had no particular desire to do so. The glamorous Estelle Mavros could scarcely have reconciled herself to becoming the second wife of a Welsh sheep-farmer. It suited her much better to maintain the affair until her interest in it might be exhausted, when she would be free to move on. Thus, her declaration lulled my concern regarding any threat to what I valued most in life, and enabled her to assume an air of humility and unselfishness, while in reality it cost her nothing.

Another device of Estelle's was to say, in a tone of appealing pathos: 'I know you'll drop me sooner or later.' According to her account, she had been dropped by almost all her previous lovers, sometimes in a wounding or even a ruthless manner. I considered it more likely that the boot had been on the other foot, but I was in no position to give her the lie direct, and some of her stories were told in a detail that made them plausible. The effect, in any case, was what she had doubtless intended: to make me feel that it would be heartless and dishonourable to abandon her. I had never 'dropped' a woman in my life, and any possible way of doing so struck me as repugnant. A letter would be cowardly, as well as cold, especially as I lived so near; a verbal announcement would lead to a painful scene. I could not justify the decision except on the grounds that I wished to be faithful to my wife, and she might reasonably reply that I could have thought of this before. Above all, it must be remembered that I loved Estelle. I was ashamed of loving her, I profoundly regretted it – yet I did love her, and I found it hard to contemplate an action which would cause her to suffer. It would be far better, surely, if she were to tire of her solemn and unexciting lover, of the inconveniences of Ty Pellaf, and of the monotonous life that she had now led for several months. I imagined opening the door of the cottage one evening to find it empty; I was sure that, however keenly I might miss her until I had recovered my balance, I should also be grateful for my deliverance.

But the chances of Estelle's departure appeared to diminish rather than to increase. Although it could scarcely be said that we suited each other, there were signs that her attachment to me was growing stronger. Perhaps, now that she was no longer young (I could only guess at Estelle's age, and a question regarding it would certainly not have been welcomed, but she must have been over thirty), she had lost her zest for a frequent change of partners. More remarkably, she seemed to be perfectly content with her place of residence. She said that she loved the Welsh landscape and found Welsh people congenial; she was even making some effort to acquire a knowledge of the Welsh language.

One might have reasonably supposed that the growing

danger of war would make any American consider a return home to be the course of prudence. But Estelle, as it happened, refused to believe in this danger. She expounded a peculiar line of reasoning, according to which 'European men' no longer possessed the degree of nerve necessary for the launching of hostilities. Martha, oddly enough, put forward the same ludicrous argument. I could only deduce that it made a natural appeal to the feminine mind.

In reality, war was coming inexorably closer as the summer advanced. This was taken to be an incontrovertible fact by all men of judgement and experience. Sir Richard Arbuthnot – who was well into his sixties, but had commanded a Guards battalion in the previous war – mentioned to me that he had written to the War Office offering his services in any capacity that might be useful. I was gratified to find that the authorities were giving more serious attention to the training of the Territorial Army. The equipment of my company was much improved, so that it included an anti-tank rifle, a Bren light-machine-gun, and a two-inch mortar. I insisted that every man should become proficient in the use and maintenance of these weapons. Taking advantage of a spell of fine weather in June and early July, we pressed on with an intensive period of training. The activity absorbed much of my energies and even diverted my thoughts, to some extent, from the trials of my personal life.

I awaited the outbreak of war with mixed feelings. I assumed that, very soon after the proverbial balloon went up, I should be in uniform; away from home for the first time since my schooldays; on foreign soil for the first time in my life; and, like my father twenty-five years before, striving desperately to stem the onslaught of superior German forces. The prospect of separation from my precious Martha and my little Ann was naturally saddening. Yet the end of normal life would also be the end of the deceit and dishonour in which I was enmeshed, for the day of my parting from Martha would also be the day of my parting from Estelle, and no comparable temptress was likely to present herself in the vicinity of the front line. It seemed that I must rely on the universal cataclysm for the deliverance that I sought. Provided that I was spared to return home, Martha and I would make a new beginning.

Meanwhile, I had to live in the present, from day to day. This meant that I had to concern myself with an immediate danger which was both humiliatingly banal – for it had confronted every adulterous husband since time began – and nevertheless immensely serious: I mean, of course, the danger that my wife might find out. I could have no doubt whatever that the effect on Martha would be devastating. She had given me, once and for all, and with the unqualified sincerity that was natural to her, all her love and all her trust. She assumed – being Martha, she must assume – that my love for her was just as complete and undivided. That I still loved her while also loving Estelle was a notion that she would find incredible, indeed literally incomprehensible.

To make matters worse, it was probable that she had heard something – Mr Stanhope was merely one possible source – of Estelle's character and reputation. It was, on the face of it, surprising that Martha had never mentioned Mrs Mavros and evidently had not met her, since she normally took a lively interest in new arrivals in the district. The explanation could only be that she preferred to avoid the dubious adventurer. It was certain that she would be not merely distressed, but appalled and revolted, if she had to envisage her husband in the arms of such a woman. I remembered, too, that Martha herself had in the past been the victim of a husband unfaithful to his marriage vow. To find me imitating her seducer would be the final proof that all men were systematically treacherous, restrained in their sexual voracity neither by conscience nor fidelity. She had imagined me to be an exception, only to be disillusioned. It would be the end of her love for me, and very probably the end of our marriage. Perhaps, out of the goodness of her nature, she would compel herself to forgive me. Perhaps she would decide to remain as my wife and to conceal her knowledge of my infidelity from others, for the sake of our child and to avoid causing pain to her pious family. But there could be no true consolation in such a reprieve. We should live together as no more than parties to a contract, sharing nothing but the bitter memory of dead love.

I have said that the thought of causing Estelle to suffer made me unhappy. I could assure myself, however, that she would recover without undue difficulty. She was hard-boiled, to use the American colloquialism, and realistic or even cynical in her view of the male sex; in any case, our affair was only an episode in her life. Infinitely more terrible was the thought of the profound, torturing, irreparable suffering that I might be guilty of inflicting on Martha, if she came to discover how I had failed her. To contemplate it filled me with horror; to brood upon it, as I did during these months, was almost unbearable. It follows that there was no action from which I would have recoiled, if it could avoid the destruction of Martha's faith in me.

But, while I dreaded discovery, I regarded it as no more than a slender possibility. Martha was the least jealous of women, and the least likely to conceive suspicions. I was certain that she took my fidelity for granted, without even posing the question to herself. To the best of her knowledge, I had been shy with girls and disinclined to flirtations when a bachelor. When I first told her that I loved her, I added that I had never loved anyone else, and she had no reason not to believe that this was eternally true. As a married man, I avoided the parties and dances which were, in Bala, the usual starting-point for such extra-marital entanglements as from time to time occurred. She knew – and this was no illusion – that my deepest affections were centred on her, on Ann, and on our home. Knowing this, why should she become anxious if I came in later than the customary hour once or twice a week?

Another aspect of Martha's character reinforced my judgement. She was inclined to be vague, forgetful of practical details, and averse to consecutive thought. If a problem threatened to make exceptional demands on her – or, worse still, to be a source of unpleasantness – she would close her mind to it. I may mention, as a fact illustrative of her temperament and of some relevance in this context, that she did not wear a watch and generally had only the vaguest notion of the time. When I returned home after the day's work, she was always happy to see me but quite often surprised – even if I was by no means early.

All in all, I considered that the worst danger to be feared was that of observation by some inquisitive person. Estelle and I did not exchange letters, nor did we meet in public. But, if Mr Stanhope's view of her was widely held, no one who saw me entering her cottage – without my wife, too – was likely to suppose that I was paying a social call. Moreover, once on the road to 'the farthest house', I could be going nowhere else. I approached Ty Pellaf, therefore, with caution and vigilance; and, needless to say, I did not leave without assuring myself that the coast was clear. I did not welcome the advance of summer, which obliged me to make my way to Ty Pellaf in daylight and even, in the long June evenings, to return before it was completely dark. I made my visits to Estelle, preferably, either when Martha was out for the evening or else at the end of a Territorial exercise, which might explain my presence at a deserted spot.

In the event, only one awkward incident occurred. I was walking along the road, and just passing Pritchard's wretched habitation, when I was overtaken by the Bala police sergeant on his bicycle. Since I was in uniform, an expedient readily suggested itself. I said that, during a route march along the road, one of my men had dropped the magazine of the Bren gun, and asked him if he had seen it. Naturally, he replied that he had not (I scarcely imagine that he would have known what it looked like) but he would keep his eyes open. I then said that someone else might well have picked it up and would doubtless return it to me next day. Abandoning my plans for the evening, I went home. I cannot say that the incident much disturbed me. The policeman was fond of wandering about on his bicycle, and he was – to put it charitably – not distinguished for any great intellectual acumen.

The scenes, and also the intense and contradictory emotions, of that summer of 1939 are indelibly marked in my memory. It was a time of mental anguish, when I was never free from the consciousness of guilt and the menace of disaster. Even so, I cannot look back upon it with undiluted regret, for it was also a time of happiness – of the last happiness that I was ever to know. More: that happiness attained a degree of concentrated perfection which I still recall, across a waste of dull and empty years, with breathless astonishment.

It was to Martha – my beloved, trusting, betrayed wife – that I owed this happiness. She behaved to me with a sweetness and tenderness that exceeded even what she had given me over the past four years. I might almost have fancied that she knew of the ordeal through which I was passing and sought to relieve the pain by her gentle and unselfish sympathy. Strange though the assertion may seem, I honestly believe that the love between us was never stronger, and we were never closer to each other, than when I was false to her.

I recall with particular poignancy the evening of Midsummer Day. The weather had, for several days, been unusual: a dry furnace-heat, generated monotonously from a cloudless sky, with none of the volatile freshness characteristic of Wales. Old Arbuthnot had remarked that it reminded him of the pre-monsoon period in India, to which I rejoined that the monsoon would be a welcome relief; and Estelle had told me that the heat was equal to that of Iowa, the American State where she had spent her early years. I was busy with the sheep-shearing, which in those days was done with real shears and not with a mechanical contraption. The exertion was considerable, and in the oppressive heat it left me in a somewhat light-headed condition. When the work was over for the day, I washed myself in a stream to remove the worst of the odour of untreated wool, and set off in the direction of Ty Pellaf. On the way, however, I remembered that it was Midsummer Day.

Ancient traditions connected Craig-derw – 'the rock among the oaks' – with this once sacred day. In a half-jesting manner, and yet with a certain involuntary reverence, Martha and I had always treated it as a special occasion. Now, the weight of my apprehensions in general, and the approach of war in particular, made me feel that this might be our last Midsummer Day together, at least for a period whose dimensions were unpredictable. To desert Martha for Estelle on this day of all days would be a betrayal within a betrayal. I retraced my steps, and was soon at Craig-derw.

Martha was not in the house. The servant had put Ann to bed, but informed me that she was still restless, a natural effect of the long daylight. I went upstairs to tell her a goodnight story and calm her. Then I went out again, for I was sure that I should find Martha at the place invested by this day with mysterious significance. I was not mistaken. As I joined her and put my arm round her waist, I was almost able to believe that nothing had ever threatened the contentment and tranquillity of the life we shared. We stood in silence, awed by the beauty of the scene, and watched the sun set in a blaze of red and gold.

At that moment, I felt my love for Martha as an eternal and immutable reality. I knew that it would endure as long as I lived; and I was seized by the belief that, even after death, something of it would remain in this earth, this air, these trees. Surely, then, it must be victorious over a corrupt and transient passion. Surely, united by a deeper loyalty, we could dismiss that passion with scorn and deny it the power to divide us. I was – or I may have been, for it is impossible to reconstruct an emotional impulse – on the verge of offering to Martha the very disclosure that I had so anxiously guarded from her, and staking everything on her compassion and her understanding. Whether that would have been the path to salvation or an invitation to immediate disaster, I shall never know.

I made one plea: the plea that, whatever the trials that the future might bring, she would believe that my love for her was as real and as deep as ever.

'Of course,' she replied. Her tone was light, indeed casual. I saw that she was in no way prepared to comprehend the gravity of my tone. I said no more; the moment passed.

She stepped from my grasp and wandered away into the recesses of the grove. In the steadily descending darkness, and under the convergent branches which at this season were heavy with leaves, she was soon lost to sight. It was, I could not help imagining, as though the grove, into whose enclosing shadows she had innocently ventured, had swallowed her up. A sudden apprehension shrivelled the hopes that I entertained a minute before. It was, I am sure, an apprehension of the catastrophe that was to separate us for ever.

I called her, on a note of desperation that she must have found bewildering. We returned to the house without speaking, and scarcely spoke until we went wearily to bed. I doubt if Martha found a place in her memory for that brief and fruitless conversation; but my mind often went back to it, with a sense of hopeless regret, during the long years of solitude.

ESTELLE

'I don't offer you happiness, I offer you love.' That was a line in a play, I think by Somerset Maugham, which was a big hit while I lived in Europe and which I saw during one of my spells in London. I remember only the basic situation and that one line. A young man is urging a married woman to run off with him. She's naturally reluctant, being quite happy the way she is and comfortably placed with a rich and tolerant husband. He then produces this tremendous line. Captivated, she puts her hand in his and they exit left. Maugham's stock is now low, I'm aware, and theatre audiences in his heyday weren't very demanding, but he did have an uncanny knack of hitting certain nails bang on the head.

David had absolutely no gift for happiness, either for achieving it himself or providing it for another. The irony is that he thought about and talked about it more than most people. 'Are you happy, my darling?' he would ask anxiously as we lay on the mattress after making love. 'My marriage is very happy,' he would state firmly when warning me not to get ideas above my station. But happiness for him was an ideal and he was constantly putting it to the test, like a man taking his temperature to prove that he's in good health. You could say with fair accuracy that he didn't know what it was.

With a lover – or it was this way when I was young – a parting was inherent in every meeting. But David was, among my lovers, the only one who was never with me all night, whom I never saw in the peace of sleep. This filled the time we had together with a breathless intensity. If every minute was precious, every minute also contained the whole difficult, searching, passionate essence of what we meant to each other. His visits, or perhaps that word should be visitations, left me exhausted but marvelling. I knew that I was loved by him as I had never yet been loved by any man. With so much love, how could I expect him to give me happiness too?

Indeed, the absence of happiness was the proof of love. I knew that he was weighed down with guilt about being unfaithful to Martha. If he could have broken with me, the relief would have been enormous. He couldn't, and the relentless force of love was the reason. Georges, who suffered from no guilt whatever, would have broken with me without hesitation to save himself a bit of inconvenience. David, enduring not inconvenience but torment, paid that price.

It could be said that we were wildly unsuited to each other. I never thought of it that way. I wasn't about to marry him, after all. I wanted no more from him than he would give me in honesty. He didn't tell me, like other men, that he cared for me more than for his wife and it was too bad he was stuck with her. No: he told me that she was the abiding centre of his life. He didn't tell me that our affair was sheer joy, or lots of fun. No: he told me that it was a burden he would not have chosen to shoulder. He never lied to me. He never lied to Martha except by silence. Amazed and awed, I realized that this was the man I had been looking for through all my years in Europe, and whom I had almost lost hope of finding.

I always knew, of course, that it couldn't last. David was perpetually dismayed and bewildered by what he was doing. The Hughes-Talbots of Craig-derw had never behaved like this; as well as betraying his wife, he was betraying his inheritance. Next week or next month, he would come to his senses – that's how it would appear to him. And then, the memory would be buried under a concrete slab. In ten years' time, if by some chance I ran across Georges, I might expect a dinner heavily flavoured with sentimental reminiscence; although in reality I had never been more than a diversion to him, he would assure me that he had loved me deeply and possibly believe it. But if I showed my face in Bala in ten years' time, David, who really had loved me, would look straight through me.

Yet I fought against believing what I knew. This wasn't just like any other affair; we had invested in it so much passion, so much striving, so much pain. It couldn't be true that it would end as others had ended and leave nothing behind. It must yield some lasting enrichment, some addition to his life and to mine. And surely it must last longer than the brief summer season. It couldn't end yet, not yet: so I thought, and so I prayed, in May and June and July.

I waited, often in fear and trembling, for the moment when David would tell me that it was all over. Having been through this before made it no easier; it always hurt, and with David it would hurt worse than ever. In certain moods, I thought that it would hurt less if I cut my losses while things were still good, and made the break of my own accord. I was too much in love, however, to act upon that arid calculation of prudence. I took one resolution: I would give him up when it had gone on too long for Martha. But I was under no pressure from Martha – quite the reverse.

Among all the unsolved and perhaps insoluble problems, there was one reason to be thankful. I had done the right thing when I told Martha what was happening – told her before she found out anyway, as I was sure by now that she would have. For me, the worst aspect of having an affair with a married man was always the thought of being the target of another woman's anger and hatred. It would have been nasty when I didn't know her, and unbearable when she had been my friend. That was what I had escaped. Martha was still my friend.

Aside from anything else, I needed a friend. Respectable society around Bala hadn't taken long to scrutinize and reject my suspect credentials. Lady Arbuthnot had stopped asking me to tea, and a hint from her was a command to the other exiles. This I didn't care about, for I preferred the Welsh. But the Welsh too had their doubts about me, I could see. Probably they'd have said that they sensed something peculiar, without being able to put a finger on it. Ironically, the longer I stayed the further I was from acceptance. Mrs Jones, the garage-owner's wife, asked me outright: 'You'll be leaving soon, I suppose?' I said I had no plans to leave; she enlarged on the threat of war, but something else was in her mind. The suspicion was that, if a woman like me (as they saw me) stayed in this improbable environment month after month, it must be for no good reason. My visions of striking roots in Wales faded. Only David held me now: David and Martha.

Mrs Jones would have been baffled, but Martha and I were bound in closer friendship after David was my lover, and because he was my lover. Most friendships are tinged by some pretence, or at all events some reserve; ours had the rare quality of utter frankness, since it could not otherwise survive at all. Martha's Welsh sense of humour – sharp, perceptive, often mischievous – did the rest. She was proud of being able to guess when David had been with me. In the bar of the Red Lion, she might suddenly say in a conspiratorial manner, but loud enough to be overheard:

'Tuesday, wasn't it, the last time?'

'That's right, Tuesday,' I would reply.

'Ha! Thought so.'

And I remember that she said, though fortunately not in the Red Lion: 'You know, Estelle, I have better loving with David since he started with you. I think you're keeping him up to the mark.'

'I'm glad you're not losing out, anyway.'

'Oh, no. Not at all.' Then she became thoughtful, and continued: 'It's like a fresh start, altogether. I think we're closer than we ever were.'

'That's great.'

'And we're closer as well, aren't we? You and me, I mean.'

'Then everybody's closer to everybody.'

'Yes,' Martha said with her open, beaming smile. 'Isn't it nice?'

Strangely – or strangely by conventional standards – Martha was the least anxious and the most optimistic among the three of us. I think she expected the juggler's balance of marriage, love-affair and friendship to maintain itself indefinitely. There was, indeed, a time when that seemed possible: a time, to make a comparison with European politics, like the period after Munich when the desire for peace was mistaken for peace itself. The weather in June was marvellous, and when you're living in the country you let it shape your mood, even your thinking. Wales was dry, a rare state. You could walk cross-country on the resilient turf, needing no road or even path. On sunny mornings, Martha would appear at Ty Pellaf and lure me on an expedition. We walked until we dripped with sweat, until I pleaded for the mercy of a rest.

On one of those splendid days, we lay on the grass high enough on the flank of Arenig Fawr to be unseen, unless by the eagles of these mountains. The young pale green ferns quivered, rather than swayed, in the gentle wind. Somewhere, a stream searched for a way to the lake. We listened to the small unvarying noises, and didn't speak for a while. We didn't need to say that we were both thinking of David. It was seldom that we didn't think of him, especially when we were together.

'He'll come to you tonight,' Martha said.

I was accustomed by now to her knowing when he'd been with me, but she hadn't yet claimed to know in advance.

'Maybe he will,' I said. 'I'm never sure.'

'I think he will. I'm bleeding.'

'You're what?' I didn't know the Welsh word.

'I'm having my period,' Martha explained in English, and then reverted to the language of secrets. 'It's late. I was hoping it wouldn't come. He wants a son, you know. I wish I could do it.'

'He wants another child, when he's expecting a war?'

'Maybe because of the war. Craig-derw has to go on, whatever. I wish I knew why I can't do it. I used to get pregnant whether I wanted or not.' It may have been at this time, or another time in that warm tranquil June, that Martha told me about the child that was lost to her. I understood why she, as well as David, wanted a son.

'I expect there's nothing to worry about,' I said. 'But you could see a doctor.'

'No, thank you. The doctor's my sister's husband. I don't like them to know too much about me.'

Struck by an idea, she moved her head to give me a grin.

'You could have it, Estelle. He'd be just as pleased. It would be his, wouldn't it?'

'I don't think it would count as a proper Hughes-Talbot. Not to inherit Craig-derw.'

'Perhaps it wouldn't. Oh well, I expect I'll manage it sooner or later. It would be nice for you, though. Have you ever had a baby, Estelle?'

'No, never. Mavros was keen, but nothing happened, thank God.'

'Don't say that. You ought to do it, really. There's nothing like it.' Martha laughed. 'It's funny, you've had all these men, but you're still a sort of virgin. You've got to have a baby to be a woman. That's what I think, anyway.'

'I'm sure you're right. It's just the way life has gone for me. Men don't have affairs' – I had to use the English word – 'to have children.'

'Oh, I don't know. What about those old kings, having dozens of babies with all their women, married or not?'

'If you're king, you don't care who knows what you're doing.'

'No, that's it, isn't it? It comes back to that, every time.'

Martha rolled on her back and gazed up into the sky, shading her eyes from the vast sprawl of the sun.

'Wouldn't it be lovely, Estelle, if David was here with us now? If we could say everything, and all of us know everything, and just be good friends together.'

'It's impossible, Martha. It wouldn't be possible with any man I've ever known.'

'No, I suppose not. I'm his wife, you're not. Once I know you're loving him it's part of my job to be horribly jealous. If I'm not jealous, I can't be a proper wife. That's what he'd think. He'd be furious if he heard us talking like this.'

'He certainly would.'

'But do you think it'll always be like this? Do you think so, Estelle? Perhaps it won't. Perhaps, when Ann's grown up, or Ann's children anyway, everything will be different. There won't be any more of this "he's my man", and "she's my woman", and "he's being unfaithful", and jealousy, and suspicion, and deceiving and pretending, and all this nonsense we think is so important. We'll remember it, we old ones, but the young ones won't know what we're talking about. They'll just love each other, openly, when they feel like it, and it won't ever be wrong so long as it's love.'

I couldn't say anything. My Welsh was good by this time but I had to listen closely, weighing each word for its charge of feeling, as one listens to poetry; so I was moved almost to tears, as by a poem of ardour and hope, a voice from the heart to the heart. I could answer only by reaching out my hand. We lay still in the sun's warmth, hands clasped on the growing grass, joined in a dream.

Soon after this, the weather broke up. The English phrase, packing a cosmic fragmentation into two curt syllables, conveys exactly what happens. In other European countries, or in America, the weather in mid-July is safe, predictable, indeed monotonous, and will remain so until the slow descent into fall. Here, from one day to the next, everything falls apart. It's always surprising because there's no warning, and dismaying because no benefit follows – both harvest and holidays are spoiled. I hadn't spent a summer in England for the past three years, and never in Wales, so the shock was absolute.

I woke one morning to hear rain drumming on the slate roof. I hadn't lit a fire for weeks, but I was still sleeping downstairs from a feeling that love must be protected from change. Coming reluctantly awake, I realized that I was cold, an unfamiliar sensation. I debated whether to get dressed well in advance of any purpose, or to dash upstairs and hunt for extra blankets; neither prospect was inviting. Framed in the square window, the sky was a watery grey. The light, though the sun must have invisibly risen three hours ago, was dim and wintry. After a moral struggle, I put on my clothes, adding a polo-neck sweater that seemed, in July, a badge of cowardice. When I ventured outside, I saw the puddles in the road filling up, the dust thickening into mud, and the grassy slopes where I had walked with Martha sodden. Arenig Fawr, pride of the clear skies, was hidden. It rained all day.

The monsoon (Lord Arbuthnot's word, so David told me) made a season of its own. It didn't rain all the time, but there was never a day when rain didn't hover, threatening or taunting, in the air. Black clouds with silver edges, dramatic in their sinister beauty, crowded the sky. Thunder boomed like the gunfire of invaders. Restless, stormy winds raced between the western sea and England. Trees tossed their load of leaves to and fro as though striving to escape, and torn branches lay in the field. Summer's serenity was whirled away; it was a second spring, but without spring's hopeful growth.

Life, which had opened more broadly under the sun, narrowed again. There were no more walks with Martha. Sorties to Mrs Bowen's shop were made in haste, because I risked a drenching on the way home. I seldom ventured to Bala, where dejected holiday-makers filled all the seats in the Red Lion. My garden became a swamp. I could do nothing but sit indoors, build up the fire, and wonder whether David would come in the evening. Except when the rain was torrential – and it was seldom that – the weather didn't keep him away. It even helped us, he believed, because the empty road to Ty Pellaf would be emptier than ever. The police sergeant, whom he'd inconveniently met on one occasion, wouldn't be so keen on cycling out to remote places. I used to fix a rope in front of the fire and arrange David's damp clothes on it, to steam muzzily while we lay on the mattress. He had brought the Welsh smell of wet grass the first time he came through my door, and he would leave it the last time.

The last time . . . I couldn't guess when that would be, and sometimes I thought that I'd rather bring it on, and get it over with, than live in daily fear. Once, I almost ran. I think it was around the time when the rain started, a time made for glum depression. Martha walked into the cottage in the morning, before I'd had a chance to rebuild my defences or fortify myself with coffee. 'Martha, I'm leaving,' I said. I tried to sound as though I'd made a considered decision, but it was no more than an impulse. Once I was outside the window and balancing on the ledge, so to speak, I was ashamed to draw back. I begged Martha to drive me to the station, and almost dashed off to pack my suitcase – the ritual ending to all my love-affairs. She coaxed me out of my panic and persuaded me to stay. I knew that I had, in reality, been saying 'Please tell me not to go' to her because I didn't dare to say it to David. 'I don't want to lose you,' she said, as though I proposed to desert her rather than to relinquish her husband. We saw, suddenly, that we had come to need each other; that what we had to fear, each of us, was being alone in a time of danger and affliction.

Something else happened in July: the sheep started acting strangely. I had never been much aware of them except as a feature of the landscape, and as material for the displays given periodically by those clever dogs. Unless they were being rounded up – for shearing, most recently – or were disturbed somehow or other, sheep stayed pretty well where they were and kept quiet. But now I saw them wandering incessantly over the grazing land, as though engaged in some compulsive but hopeless quest. Frequently, they raised their faces to the grey indifferent sky and uttered a plaintive 'Baa!'. This sound perfectly expresses the nature and the predicament of sheep – pathetically limited in resources of intelligence and character, never able to grasp what's happening or why, always a step behind the game. You hear it, as you might hear the repetitive questions of a backward child, with a mixture of pity and exasperation. What the hell, I asked David, was the matter with the sheep?

'The lambs have been taken away,' he said.

True: the lambs, which I had first noticed with pleasure in the early days of our affair, and whose growth had followed spring into summer, didn't seem to be around any more.

'Why?' I asked foolishly.

Instead of an answer, he lifted my chin with a kindly forefinger and kissed me. I got the message. How odd, how stupid, how shameful: between lamb, as a tasty substance that I might consume for dinner, and lambs, as creatures hurried through a brief doomed life, I had never made the connection.

A few day later, when I was using a break in the monsoon to restore my ravaged garden, a troop of sheep appeared to fix their melancholy gaze on me. 'Baa! Baa!' Or rather: 'Baa? Baa?' I stared back at them for a short minute, trapped in a dishonest sympathy. Then, waving my hoe, I plunged them into the terror to which they were always so close, and chased them away. I found myself shouting: 'It's no use, can't you understand? It's too late! I can't do anything! It's not my fault, anyway! I'm an American citizen! I'm just renting this cottage! I've got my own problems, damn it!'

David, by now, was thinking far more about his war games than about his work as a sheep-farmer. Despite the bad weather, the Territorials were given no let-up in their training. Combat, David told them sternly, wouldn't be adjourned for rain like a cricket match. There was a major exercise, lasting for hours, every Saturday; he would have called the company out on Sundays too but for the denunciations of the devout. By pestering the regional command, based at Chester, he had succeeded in acquiring quite a range of weapons. There was a machine-gun (whose brand-name I knew, but have forgotten) capable of firing six hundred bullets a minute. Totally unmechanical as I am, I couldn't grasp how this was achieved. The idea of six hundred potential deaths in that inconsiderable time struck me as a black miracle.

I could recognise the guns by their sound, and if they were close enough I could follow the whole relentless sequence. First, I heard the single sharp crack of David's revolver, which he fired as a signal for attack. Then the rifles; each shot reached me as an expletive, a vengeful release of anger. Then the machine-gun, introducing a note of sheer crazed hysteria. The mortar, finally; it made a deep reverberating thud, the solemn voice of destruction. Though it wasn't big, the mortar fired what was correctly called a bomb, not a bullet or a shell, so it called to mind the worst threats of war as then imagined. Alone in my cottage, I listened to the sounds of war with loathing. Each shot seemed to strike into the crumbling defences of love, and to invade the time that was left to us.

The war was David's future; he saw no other. By July, it could almost be said that he was already living in the future, so certain was he of its inevitability. He preferred not to speak of it with women – either Martha or me – but a question could set him off. There was no safety, he considered, in a defensive posture on the Maginot Line. The right strategy was to engage the Germans in mobile battle at the outset, while their best divisions were committed in Poland. We, his women, began to call him 'the General' between ourselves.

I still refused to believe that war was coming. Why shouldn't they all back away, as they had the year before? But I must have known that I was blinding myself to what, out of common prudence, I should be preparing for. Anyway, everybody else was resigned to war. There was a trend toward building stocks of food, according to Mrs Bowen, and filling barns with cans of gasoline, according to Mrs Jones. My father, once again, urged me to leave the doomed continent. Rosemary wrote inquiring whether I knew of any 'possible' houses around Bala. She had two young children, she would naturally quit London when the war began, and it was sensible to make arrangements in advance. I'd have needed to be either very vain or very brave not to be influenced by all this. I was influenced most of all by David; his certainty seemed to come less from knowledge or judgement than from a dark, awesome intuition. Wars began in August, he said. As the end of July came in sight through the damp mists, every day was a gift.

22 July was a Saturday. It was a day that might have lost its way from spring or fall: not raining much, but gusty and chilly. The guns quarrelled and threatened and chased one another all the afternoon. I thought of David out there, crouching among the dripping ferns, straining to peer through the low drifting clouds. I expected that he'd come in the evening, but I could never be sure.

The guns ceased, leaving a silence that wasn't peace but a pause for questioning, an emptiness in the air. The light dwindled, though it was hard to tell where the dimness of the overcast day met the twilight. It became too dark to read, but I didn't light the lamp, seeking to remember if not revive our discovery of each other.

I had given up hoping for David when he suddenly walked in. I ran to him and pressed myself, in a silk blouse, against the rough serge of his uniform. It was wet through; he must have been lying on the turf.

'You're soaked.'

'I'm afraid so.'

'And you're shivering.' So he was; and there was something unnatural about it, more of a trembling than shivering.

'Am I? I may be sickening for something.'

'Come by the fire and get out of these wet things. We'll have to get you well. You don't want to miss the war.'

'A drink would do me good.'

'Sure.'

The whisky was low. I said: 'I'll have to get another bottle.'

'There's enough. It'll last out.'

He sat down and talked about the war, as he did more and more often these days. Not exactly the war, but the training and his company's state of readiness, in which he took great pride. The day's successful exercise was already a victory; no defeat could wholly cancel it. I didn't try to listen. I was impatient to make love. There wasn't much time for us – literally; David had never arrived at Ty Pellaf so late in the evening, the guns had been silent for an hour or more, and Martha would be expecting him home.

Suddenly, my wandering mind grasped that he'd stopped talking and was gazing intently at me.

'Estelle, Estelle,' he said in a strained, cracking voice.

I don't know, but I believe he wanted to tell me something. I don't know, but I imagine he changed his mind. What I thought at the time was that he wanted me as I wanted him. I locked his lips with a kiss.

We sank to our knees and crawled to the mattress. Above the rise and fall of his body, I watched the firelight flickering on the ceiling. And so, we ended as we began.

He dressed methodically, like a soldier going on duty. The uniform, dried by the fire, still steamed a little. When he was ready to leave, I got up, somewhat weakly, and slid into my kimono. I handed him his cap, then his belt and the revolver in its hoster. We kissed for the last time. We didn't speak.

I went slowly back to the mattress and lay down alone. Perhaps I slept, perhaps not. The next thing that I was aware of was a single shot from David's revolver, like the shot that signalled his company into action. Nothing followed it; in my dozing state, that seemed strange. I tried to persuade myself that I had imagined it or dreamed it, but I was sure that I hadn't.

I knew that I couldn't rest until I found out what had happened. I dressed and set out to walk along the road – the shot, I thought, had come from that direction. The rain had started again, or at least the damp miasma of a Welsh drizzle. Curiously, it was easier to see than it had been earlier. A full, or almost full, moon had risen; though it was cloud-hidden, it coloured the darkness. And of course, I knew every stone and every puddle.

I understood nothing. It was practically out of the question for David to have met anyone on the road at this time of night. When I thought of that, my heart went cold. In my blackest fears, it had never crossed my mind that David might kill himself. Yet, did I know the depths of the guilt and torment that he endured, or the point where endurance could become impossible? I walked faster, as though that could make any difference.

I was halted by a beam of light full in my eyes. After a moment, it was diverted mercifully to the ground and I saw that it came from a bicycle-lamp. The man standing by the bicycle was Craddock, the police sergeant. I said 'Good evening', though it sounded foolish. As well as knowing his wife socially, I had met him a number of times when I was walking to Parc and back; he went in for conscientious patrolling.

'Good evening, miss,' he said. He always called me that, doubtless taking the view that a young divorcee reverted to single status.

'May I ask where you're going?'

'For a walk.' It didn't sound very credible, so I added: 'I quite often have a breath of fresh air last thing at night.'

'In the rain?'

'It's only drizzling.'

He didn't pursue the point; it was of minor importance to him at that moment.

'Have you seen anybody on this road, miss? Think carefully.'

I couldn't see why careful thought should be required, but I allowed a half-minute to pass and then said: 'No, nobody.'

'Or have you heard anything unusual?'

'What sort of thing?' I parried. 'What d'you call unusual?'

He raised his lamp again to examine me. I must have been vacuously smiling. He said: 'Please take this seriously, miss. A man has been murdered.'

'Who?' I yelled – or I felt that I was yelling.

'The man who lived in that house there.' Craddock pointed with his lamp. 'Samuel Pritchard by name.'

I almost said 'Oh, is that all?' I hadn't given a thought to Sam Pritchard for weeks; the world had contracted to David, Martha and myself. Indeed, I had virtually forgotten that there was another house between Ty Pellaf and Parc.

'How d'you know he's been murdered?' I asked.

'I've just found him. Shot in the head. There's no possibility of an accident, that I can see.'

'How extraordinary.'

'Never seen anything like it, not in Bala,' Craddock said with some feeling. 'Still, there it is. Well, I must get busy. I think you'd better return home, miss, and bolt your door. Unless you'd be happier under protection? My wife would give you a bed.'

'No, I'll be all right, thanks.'

'If you're sure. And you may be interviewed tomorrow, as the nearest neighbour, so please be available.'

I promised, and we said goodnight. The sergeant pedalled off, presumably to the nearest phone. When I got back to my cottage, I sat down by the dying fire and poured myself some whisky. There was no point now in making it last, so I finished the bottle. Later, I heard cars stopping, starting up again and turning by Sam Pritchard's barn – the greatest activity ever known on my road. It was two o'clock before all was quiet.

In the morning, it was raining hard and unpleasantly cold. I was far from at my best: tired, hung-over, and battered by anxious uncertainties. I still understood nothing, or not much. There didn't seem to be any reason why David should kill Sam Pritchard. But Pritchard was fairly crazy – perhaps, after all, crazier than I knew – and David was in an overwrought state, so a collision between them could have led to a stupid, blundering fight. It was also possible that Pritchard had been killed by someone else, but I couldn't make myself believe that. Only one thing was clear: I had to talk to Martha, and preferably before the police talked to me. I gulped my coffee, put on my warmest clothes with a hat and raincoat, and tramped across the soaking landscape to Craig-derw. A scared-looking maid opened the door and ushered me into the room dedicated to Hughes-Talbot history. Martha appeared. We looked at each other for a helpless minute, then kissed.

'They've taken him away,' she said.

'Already?'

'Well, it was nice they waited for him to have breakfast.'

We spoke English, the language of the outer world, of cold truth and cold justice. I didn't see how they could have traced the killing to David, or be positive enough to make an arrest. As I learned later, this was fairly simple. The body was given an immediate post-mortem and the bullet was extracted; only one man within miles carried a Service revolver. Footprints in the soft earth matched a tall man's army boots. Besides, Craddock had found David loitering near Pritchard's dwelling on other occasions, and inventing a poor excuse for it.

I said 'Maybe he didn't do it.'

'Oh, he did it,' Martha answered at once. She had a sheet of paper in her hand. 'Look at this.'

It was a letter from Sam Pritchard to David, written on cheap ruled paper and all in laboured capitals. The moment I read it, everything made terrible, hopeless sense. It said:

TO MR. D. HUGHES-TALBOT. SIR. THE LORD SEES ALL AND I AM HIS MESSINJER AMONG THE PEEPLE. I KNOE YOU GO TO TY PELLAF TO THE AMERRICAN HOARE. I KNOE YOU SIN AGENST THE WORD OF THE LORD. FOR THE LORD HAS COMMANDED US SAYING. THOU SHALT NOT COMMITT ADULTERRY. YOU THINK YOUR WIFE KNOES NOTHING BUT HERE ME. YOUR WIFE SHAL KNOE. THE WICKID SHALL NOT GO FREE. THAT IS THE WORD OF THE LORD. HOWL YE FOR THE DAY OF THE LORD IS AT HAND IT SHALL COME AS A DESTRUCSHAN FROM THE ALLMIHTY ISAIAH XIII 6. BELEEVE THIS MESSIJE. FROM SAMUEL PRITCHARD.

'Where did you find it?' I asked.

'In his study. What he calls his den. I'm not supposed to go in there. But after they arrested him, I thought I'd better have a look. The police could search the house.'

'You're damn right. Thank God you found it. Now you'd better burn it.'

Martha hesitated. She must have had a feeling that the clue ought to be preserved, for our memories, or for history if you like. Or perhaps that even wretched Sam Pritchard had a right to comprehension, and a right to leave something behind him, other than his junky pictures. Anyway, she said: 'You have it, Estelle. You won't be searched.'

'All right,' I said. When I got home I put it inside – I still remember – a good leather-bound edition of Ronsard's poems given me by Georges, which was one of my favourite books and which I wasn't likely to lose or leave around. Months later, back in Toledo, I started re-reading Ronsard and the letter fell out, and then, my disgust renewed, I nearly did burn it. But I thought: if Martha wanted it kept, it ought to be. That's why it still exists.

Disgusting it really was, when you put together the vile intrusion, the disruption of a harmony far beyond the man's understanding, and the sanctimonious claim to moral superiority. I saw how it had made David, to take a phrase from another context, reach for his revolver. The most you could say for Pritchard was that it wasn't blackmail; he was determined to do what he said, to tell Martha, and he had a hazy notion that a warning was the correct procedure. We gazed sadly at each other. It had occurred to us that someone – though we'd never thought of Pritchard – might get wind of the affair and tell Martha, and we had tried to figure out how she could best deal with that ludicrously embarrassing situation. What had never occurred to us was that David might be warned.

'If only he'd told me,' I said.

'Well, if only he'd told me. But there, it was too much to expect.'

'Did he seem strange, when he came in?'

'Depends what you call strange.' Martha attempted a smile. 'He was in the mood, if you want to know. So we did it. It's the only time he's ever wanted to do it after he's been with you. I ought to have worked out what it meant. It was farewell, wasn't it? But I was sleepy, so I didn't think about it.'

'What shall we do, Martha? There must be something.'

'I don't know. Perhaps I'll get an idea. I'm not at my best this wonderful morning.'

'Nor am I. Not at all.'

'This bloody rain, too,' Martha said, staring angrily out of the window. 'You know, it's our wedding day tomorrow. David was going to take me to Llangollen, have a nice day out. But I expect it would have rained. When we were married it rained all day, never stopped. I didn't enjoy anything, not till we went to bed. Even then, it wasn't . . .' Martha's face suddenly crumpled; she began to weep.

She soon had to compose herself, at the sound of an approaching car. It brought her sister Ruth and Ruth's husband, Dr Probert. I don't know how news travels so fast in country places.

'Martha, my dear, this is incredible,' the doctor said. It was an inane remark, and yet it was helpful. It showed Martha the outline of a body of opinion friendly to David, reluctant to condemn.

After a few minutes, Ruth looked at me and said: 'If you'd excuse us, Mrs Mavros. . . '. Martha was being absorbed into the stockade of her family, where I had no place.

'Yes, of course,' I said. 'I'm so sorry I came at a bad time. I'll see you later, Mrs Hughes-Talbot.'

'I hope so, Mrs Mavros,' said Martha.

The doctor offered to drive me home. I declined, but he insisted. He preferred, no doubt, to leave the sisters together for a while; and it really was, as he said, raining cats and dogs.

We drove in silence until we were bumping along the

rough road. The doctor cast a hurried glance at Pritchard's barn, like a man passing a place of ill omen and anxious to assure himself of his freedom from superstition.

'You know what's happened, Mrs Mavros?' he asked abruptly.

I said 'I've some idea.'

'You may as well know it all. Everybody soon will. Mr Hughes-Talbot has been charged with murder.'

MARTHA

David was in prison in Chester, where the trial was to be held. He might as well have been given bail, for he was in the full clutch of fate and wouldn't have thought of escape; but bail was out of the question in murder cases, especially in those days when the punishment was hanging. I was allowed to visit him once a week. The obvious way of making the trip was by train, but there was always someone in the compartment who knew me. I was exposed to a variable mix of emotional sympathy, religious consolation and alert curiosity, which I could sustain well enough for five minutes in Bala High Street but not for a train journey of over an hour. So I switched to using the car, and launched myself on a forty-mile drive of mountain climbs, twisting roads and blind corners, in the midst of the holiday traffic too. Our old car wasn't made for such work, and I had never driven outside the neighbourhood. Every time I made the journey, I came home worn out.

I might have faced it more bravely if I hadn't felt that these visits were essentially pointless. They were a duty performed toward public opinion and the notion of a loyal wife, not toward David himself. We had always found it difficult to talk frankly; in the trough of disaster, it was almost impossible to talk at all, and painful to admit the impossibility – to let minutes that should have been precious pass in awkward silence. I've never been able to converse naturally in any institutional atmosphere; I dry up wretchedly, I must admit, in hospitals. The final dampener was the obligatory presence of the warder. He was a man with a beaky nose, a thin moustache and thinner lips, who looked as though he had never kissed a woman, nor even committed himself to a trusting handshake, in his life. He made me fear that any word of love would be noted as a breach of the rules. Once, in a desperate attempt to warm the frozen air, I tried speaking Welsh. David and I had never used it in better times, but he could handle it readily enough and I thought it might bring him a whiff of the free life across the border. The warder at once intervened: 'Now then, none of that.' The device couldn't have been new to him, since the offenders entrusted to his control must have included, over the years, quite a number of the cunning peasants of North Wales.

What I brought to David was a report; that's the best word, for it emerged without animation or colour and didn't even fill the permitted time. Ann's welfare was of course the principal item. Others were the state of the farm, so far as I was capable of describing it, and – not least – the dogs. In fact, we talked very much as though David were in hospital, maintaining his links with his normal environment and avoiding allusions to the unpleasant circumstances which had removed him from it. It would have been merely embarrassing for me to say: 'David, I wish you hadn't committed this murder'; and if I could have said it at all, I certainly couldn't in front of the warder. In particular, I couldn't dream of telling him – face to face, in his present extremity – that the murder had served no purpose because I had known for months what Sam threatened to tell me. I never dared to reveal that I'd read Sam's letter. For one thing, David would have been furious with me for infringing the privacy of his den.

At Craig-derw, I moved about the house like a trespasser. It could never belong to me, I knew, as it had belonged to David, to the stern old Major, and to the line of Hughes-Talbots. Without David, everything was too big for me – the rooms, the dining-table, the bed. Sometimes I took Ann into that double bed with me, not for her comfort but mine.

However, my family had decided that I mustn't be left

alone to brood. I was grateful, except that I had to scheme to be with Estelle. The family didn't much approve of her, and I couldn't have explained why this alien should be my confidante in time of trouble. I spent much of my time in my old home over the bakery. Ruth was often there, and we could succeed on a good day in being as close as when we'd shared a room and giggled about boys and kissing. The drawback was that Jacob was there too. He had secured a job at Tarporley, in Cheshire, prudently establishing a niche ahead of the bombs. During the school holidays he was staying under the parental roof, with Margaret and their children, while looking for a house. Clearly, he wasn't surprised that Martha was in difficulties again.

Ann was, of course, my gravest responsibility. From the moment of David's arrest (which she didn't witness, thank heavens, being hustled to a back room by the maid as the police arrived) I decided that there was one sure way of inflicting real injury on her, and that was by telling her lies. 'Daddy's gone away,' I said, giving the words an unflinching finality. If David returned at all, it wouldn't be within a time that a child could foresee. Ann grasped that it was true and it couldn't be helped, and looked for compensations. These, she soon found, were real. It was exciting for her to be shuttled between Craig-derw, the bakery, and the lakeside house where John and Ruth lived. She played with her cousins, a delightful novelty for an only child. Though she didn't know it, she was equipping herself for the life of temporary homes, strange faces, surprises and adaptations that was to be her childhood.

Beyond caring for Ann, and visiting David when permitted, I could do nothing but wait. It was a strange interregnum; the trial, like the coming war, impended but gave nothing away in advance. Bala lived in uncertainty, a condition unsettling for any community and exceptionally frustrating for the Welsh. In an atmosphere that demanded some outlet for the emotions, I was deluged with pity. Young women who had been at school with me, and young men for whom the warmth of my kisses had cooled into sentimental memory, squeezed my hands and declared: 'We'll stand by you, Martha.' Older people made the same pledge with greater solemnity. It was sincere, I'm sure, but it was also reasonably safe. If David turned out to be blameless, or relatively blameless, I deserved sympathy. If he was a maniacal killer, my love and trust had been cruelly abused and I deserved all the more sympathy.

One of my friends gave me a candid account of the talk in the White Lion bar during the weeks before David's trial. There was a mystery, so it was agreed – the mystery of why a man should suddenly kill another man whom he could be expected to regard with distant contempt. But the question led into a larger mystery: that of David's character, the character of a withdrawn and secretive man whom no one fully understood. Such a man could, perhaps, be imagined shooting down someone who crossed or insulted him. If we all walked around with guns, said my friend reflectively, there would be as many murders as lost tempers.

The conclusion reached by closing time in the White Lion was that the whole story hadn't been told, not by a long chalk. There would be plenty more to come out at the trial; David's inexplicable act would receive a rational shape, if not a justification. But Estelle and I knew that there was nothing to come out, except what David was determined to conceal.

The next event was the hearing in the magistrate's court. I went, of course, and tried to encourage David with brave smiles, to which he responded with a grave look that clearly warned me not to be hopeful. The procedure is that the prosecution outlines its case, giving the magistrates proper cause to send the defendant on for trial, but the defence doesn't have to say anything. The prosecuting counsel said nothing about motive, thus giving no guidance to the specualtion in the White Lion bar, but produced plenty of factual evidence – David had last been seen at the Territorial exercise near the scene of the crime, the bullet extracted from

Pritchard's skull fitted his gun, the time of death fitted, and so forth.

It looked pretty grim, but I had – like most people who know nothing about legal matters – the idea that a clever lawyer could achieve a Houdini escape. The local solicitor, who was acting for me with much sympathy and energy, managed to retain a KC who, I gathered, could do the trick if anybody could. His name, a good omen, was Mr Quick. I took to him as soon as we met. He was younger than I'd expected, which indicated that he'd done well to become a KC. The solicitor assured me that he was bound to end up as a judge, and so he would have, I suppose, if he hadn't been killed in Sicily.

At our first talk Mr Quick was quite optimistic, whether because that was his temperament or because he wanted to cheer me up. Then he saw David and his optimism vanished. A lawyer, he explained, has a right to expect that a man facing trial for murder will search his memory for facts and details that may be useful to the defence. David did nothing of the kind. He said that it was up to the prosecution to prove him guilty, and that was that.

'He's correct, strictly speaking,' Mr Quick conceded. 'But it's not helpful, not helpful at all. I'm sure you can see that, Mrs Hughes-Talbot.'

'It's very like David,' I said.

'I daresay. Let me state the position as I stated it to him. The prosecution have what must be described as a strong case. I could get a verdict of manslaughter if I could describe a struggle between Pritchard and your husband, but he's giving me no help in that direction. The only other verdict is one of murder.'

'You're saying he's sure to be found guilty.'

'At present, I've no reason to think otherwise.'

'What will happen then? They'll hang him?'

'Don't think about that, please. We haven't had the trial yet – not even the date for it. If there's a conviction, there may be grounds for appeal, perhaps on a point of law. If not, there may be grounds for a reprieve.'

I could see that he said this out of compassion, not confidence. I had managed until this time not to think much about David being hanged. That fear had seized me only when I was alone at Craig-derw, in timeless stretches of the night, and with daylight I fought my way free of it as from a nightmare. But now I recognized that it was within the scope of cool, informed calculation. David would be found guilty, and David would be hanged; there was 'no reason to think otherwise'.

It was a horror, and a horror to which I knew that I could never resign myself. I admitted no justice in it, not even the stern equality of retribution. The victim of murder dies once, in a single dizzy rush of incredulity. The man who waits for execution dies many times, across the dragging and halting of the days and weeks; and those who love him share in this death. Twenty years later, in the heat of the controversy over capital punishment, I ruined dinner parties by declaiming on this point. I was constantly amazed that there were people to whom it hadn't occurred, and others who couldn't see its significance. Perhaps one needs to go through the experience, or to come close to it.

Especially, I found it outrageous that David's life should be taken as the forfeit for Sam Pritchard's. To say this is to reverse the values established by the legend, which places David in a class with the man (whatever his name was) who killed Pushkin in the duel. But what I saw was a man of noble stature matched against a grotesque: a man passionately loved against one who would be little missed and soon forgotten.

Soon after this talk with Mr Quick, the war began. It was on a Friday that Hitler launched his *Blitzkrieg* (one of the new words) against Poland and thus extinguished the last hopes of those, like Estelle, who had believed that it wouldn't happen. I was at the bakery on Saturday. My Dad didn't appear, as he was working hard on his sermon for Sunday. Befitting the occasion, it would be one of his most awe-inspiring performances.

We gathered that the declaration of war would be announced in a broadcast by Chamberlain. A war in those days had to be formally opened, like an exhibition or a bridge. The broadcast was set for eleven o'clock on Sunday morning. I was undecided between it and my father's sermon, but Estelle came round while I was having breakfast at Craig-derw.

'Can I listen to the Prime Minister with you?'

'You wouldn't believe it otherwise?' I asked.

'That's it, I suppose.'

Chamberlain had a harsh, grating voice which reminded me of the warder at Chester prison. Eloquence was beyond him; for that, I'd have done far better to go to chapel and hear Dad. But perhaps his flat tone was right, to bring in a grey and weary time.

'What will you do?' I asked Estelle. 'You'll go back to America?'

'I don't know if I can. Won't they stop the boats?'

'I shouldn't think so.'

'I'm not going now, anyway. I'll stand by you, Martha.' We smiled, as best we could; this phrase had become a quotation.

Like a production too long anticipated and too dramatically advertised, the war opened as anti-climax. Prophetic films had shown the cities ripped apart by bombs and poison gas covering the fields, but nothing happened except in far-away Poland. In this eerie calm, the departure of the young men had the sinister portentousness of a Biblical plague. The Territorials were mustered in the first week and went to a camp somewhere in England. A number of other men went as volunteers. I took it as an additional insult that David should be debarred from this forming of the ranks, for which he had prepared more devotedly than anyone else. Willing for heroic sacrifice, he was to be set aside for a nasty and useless death.

It was hard to believe that, amid the universal catastrophe, a special doom was being found for us. It was like dying of cancer during an earthquake. I entertained wild – yet, to my mind, logical – hopes that David's transgression would be overlooked in this time of national reconciliation and national need. There was a yawning disproportion, surely, between the loss of Sam Pritchard and the wholesale losses now in contemplation. It didn't make sense, either, to devote scarce resources of skill and effort to one small individual murder. Mr Quick, for instance, mentioned that he planned to get into uniform when he was set free from current commitments.

When I came down to earth, however, I wasn't in serious doubt that the trial would go ahead. The effect of the war, I imagined, would be to speed up the timetable. But I was wrong about that; it would take more than Hitler, Mr Quick said sardonically, to get the judges back from vacation early.

Eventually, the date for the trial was fixed. By this time, Jacob had started teaching in Tarporley, with mixed classes of local children and evacuees, and moved into a house there. It was decided that I should stay with him during the trial, because Tarporley was only ten miles from Chester.

The last weeks before the trial – late September, early October – are indistinct in my memory, naturally enough since they were weeks of grim and hollow vacancy. I continued to visit David once a week, to spend time with my parents or with Ruth and John, to join Estelle for a walk through the brown, crackling bracken whenever it could be managed. I occupied myself, too, in tidying up Craig-derw. I was pretty sure that I shouldn't be living there any more – not for a long time, perhaps never again. I was impatient to reach the trial and get it over, and yet I was calmer than in the black time after David's arrest. I had decided what I was going to do.

I said to Mr Quick: 'There's something you ought to know. I should have told you before, but . . . well . . I just couldn't.'

I took out a handkerchief and twisted it nervously in my

hands. The handkerchief was a prop, distinctly useful from now on, but I really did feel nervous.

'Go on, Mrs Hughes-Talbot.'

'It's about Sam Pritchard . . . Sam Pritchard and me . . . you see . . . well, we were having an affair.'

Unable to look Mr Quick in the eyes, I gazed at his superbly polished right shoe. I was scared that he would say: 'Come, come, Mrs Hughes-Talbot, you won't get anywhere with this nonsense.' However, he didn't. He had never known Sam, of course.

'When did this begin?' he asked.

'March this year.' I hadn't expected the question, and I plumped hastily for the month the real affair had started.

'Did you go to his house?'

'Yes, Early evenings, before David would be coming home.'

'How often?'

'Once or twice a week. There's nobody on that road, as a rule. But I suppose we got careless, especially in the light evenings. David must have seen me when he was out with his Territorials.'

I ventured to look at Mr Quick. He was smiling, in a way that I wasn't meant to see. It was partly a smile of intellectual satisfaction; dealing with a murder devoid of apparent motive or explanation was what had irritated him all along. But it was also an appreciative smile, which might have been rendered in words as: 'Well, fancy that. And very nice too.'

I said: 'The reason I'm telling you is . . . if this comes out, I mean at the trial – would it make a difference?'

'Not to the verdict, I'm afraid. Murder is murder, whatever the provocation.'

'But they wouldn't hang him? That's what I meant.'

'No, in that respect it might very well make the vital difference. One can't be positive, but I should say that a reprieve would be highly probable.'

There was a short silence. Then he asked: 'Would you be

willing to repeat what you've just told me in the witness-box?'

I twisted the handkerchief again and said in a faltering voice: 'It wouldn't be easy.'

'I appreciate that.'

'But if it's like you say, I've got to, haven't I? I couldn't live with myself otherwise.'

I told Estelle what I was doing, but no one else. For anyone around Bala, I thought, the idea that I would ever have let Sam Pritchard touch me was blatantly ridiculous. I couldn't see myself telling that story, face to face, to any of my family. Ruth would laugh and tell me not to be silly; my Dad would lecture me sternly on the sin of lying on the Bible, and frighten me out of the whole plan. In the court, I could avoid looking at people who knew me. Even so, I wondered whether I could put on a convincing performance.

I went off to Tarporley, with Ann, the weekend before the trial started. It was a dull place, set in depressing flat country that reminded me of Saxby. Ann was cheerful, and pleased to be with Jacob's children, but Jacob was the last person whose guest I'd have chosen to be at this time. Characteristically, he had found the ugliest and gloomiest house in Tarporley, all chocolate-brown panelling and creaking staircases. We were give a room with just the space for two beds, and lived out of suitcases. I wished that I was in the hotel in Chester where Estelle was staying, but I hadn't dared to challenge the family's decision. In any case, from now onward I was sure to need all the money I could save.

Mr Quick explained to me that he didn't propose to put David in the witness-box. I was surprised – I imagined that, if you were on trial, you were obliged to tell your story and answer questions – but also relieved. David would have been certain to say something that set him on the way to the gallows. On the other hand, it was a surprise to the family that I was to give evidence. 'What are you going to say?' my Mam demanded. I put on a teasing smile and replied: 'You'll see.' She sniffed, to indicate her view that I would make a mess of it one way or another.

The articles that get written nowadays about Sam Pritchard describe the Hughes-Talbot trial as a sensation of the period. That's an exaggeration; with the nation at war, people had other things to think about. Still, you could sense a nostalgia for anything so redolent of peacetime as a single killing for personal reasons. It happened, too, that there was a shortage of news; Poland was buried in the silence of defeat, there was no action elsewhere, and the war had gone into the curious state of suspended animation that lasted until the next spring. The penny papers gave the trial a fair amount of space, and on the day after I gave evidence my picture was on the front page of the *Daily Mirror*, with the caption: 'HE KILLED FOR HER.' The courtroom was always packed, but I believe that was normal for a provincial assize court that saw only occasional murder trials. In Bala, I've no doubt, people talked of nothing else.

As a witness, I wasn't allowed to attend the trial before my own appearance. I went to Chester each afternoon, leaving Ann with Margaret, and was given a summary by Mr Quick. After that, I had a drink with Estelle and received a rather more vivid account. The prosecution piled up the evidence laboriously. A lance-corporal in David's company testified that David hadn't gone home after the exercise, but had headed in the direction of Pritchard's house. The man gave evidence in a distinctly shamefaced manner, Estelle said; presumably he hadn't been able to resist a break from Army life and a night at home.

My turn came on the third day. I went into the witness-box and looked briefly at David, this time without trying to smile. Then I turned to face the judge, which was the proper thing to do, I imagined. He was a very old man in a red robe that seemed to be much too big for him. Perhaps he'd borrowed it from some other judge. The effect wasn't dignified, anyway.

I took the oath and gave myself a quick mental run-through of what I had to remember, as you do when you're taking an exam and waiting for the questions. The answer to

'What was your relationship to Pritchard?' was 'I was his mistress'. What a silly word for it, I thought. I hoped desperately that I wouldn't giggle when I had to utter it. Most likely, everybody – even the decrepit old judge – would be able to see what a feeble act I was putting on. But it was too late to worry about that now.

I got through it, somehow or other. My voice was reduced to a brittle croak, and it was only by luck that it gave a touching effect of emotional stress. Two or three times I dried up, like a bad amateur actress (which indeed I was), and had to be patiently prompted. Halfway through, I suddenly remembered about the handkerchief and started twisting it like crazy; this helped a bit, but I was afraid that it was too obvious. I didn't dare to look at the public benches, where the Hughes family filled the front row. The jury stared impassively at the wall behind me, rather than at me, like people compelled to sit through a boring lecture; perhaps juries always look like this. The judge was calmly writing. I didn't know that judges took their own notes, and it looked as though he had lost interest in the trial and was catching up on his correspondence. Anyone accustomed to what's called 'courtroom drama' knows how completely undramatic it is, but I was just finding out.

When I finished, there was an uncomfortable silence. I didn't know whether I was allowed to leave the box or not; the judge was still writing. I looked, just once more, at David. Although Mr Quick had certainly told him what I was going to say, and although of course he knew that it wasn't true, he looked absolutely shattered. I saw, as I hadn't seen before, the despicable ugliness of my invention. It occurred to me that perhaps I had done it for myself – or myself and Estelle – more than for David. To my surprise, I found that I was crying.

I was allowed, now that I'd given my evidence, to sit in the courtroom, but I didn't feel equal to joining the family. I went back to the little room where witnesses waited. It was empty, since I had been the last witness, and very quiet.

Here, I made a discovery. It was as absolute, as irrevocable and as dismaying as the discovery that you have lost your religious faith. What I discovered was that I had stopped loving David. It wasn't because of anything he had done; it was simply that I had given him all that was in me to give. I realized that, even if by some quirk the court set him free tomorrow, we couldn't return to living together as though we were still clasped in the same intense, absorbing, ever-striving love. And I realized that a part of my life was over: my youth, burned up in the fire of my love for David. The rest of my life stretched before me, a bleak wasteland across which I should have to make my way.

An official of some sort came to tell me that the court had risen. I went out to the foyer, or whatever they call it. Estelle was the first person I saw. We almost threw our arms round each other, but restrained ourselves.

'Was I good enough?' I asked her in Welsh.

'You were very good, really you were,' she answered. I turned to find Mr Quick standing close to me. He gave me a funny look – the sort of look that, in my childhood, my Dad used to give me when he suspected me of telling a fib, but couldn't prove it. But Mr Quick couldn't have understood Welsh, surely.

One other person spoke to me: my sister Ruth. Her face was white, and a frown dug lines between her eyes, so that I suddenly saw her as a middle-aged woman. She said: 'How could you? Martha – how could you?'

It was clear that she believed my story. I felt this as a severe injustice, but an injustice of which I couldn't complain since it had been my aim to convince. And if Ruth, who had been so close to me all my life, believed it, then everybody else would. I saw that I'd been hoping to have it both ways, and I wasn't to get off so easily. I had supposed that, while my story would go across with the English judge and jury, people who knew me would catch on to the device. It struck me for the first time that the Welsh weren't quite so clever as they believed themselves to be.

It was clear, too, that Ruth was deeply shocked, for reasons not so much of moral principle as of personal sensitivity; that she considered an intimacy with Sam Pritchard as something ineradicably demeaning, disgusting, unclean, of which she would never have suspected me and which she could never condone. I felt miserably ashamed, exactly as if it had been true.

A policeman said to me, not hiding his dislike and contempt: 'There's a bit of a crowd out there. You'd better go out the back way.'

The next day, the trial reached its conclusion. I stayed in Tarporley. Mr Quick made a brilliant speech, by all accounts, laying stress on David's high moral code, his profound love for his errant wife, and the unbearable strain which had driven him to his desperate act. The jury took little time to bring in a verdict of guilty with a recommendation to mercy. The judge, as required by law, sentenced David to death.

The day after that, I had a letter from Ruth. 'I won't make any comment on what you have admitted,' she wrote. 'I have no wish to add to what you must be suffering from your conscience.' Her reason for writing was to tell me that our parents were taking it very hard. 'They say they never want to see you again. I hope they'll come round in time, but Dad is very positive now – you know what he can be like. You can imagine, too, that the general feeling in Bala isn't friendly to you. In the circumstances, I strongly advise you not to come back at present. If anything needs to be done about Craig-derw, write to me.'

I had no choice but to follow this advice, but I hadn't envisaged staying on at Tarporley after the trial and it was decidedly no fun. Jacob called me into the gloomiest room in the gloomy house, which he had selected as his study, and subjected me to a long and merciless speech. He didn't forget, of course, to rake up my first steps on the downward path years ago in Camden Town when, as he amiably put it, I 'offered myself to the first man who was fool enough to take

216

an interest'. Nothing – not even marriage to a man far above my deserts, not even responsibility for an innocent child – stopped me from sinking again to my abysmal level. How our family could have produced a creature like me, Jacob failed to understand. What would become of me, or how I could ever make up for the havoc I had wreaked, he understood still less. I was thinking that the Baptist Church, though long on the vocabulary of condemnation, was short of a useful institution. Had we been Catholics, I'd have been just the candidate for the lifelong atonement of a convent.

Margaret, a woman who shrank from all forms of unpleasantness, tried to soften the atmosphere. She was really the one who failed to understand; it puzzled her, I believe, how anyone could be so keen on sex as to incur risks for the sake of it. Politeness was important to her, and she treated me as a relative paying a visit. When Jacob was out of the house, we chatted blandly enough about children, clothes or the novel complexities of rationing. The evening meal, however, passed in a grim silence and I always went up to my room directly after the nine o'clock news.

It was a hard time for me – harder, in some ways, than before the trial. I hadn't allowed myself to think beforehand about the disgrace that I was inviting. Now that it was a reality, it hurt. Dad and Mam had forgiven me for my lapse with Peter Morshead, but they wouldn't forgive me this time. Friends in Bala, who had sentimentally pledged themselves to stand by me, would condemn me with all the greater vehemence from a feeling of being deceived. So I was all alone; and I no longer had any battle to fight, any heroic posture to strike, or any devoted love to inspire me. Worst of all, David was under sentence of death. Despite Mr Quick's judgement of the probabilities, I couldn't be sure that there would be a reprieve. Perhaps the war had generated a new ruthlessness, and one life more or less no longer mattered. The hanging was still a horror to me, or a worse horror now that I could do nothing to avert it. Waking early on those dark, rainy autumn mornings, and shivering under the blankets (my room under the roof was draughty and cold), I imagined the vile ritual in the prison yard and wanted to scream from helplessness.

I thought of Estelle, too, going through the same misery in the loneliness of Ty Pellaf. She 'phoned me, speaking in a guarded manner from Mrs Bowen's shop, and we arranged to meet. I was to drive to Wrexham, a place where I hoped not to be recognized, and she would get there by train. Before the time came, however, Ann went down with a nasty brand of 'flu which was going the rounds in that sad season. When she was on the mend, I caught it; I had a temperature of 104, and was barely able to stumble to the lavatory. These illnesses, which prevented me from seeing Estelle, also kept me from what would have been my last visit to David at Chester. I confess that I was relieved. It would have been the most difficult of all.

While I was in bed with 'flu, Jacob appeared in my room and said: 'David's lawyer has telephoned. He has been informed that a reprieve has been granted.'

I didn't take this in at once. My hold on any reality outside my burning, aching body was fairly weak, and Jacob had spoken in a mournful tone, as though bringing bad news. When I grasped it, I had a strange feeling of being lost, with no focus for my emotions left to me. I would never, it seemed, care so much about anything again.

I wasn't going to give anything away to Jacob, so I said: 'Oh, it's nice of Mr Quick to ring up. I never had any doubt about it, of course.'

'You should thank the Lord for His mercy,' Jacob told me.

'Oh, I do. Let Him know, won't you?'

David was taken to Dartmoor to begin serving a sentence of life imprisonment. It would mean about ten years in practice, Mr Quick said. I got over the 'flu and resumed what passed for normal life. Estelle and I revived our plan and met in Wrexham. We had lunch in a foul little snack-bar opposite the station; then we drove a couple of miles out of the town and went for a walk. It was unpleasantly cold, or perhaps I hadn't fully recovered. I remember every day in that first autumn of the war as grey, sunless and bone-chilling.

I asked Estelle: 'Are you still sleeping in front of the fire?'

'I am, yes. I'm used to it. Sometimes it seems that nothing's changed. Sometimes I can't believe what's happened. It's nothing like what I imagined. I was sure he'd drop me by this time. But he never did.'

She halted in the road and looked directly at me.

'I still love him, Martha.'

'I'm glad,' I said. I didn't say that I had stopped loving him; and I thought, sadly, that I was hiding something from Estelle for the first time.

'Perhaps you ought to take up with him again when he comes out, Estelle.'

'Oh, no. We'll all be too old for this kind of thing.'

'Are you going back to America now?'

'I guess I am. There are ships, after all. And I don't care about this war, now David's not going to be in it.'

'Nor do I.'

'All the same . . . I can't decide. I don't know if I can face America, either.'

'Oh, nonsense. Once you're in America all sorts of exciting things will happen to you, I'm sure they will.'

'I don't believe anything will ever happen to me in my life again – anything that matters. I'll feel different in time, maybe. But that's the way I feel now.'

She seemed so irresolute, so sunk in lassitude, that I took her straight to a travel agent in Wrexham to ask about ships. The man was delighted to see a customer, with his business extinguished by the war, and spent the whole afternoon making long-distance calls to shipping lines. While he was on the phone, Estelle suddenly said to me: 'Why don't you come with me, Martha? You and Ann. You don't have to go through this damn war.'

The idea was tempting. I was exiled from Bala, anyway: homeless and friendless anywhere in Wales or England. I had always heard that it was easy to make friends in America, where everybody moved around so much that strangers couldn't be suspect. It was likely, too, that I might be doing Ann a good turn by making her an American, considering what the war would do to the Old World. And yet I felt, deep down, that I must go forward on my own, without anyone linked to me by the memories of this transforming year – without David, and without Estelle.

I might have been persuaded; it was a time when no choice was clear. But the agent, his hand over the 'phone, called to Estelle that there was just one berth left on a ship sailing in five days' time from Liverpool. I shouted at her: 'Take it!'

I went to Liverpool to see her off. I took Ann with me, from some stupid notion that it would be a treat for her, and of course this was a mistake. The crowds of strange people, the voices emerging from loudspeakers (which she'd never encountered before), the hours of hanging about in the cold – the whole thing was too much for her. After being good and brave all day, she started to cry miserably just when it was time to say goodbye. But without her, the tears would have been mine and Estelle's. We had no cause to believe that we should ever see each other again.

The rest can be told briefly.

When Estelle had gone, I gave thought to the future for the first time. I had no grounds for hope, but no excuse for despair. One way or another, I had to survive and to clear a path for Ann.

I stayed at Tarporley for another couple of weeks. I'm sure I do the town an injustice, having struck it at such a low point in my life, but I don't think I could have made it my home in the best of circumstances. It's an amorphous, undefined part of the world – not quite Northern, not Midland, not Welsh. However, I hid in the house most of the time and my contacts with the local people were minimal. They knew all about me, I'm sure, and tracked me along the streets with a sly, whispering curiosity. I decided that the chances of escaping notice would be best in a large city. I had no happy memories of London, and it was out of the question to take a child there because bombing was still expected at any time. I read the ads, and found a job in Manchester.

I needed the job because I needed money. After Mr Quick had been paid, the Hughes-Talbot bank account was at a low ebb (I might just have bought tickets to America and arrived there as the traditional penniless immigrant). I sold the car, but it was five years old, and anyway no one was thrilled to acquire a car with petrol rationing in force, so I didn't get much for it. Craig-derw was full of valuables, but I didn't want David to come home and find the heritage looted.

The house was locked and bolted; Ruth paid somebody to sweep up the dust a couple of times a year. The Council had powers to install evacuees in it, but never did. A neighbouring farmer rented the land and kept it from going back to wilderness. He considered that he was doing a favour, so the rent was a token amount. I believe that the sheep were slaughtered, though the meat left no record in the official rationing scheme.

I didn't visit David in Dartmoor. There were plenty of excuses: the journey was long and difficult in wartime, I had no one to whom Ann could be entrusted, work tied me down (in the war, you were entitled to one week's holiday a year). In reality, we had already parted. Between me and this man, either there was a passion throbbing at the core of life or there was nothing. I wrote once a month, sending news. He replied, sending what passes for news in a prison. When I decided to get a divorce, I wrote a carefully phrased letter of explanation. He made no answer except to sign the papers.

Sadly, I was never reconciled to my parents. Trouble aged them quickly, and they both died before the war had lasted two years. It made no sense for me to attend the funerals. Ruth sent me an olive-branch letter when I got married, saying that she hoped to meet Alex when the war was over and things in general were easier. It wasn't impossible to meet in wartime, but I took this to mean: don't rush it.

Things had started to get easier for me, in fact, from the suumer of 1940, the very time when the war was blazing up. Just as though nothing were happening, I passed tests in typing and office procedure and got a rather good Civil Service job. I moved into a nice flat, with a day-nursery for Ann down the street. As well as security, the job brought an end to loneliness. I was in a large office, working with women who for the most part were easy to like. They weren't regular civil servants and regarded the formalities with amused tolerance; they were better educated than I was, and took pleasure in lending me books or inviting me to listen to records. They also gave good and frequent parties. It wasn't until later in the war that liquor ran short. These parties were attended by men in adequate numbers, although the irregularities of Service leave meant that you could never be sure who would be there and who wouldn't.

I didn't consider myself a married woman, and I wore my ring only because the existence of Ann had to be justified. Among my friends, I encouraged a vague impression that my husband was overseas. I was inclined, nevertheless, to evade the recurrent male demands. I had travelled further than I'd imagined from my girlhood, and from the time when going to bed with a man was an excitement in itself. What I wanted, in principle, was to love someone; but I didn't expect it, and in truth didn't care a great deal. I was passing, indeed, through a period of emotional exhaustion. Two other factors worked in the same direction. One was Ann, who directed looks of searching inquiry at the men who, now and again, called at the flat to take me to a film or a concert. I didn't wish her to grow up, like some other children in wartime, with a bewildering series of 'uncles' in place of a father. And then, I was reluctant to attach myself to a life that might be endangered. David, against all expectations, was barred from the chances both of glory and of sacrifice; that should be a sign, I felt. To bomber pilots and parachutists, I refused so much as a kiss.

Alex and I first met, probably, at a party where he took no

special notice of me, nor I of him. It was typical of our gradual approach to each other that the occasion carved no mark in our minds. He was a sergeant in the Air Force, in charge of the cookhouse at a training depot. We became friends, and thought cautiously about becoming lovers. Guessing what concerned me – he has always been good at that – he assured me that there was no risk of his being sent abroad or switched to some more belligerent activity, and that his sole aim was to get through the war as comfortably as possible. From the military aspect, his talents were those of Schweik. He was in the city often, whether officially on leave or unofficially but safely absent. At my flat, he made delicious meals from ingredients believed by others to be unobtainable. This endeared him to Ann, who never found it odd that he was a better cook than her mother.

We talked late, and Alex slept on a couch, generally departing to reach his depot before morning. One night, he informed me that he'd had enough of the couch. He made love with deft, unerring competence, as he cooked. I enjoyed it, like a good dinner.

A couple of months later, huddled warmly in his arms, I told him about David. Since my exile, I had told no one else. He stroked my back consolingly, made no comment, and went to sleep. I stayed awake, trying to work out what had changed for me. Listening to his calm, strong breathing, I found myself weeping: tears of release, tears of gratitude.

Alex woke up, wiped my face gently with the sheet, and asked: 'What's the matter?'

'Nothing's the matter. I've realized I love you.'

'About time,' Alex said.

We were happy to go on like this, but in the spring of 1942 he was transferred – 'posted', as the jargon went – to another RAF station away in Suffolk. His depot was being closed; nothing less could have prised Alex from a cushy billet.

'I don't know what I'll do,' I said.

'I think you'd better get a divorce and marry me.'

'Yes, I'd better, hadn't I?' I wondered why I hadn't

thought of it before.

We had three homes before the end of the war. Alex always managed to find a pleasing flat or house. We settled, finally, into a roomy late-Victorian house with a conservatory that made a studio for his weekend painting.

'Can we stay here a long time, Mummy?' Ann asked.

'Yes, I hope so.'

'Then I think you ought to have a baby.'

The baby – Ralph – was born in time to give his first smile for the coming of peace.. The war had been like a relentless exaction of tribute, and shopkeepers uttered scornful laughs when asked for safety-pins. But with Alex, nothing was really unobtainable.

When we first met, Alex had told me that he was a painter by vocation and a cook only by wartime necessity. I didn't take this seriously, even after we were married. I couldn't imagine that anyone who was practical, even-tempered and amiable could be a real artist. I liked his paintings – they were a lot better than Sam Pritchard's, obviously – and it was nice for him to have a hobby that gave him pleasure, as well as a skill in which he could guide Ann and our future children; but being a cook was serious. People needed to eat, whereas they didn't need pictures, and restaurants would improve after the war, so Alex would always be able to get a job. So I was alarmed when, having been given a date for his release from the Air Force, he announced that he proposed to qualify as an art teacher and we would live on a student grant while he took the course. I was alarmed, too, when he spent the whole of our savings on a house in Hampstead. I told myself that Alex usually knew what he was doing, and so he did. He came top in the course and got an excellent job, and the house was destined for an increase in value that only a third world war, I suppose, will ever check.

We made new friends, especially when Alex began to sell his pictures and sow the seeds of a reputation. At first, I found it breathlessly exciting to be on first-name terms with artists, writers, actors, film directors; after a while, I took it for granted. In the early days when we were all just raising our heads from the war, we met at the 24 bus stop, sat on the floor at bottle-parties, bought cheap-day tickets to go walking on the South Downs, and 'phoned to congratulate a friend on a mention in the *Ham and High*. Twenty years later, the people we knew drove bulky cars and complained about parking, planned their dinners like election campaigns, had second homes in the Dordogne, and found it a bore to give interviews. By that time, Alex was able to give up teaching. We moved to Cornwall.

We see Ruth and John from time to time. After some negotiation, they came to stay a week with us in London in the summer of 1949. It was ten years, or nearly, since we had seen each other; I was amused to find that slender Ruth was more solid than I was. Her accent struck me as overdone, and she remarked that I'd lost mine. We spoke Welsh a little, but it sounded artificial and we reverted to English.

One quiet morning when we were alone in the house, I mustered my courage and asked about David.

'He keeps by himself, very much so. John sees him professionally. He gets a bad cough when it's wet. He won't make old bones, John says.'

'I was hoping he'd marry again.'

'Oh no, I don't think so.' Ruth hesitated, then said: 'You shouldn't feel bad, Martha – not now. I'm glad to see you so happy with Alex. David was never the right one for you. Our Mam always said that, from the first.'

'Did she really? She didn't say it to me.'

'Well, nobody could tell you anything then.'

When Ruth and John left, we said: 'You must come every year.' Sometimes they did, and sometimes they had other holiday plans or didn't choose to leave Bala. A return visit wasn't suggested. We haven't tried, my sister and I, to reconstruct the old closeness. It's wiser to be content with an intermittent friendship between people whose lives have diverged, sustained as much by our husbands – Alex and John like each other, and both play golf – as by ourselves. My joking brother Gideon couldn't settle to home territory after the war, and made his way to Australia. With Jacob, I never came closer than Christmas cards. He became an Inspector of Schools, and died soon after his retirement.

When the Pritchard boom started, and the legend reverberated like one of those echoes that guides demonstrate in caves, my first thought was that it would be better if David were dead. It was embarrassing for me to be the romantic heroine, but it was worse to be the villain. Ruth said, however, that he took no newspapers and didn't have television, so I hoped that he didn't know much of what was going on. Nobody, so far as I'm aware, ever had the nerve to try to interview him.

My impulse was to divulge the truth, but I was afraid that I'd be liable to some dire penalty for perjury. Eventually, I put the situation in carefully hypothetical form to a lawyer whom we knew, and he told me that this couldn't be so. But by that time I had been badgered into giving tacit assent to the legend, and I didn't see how to change my line.

One day, the phone rang and I heard: 'Martha, is that you? It's Janet Bullard – remember?' Naturally, I said I remembered. She went on to say that she was in Cornwall on holiday with her husband – 'I don't think you ever met him' – and if it wasn't too much of an imposition she would dearly love to see me again.

By this time, I'd succeeded in placing her. We had worked together in Manchester. She had been, like me, an enthusiastic apprentice to culture, seeking relief from the war in learning what she ought to think about Virginia Woolf, Stravinsky and Modigliani. She also gave parties; it was under her roof, more likely than not, than I met Alex. Her husband had spent the war in the Middle East and Janet had hurled herself into a succession of affairs, but apparently the marriage had survived.

I invited the Bullards to lunch, explaining that Alex was unfortunately away at the opening of his first show in New York. Mr Bullard turned out to be a hearty fellow, an engineer by profession. He eyed me appreciatively while his wife talked, conveying the estimate that I must have been a juicy piece at my best and still wasn't wholly without interest. I was well past fifty at the time, so this was gratifying.

After lunch, I offered Janet a visit to Alex's studio. Her husband, admitting breezily that he was an ignoramus in the arts, said that he would take a stroll in the garden.

She admired Alex's work, but I saw that it wasn't what she had come for. Gripping my arm (this had always been a habit of hers), she demanded tremulously: 'Martha – you haven't got any Pritchards?'

'I'm afraid not.'

'Oh. I went to the retrospective, of course, but the catalogue said it wasn't complete. I thought he might have given you some.'

'No, he never did.' I refrained from mentioning that Sam had sold me one for three pounds and I had junked it.

'That's a shame. I'll have to be content with what I've seen. But that was marvellous, simply marvellous. My God, what an artist!'

I said nothing.

'You know, I had such a shock when I saw your face in the colour mag. I said: "My God, that's Martha!". Then it all made sense. You called yourself Mrs Hughes, didn't you? And you pretended you didn't know anything about painting. You're a deep one, Martha.'

'Not deep. Merely evasive.'

'Well – I can understand, of course, at that time. People were so bigoted. The world has progressed, say what you like.'

'I sometimes wonder.'

'Oh, so do I. But at least we know how to appreciate Samuel Pritchard. Martha – when you look back, you must be so proud.'

'Yes,' I said, 'in a way, I do feel proud.'

When the Bullards had gone, I dug out the colour mag

which Janet had spoken of. I stared at the photo of myself, the same photo which had appeared on the front page of the *Daily Mirror* the day after the trial, and I read what the article said about 'The woman who gave Pritchard love – and death.' First I smiled, then I chuckled, then I giggled, then I dropped the mag on the floor and started laughing hysterically. Justin, my youngest son, came into the room and asked me what was so funny. I told him that I would explain to him – some other time. I'm glad that, finally, I can.

DAVID

I was released from prison on the fourteenth of October 1948, almost exactly nine years after I had been taken to Dartmoor to serve my sentence. I do not wish, as I thankfully approach the end of this narrative, to compose a chronicle of those years. I learned at an early stage that, if he hopes to minimize his suffering, the prisoner is well advised to cultivate a numb indifference to his surroundings. In particular, he must endeavour to be blind and deaf to whatever evokes memories of a better time. Sometimes, when the wind was in the right direction, the bleating of sheep and the barking of dogs recalled my former life. The swift onset and cessation of rain, the drifting mists, a western freshness and dampness in the air – each of these could, at any season, bring the illusion that I was at home at Craig-derw: that I was free to take my cap and my stick and set off for a tramp round the fields. Dartmoor is the cruellest of prisons, because it keeps alive the sense of freedom.

One other sound was audible at times: the crackle of shots on a rifle-range. It is still audible today, I believe, for a part of the moor is permanently delimited as a military training area. I was often reminded, therefore, of the mighty conflict in which I had expected to render service to my country and to find a fulfilment of my destiny, but from which I had excluded myself by a single fatal act. In 1940, when the nation was in mortal peril, I sought an interview with the Governor and petitioned to be given an opportunity for some kind of active service, no matter how perilous or indeed suicidal. The Governor, a humane and patriotic man, sympathized with my plea, but it found no favour with more remote authorities. As the war progressed, the Governor instituted the custom of assembling the prisoners for an announcement, and relaxing the severity of the daily routine, to celebrate the grand occasions: Alamein, the surrender of Italy, the invasion of Normandy, and the final victory. While I attempted to rejoice, I could not help reflecting bitterly that I had made no contribution to the achievement.

I sought no friendships in Dartmoor, and I made none. In the prison, as in the world outside, I had the reputation of being a solitary and self-sufficient character. I was also a murderer; one has to be in prison to know that among other law-breakers, quite as much as among blameless citizens, the murderer inspires a powerful and almost superstitious repugnance. I had in any case no common ground with the professional criminals, who formed a majority of the inmates and belonged to a self-contained community, with its own codes of conduct, its recognized leaders and its incomprehensible slang. They did not consider it surprising, much less disgraceful, to spend varying periods of their lives in prison; and their sentences were enlivened by the arrival of acquaintances who brought news of successful or unsuccessful criminal enterprises, just as prisoners of war might take an interest in accounts of recent campaigns. It is an ironical truth that imprisonment is a searing experience, and a deterrent to further offences against the law, for everyone except a criminal. Thus, I had neither desire nor opportunity to converse with the burglars and forgers; and it may well be imagined that I held aloof from such reprehensible characters as embezzlers who had betrayed an employer's trust, profiteers of the wartime black market, rapists and sexual perverts. During the entire span of my incarceration, I encountered only two men who appeared to share my social background and my standards of personal integrity. Both were, like me, convicted of murder. I did not inquire into the circumstances which had impelled them to the taking of life, and they preserved an equivalent discretion toward me.

Most of the prisoners received visits, but I did not. Probably this accentuated the aura of solitude that was attached to me, and perhaps it inspired a belief that I had committed a crime so atrocious that my nearest and dearest had turned their backs on me. I did not feel that I had a right to urge Martha to visit me. She had conferred on me the greatest of gifts – that of life – at a heavy and painful cost to herself; it would be intolerably churlish to repay her by a demand that she should do more for me. Moreover, I had no means of evaluating the practical difficulties. Martha wrote to me that, living among strangers as she did, she knew no one who could be trusted to care for Ann, and it was plainly undesirable to bring the child to the prison. Martha's letters, which arrived regularly, gave me a punctilious, though not exactly a reassuring, account of her circumstances. Furnished flats in Manchester and routine tasks in administrative offices were a sad substitute for the life she had enjoyed at Craig-derw. It was hardly to be wondered at that the task of 'carrying on' left her no strength for further exertions.

Nevertheless, I yearned passionately for even a moment of her presence – one glance from her eyes – one word in her soft voice. Time passed; she wrote that she had a better job and a circle of 'interesting' friends; yet she still did not propose a visit. Alone in my cell, in the anguish of interminable wakeful nights, I confronted the cruellest of questions: had Martha ceased to love me? I could not assume that, because she was my wife, she was immune from the universal reprobation toward the murderer. I remembered that, in our prison interviews between my arrest and my trial, she had found it difficult to talk to me even on subjects as natural as, for example, Ann's welfare: difficult, I had felt, to look at me. It was possible that she had resolved on her sublime falsehood from a sense of conjugal duty or of pity, and not from love. She was justified in resenting the onerous burden that I had placed upon her, my wilful destruction of our happiness, and the trials that she – and Ann – had endured through my fault.

Love, surely, could not survive such resentment. And, once I guessed at this resentment, it was more and more clearly revealed in her letters. They were cold, distant, and patently written in reluctant conformity with an obligation.

In those Dartmoor nights, I had to suffer another torment. I knew that, in the ultimate sense, Martha's innocence was inviolable. But I also knew that her physical passions, when aroused, were of considerable intensity. I had ample evidence of this from memories of our married life; and it was the only explanation of her vulnerability to seduction when she had lived in London as a girl. Now, she was again living in a large city, but this time without a brother's protection. It was not hard to imagine the erosion of conventional restraints in the atmosphere of wartime, when long separations between husbands and wives were the rule. Her letters indicated that her new, 'interesting' friends were united by enthusiasm for the arts, and this was scarcely a guarantee of moral strictness. She was sundered from her husband for, probably, ten years, a daunting span of time for a young woman at the peak of health and beauty. It was a fair presumption that another man would establish himself in the place that I had relinquished. Very likely, it would be a man whose attractions were enhanced by the distinction for which war provided an opportunity. It might well be a fighter pilot, I thought, miserably contemplating my own dishonourable uniform.

I knew Martha well enough to recognize that she could not, like certain women in her position, indulge her physical needs as a matter of cool calculation. When she yielded to a man, she would love him – or persuade herself that she loved him, which amounted in effect to the same. Indeed, not even the disastrous consequences of her seduction had (according to Jacob) shaken her insistence that she was in love with the man in London. It was her nature, moreover, to give a man her entire confidence when she gave her love. Once she had told her story to the airman – I already called him that in my mind – he would surely be able to persuade her that she owed nothing to the husband who was the cause of her misfortunes. The increasingly indifferent tone of her letters was readily explained by this influence.

In 1942, Martha wrote to inform me that she wished to obtain a divorce. She proposed to marry a man whom she had known for some months, and with whom she was in love; I almost smiled when I read that he was in the Royal Air Force. The news came as a grievous blow to me, but it was not, for the reasons which I have set out, a complete surprise. The surprise was that she was citing as grounds for divorce my adultery with Estelle Mavros.

I was aware that Estelle had returned to the United States shortly after the outbreak of war. (I wondered why Martha, in her first letter to Dartmoor, mentioned the depature of Mrs Mavros; now I understood.) The certainty that I should never see her again, and the virtual certainty that she had already forgotten me as she flitted from one new affair to another, purged me of the last remnants of my love for her – if love had ever been a permissible word for that strange infatuation. She still appeared to me in disordered and disturbing dreams, but she had no place in my waking thoughts. I did not know whether, after my release, I should have the good fortune to resume my life with Martha, but at least I believed that the memory of Estelle would present no obstacle.

Now, I was confronted with the knowledge that the secret which I had sought to protect by desperate measures was no secret at all. It was possible that, when closing our home, Martha had searched my desk for valuables and come upon the letter which I had unwisely deposited in it. I became convinced subsequently that this was the case, since the letter was not there when I returned to Craig-derw. But it was also possible – and in my Dartmoor meditations it appeared more likely – that Pritchard had been able to carry out his intention to disclose my infidelity to Martha, presumably on the last afternoon of his life. This would account more than adequately for her altered manner when she came to see me in Chester, for her refusal to visit Dartmoor, and for her ability to transfer her affections to the airman without reproaching herself. I recalled the text of Pritchard's letter. He had not urged me to reform my conduct, nor had he hinted at blackmail; he had written, flatly and inexorably: 'Your wife shall know.' For this, I had killed him. But, worthless creature though he was, his was the ultimate victory. I had lost all that was dear to me, and I had achieved precisely nothing.

Cruel though the discovery was, I could not blame Martha. She had her own life to rebuild; she had simply taken the most expeditious means to secure the divorce, which of course I did not contest. All the guilt was mine, and all the blind, stupid blundering was mine too. I had only one crumb of comfort. The newspapers, at this tense midway point of the war, could have no interest in reporting an undefended divorce nor in reviving a stale sensation.

In memory, the first three years of my imprisonment, when I received letters from Martha and bruised my mind constantly on doubts and fears, seem longer than the remaining six years, which were like the infinite repetition of a single empty day. I submitted passively to the prison routine, like a beast of burden plodding along its accustomed track. I obeyed the rules and gave no trouble, not because I cared about earning the Governor's approval and the chance of an earlier release, but because there was no purpose in doing otherwise. Like everyone who has been in prison, I can testify that it seldom or never induces repentance or moral improvement, but it bestowed on me the neutral blessing of resignation. Had I been told that I must remain in Dartmoor for the whole of the life sentence that I was officially serving, I should have accepted the information with genuine indifference.

I received one letter a year, or approximately so; it arrived on no particular date and always took me by surprise. It came from Dan Williams, a farmer in the vicinity of Craigderw, who had made himself responsible for my land and was paying an appropriate sum into the bank account which was still maintained in my name. Although the unfamiliar effort clearly gave him some trouble, he considered it his duty to report on his stewardship. It was to Williams, therefore, that I wrote when I was notified of my approaching release. He replied in unexpectedly warm terms, saying that 'all in Bala' would be glad to see me back. I was surprised by this indication that I might expect an attitude of forgiveness, perhaps even of sympathy. It would make, on the practical level, little difference to me, for I had never sought popularity or social intimacy, and intended to do so even less in the future. Had my neighbours shown a disposition to shun the returning murderer, I should not have challenged or resented it. Yet I could not help being touched by this sign of human kindness, the first that had reached me for nine years.

I arrived in Bala by a morning train, having spent the night at a cheap lodging-house in Shrewsbury. In order to evade any kind of reception – be it friendly, hostile or simply curious – I had refrained from informing Williams of the exact date of my release. I ventured to pass along the High Street and received a few glances of inquiry, but not of recognition. The bakery had been acquired by a larger firm, reminding me that Martha had lost her parents at the time when she was still writing to me, but I observed few other changes. Leaving the town, I walked beside the lake as far as St Beuno's Church, where my ancestors are buried. Beside my father's grave, I paid the respects of an unworthy son. Then I made the steep ascent (a rise, as I mentioned earlier in this narrative, of five hundred feet in half a mile) to the plateau that is my native ground. On completing the climb, I was obliged to halt and recover my breath; this had never happened before. But I was aware, from an increasing tendency to coughing in the last few years, that my lungs were no longer in first-rate condition.

My home was now within sight. I knew that I should soon be able to regain its tranquil shelter, and I vowed that I should never leave it again. From the point where I stood, it was no longer possible to see the lake or the town, and the eye was irresistibly drawn westward to the soaring mass of Arenig Fawr, which appeared indistinctly through strands of low cloud. A fresh wind stirred the long grass in the fields and picked leaves from the trees. Rain had fallen recently, probably in the night, and my countryman's nose scented more rain on the way. It was, indeed, a day very like my last day of freedom. In the crevices of the stone walls along the road, the moss and the small ferns gleamed bright and green. A stream – one of the many nameless streams that rushed to join the Afon Llafar – welcomed me with the characteristic, incessant, inexhaustible sound of my homeland.

I went a little farther, opened a gate, and began to walk on my own land. The fields were, for the most part, empty; the number of sheep had been drastically reduced during the war. But, thanks to Williams' care, the drainage was in reasonable condition. Having made a cursory inspection, I directed my steps to Williams' own farm. I found two men in the yard, intent on making some repair to the engine of a tractor. Upland farmers had not owned tractors in 1939, but I was to learn that they were now regarded as normal equipment. One of the men was Dan Williams. Middle-aged at my departure, he was middle-aged still; his ruddy countenance and the flecks of grey in his hair were just as I remembered them. The other man was much younger, and I guessed that he was one of Williams' sons. They had been children when I last saw them.

'Good morning, Williams,' I said.

Straightening up from the tractor, he stared at me for a short space before responding. it was a rare event, doubtless, for a stranger to enter his yard and greet him by name. 'Morning,' he said at last, politely but warily.

It had not occurred to me that he would fail to recognize me; yet I could not be altogether astonished. When I identified myself, he apologized with some embarrassment. I had, in truth, aged so much – as a scrutiny in a looking-glass, later in the day, confirmed – that I might well have been taken for an older man than Williams, who was actually ten or a dozen years my senior. His son, certainly, would have had some difficulty in believing that I was only thirty-nine.

I should have said, at this period, that I could expect to live to about the age of fifty, like my father. Dr Probert, who gave me a thorough medical examination soon after my return, would doubtless have concurred in this estimate, for he advised me gravely to take care of myself. I should not have been cheered if I had been able to foresee that I was destined to drag my way on to sixty, then to seventy – perhaps to eighty. Life, in its true sense, was already over for me. Its long aftermath has been neither merited, nor desired, nor valued; it has been imposed on me by a Power possessed, I can only think, of infinite resources of irony.

With the natural tact of his class, Williams refrained from putting any questions to me, even about my state of health or the details of my journey. He told me that his wife had swept and dusted in Craig-derw, lit fires, and filled the larder with essential provisions, so that I could resume my residence without delay. He expressed the hope, however, that I would take some refreshment in his home, and I naturally accepted. Then he smiled and said: 'There's somebody here you know.'

'Who is that?' I asked, not without anxiety. It was inevitable that I should encounter former acquaintances, but I was in no hurry to begin.

'Why, it's Nellie, Mr Hughes-Talbot.'

And my dog – the best dog I ever had – came trotting across the yard when she heard her name. She had lost her beauty and her vibrant energy, but her alert intelligence had not deserted her. I hesitate to affirm positively that she remembered me; perhaps, when she affectionately licked my hand, she was making an instinctive response to the pleasure that she sensed in my touch and my voice. It was, in any case, a gratifying moment for me. I had thought of Nellie during the years in prison, and hoped that Dan Williams would care for her, but had not ventured to make the request.

'She's too old for work,' he said, 'but I knew you'd want me to keep her going, Mr Hughes-Talbot.'

An hour later, I set off across the fields with the key to Craig-derw in my pocket and with Nellie by my side. When we came to a field containing a dozen sheep, she intimated by an eager whine her desire to practise her old skill. I do not know which of us was happier to find that we remembered the traditional signals. Our performance would have won no prizes, but we succeeded eventually in moving the sheep from one corner of the field to another.

Nellie hesitated, and needed my encouragement, before entering the front door of Craig-derw. Welsh sheepdogs are not pets, nor is it customary for them to be indulged with the comforts of the house. But, although I had prepared myself for solitude, I was grateful for the company that Nellie provided. She had an established place at the fireside, and slept in a basket ouside my bedroom door, during the eighteen months of life that remained to her.

Craig-derw is now, and has been for many long years, a lonely house. So it was in my childhood and youth; I think of my four years of happiness as a magical, and at this distance almost unbelievable, gleam of light in the darkness of my life. Sometimes, when I return from the fields, I still imagine that I see Martha coming to greet me with her sweet and loving kiss, or hear little Ann's excited cries. But I try to forget; what is lost to hope should, for peace of mind, be lost to memory.

I have never, since my last parting from Estelle Mavros, walked along the road that leads only to Ty Pellaf. I learned after I came home that the cottage was empty throughout the war and suffered serious deterioration. The owner, Mr Barker, was trapped in Singapore by the Japanese occupation and endured hardships which ruined his health, so that he had no desire after the war to keep possession of a residence at such a distance from London. He sold it for a small sum to an energetic young couple who repaired and modernized it, and they undoubtedly showed considerable prescience, since it was connected in the early 1950s to the electric grid and the water mains. Ty Pellaf has the reputation of a place where nobody stays long; it has changed hands several times, always serving as a second home for people with no local roots. The wife of one owner, with the excessive neighbourliness often manifested by the English in Wales, pressed me to come in for a drink on any evening that suited me. I thanked her, but did not avail myself of the opportunity.

The cottage, or rather barn, in which Sam Pritchard had lived also fell into a dilapidated condition when it was left empty. The general opinion was that, whether because of its clumsy structure or its unfortunate associations, no one would ever wish to live in it, and the District Council therefore authorized a contractor to demolish it and dispose of the stones. No trace of it remains, doubtless to the chagrin of those who, in recent years, might have profited from pilgrimages to the home of the artist.

I think of Martha, as I have said, as little as possible; but there is one day in the year when memory and regret hold me in a grasp that I cannot evade. On Midsummer Day, either in the morning or the evening, I always walk up to the place of ancient belief that gave its name to my home. Sometimes it is raining; more often, the best of summer confers a sustained and tranquil warmth; but always the ample length of the day, the slow and almost imperceptible transformations that begin so early and end so late, make a frame for meditation. At our last Midsummer, though disaster was so close, Martha and I loved each other as we had never loved before. If we could ever have been saved, that was the time.

I found when I came home that one of the oaks had been split by a storm-wind, or perhaps struck by lightning. I cleared the space and planted a sapling to restore the symmetry of the grove. It seemed foolishly weak and pitiable; but, thirty years on, it is a tall and sturdy tree. Those who, in old times, stood here at Midsummer are forgotten and nameless. I, in my turn, await the day when a merciful oblivion will cover me together with all my failings, my offences and my sufferings. The name of Hughes-Talbot will expire with me. The house that was proudly raised by my great-grandfather may, at the dictates of changing taste, share the fate of its predecessor. The oaks and the rock will remain.